I0615936

The Advice of Dreams

The Advice of Dreams

A Novel of the Ancient World

DAVID MARGARETSEN

RESOURCE *Publications* • Eugene, Oregon

THE ADVICE OF DREAMS
A Novel of the Ancient World

Copyright © 2024 David Margaretsen. All rights reserved. Except for brief quotations in critical publications or reviews, no part of this book may be reproduced in any manner without prior written permission from the publisher. Write: Permissions, Wipf and Stock Publishers, 199 W. 8th Ave., Suite 3, Eugene, OR 97401.

Resource Publications
An Imprint of Wipf and Stock Publishers
199 W. 8th Ave., Suite 3
Eugene, OR 97401

www.wipfandstock.com

PAPERBACK ISBN: 979-8-3852-0428-1
HARDCOVER ISBN: 979-8-3852-0429-8
EBOOK ISBN: 979-8-3852-0430-4

12/12/23

To Stacy, my best friend and first reader

Contents

Prologue

LATE IN THE FALL of AD 127 a horde of tribesmen swept across a remote enemy military outpost, massacring the garrison, burning what could be burned, and destroying the small stone fort so completely that every stone was thrown down and carted away section by section, brick by brick, stone by stone, so nothing remained but a small open space in the midst of the forest glade that grew up around it. As a memorial and so as not to forget one of the few victories over the invaders, the tribesmen salted the site so as to remain uncultivated and set up—much later—a monumental carved stone lion pierced with many spears.

What the tribesmen didn't know was that amid the ruin in a remote corner of the fort, behind a small, heavy oaken door at the bottom of a long flight of stairs, which the day before had been buried and covered over with soil, rock, and debris, was a small stone chamber, which held both the strongbox of pay and legal documents of the troopers—a type of bank vault—but also another and possibly vastly more important treasure: the records of the civilization that the enemy invaders had encountered when they had entered the land more than one hundred years before.

More than fifty heavy ironbound wooden crates had been hastily pushed into the strong room: fifty crates of papyrus, vellum scrolls, wooden and clay tablets, thin metal sheets, and early-form codex-bound volumes, all written in an unfamiliar language that were to be preserved and shipped to the capital for decipherment and translation. The heat from the fire that was raised over the strong room caused the stone and timber to fuse, sealing the room in an air-tight, water-tight time capsule, unique in the history of the land.

The tribesmen were also unaware as they hauled away broken stone, leather, iron nails, stores of grain and dried meat, and weapons that they had buried something that would remain hidden in a deep silence, a silence that settled over the site and would remain unbroken for nearly twenty centuries, burying for almost two thousand years one of most incredible tales told since the days of the Trojan War.

This book is the first of a projected three volumes, which are the result of another ten years of painstaking translation, archaeological detective work, and the weaving together—in a similar vein to the Dead Sea Scrolls—of all that was buried that day, an effort which has involved dozens of scholars of various disciplines from nearly every continent on the globe. The story that has been unearthed and restored follows.

CHAPTER 1

The High Fields

ALL AROUND HIM LARKS rose and fell across the meadow of horse-gold, pouring out a torrent of song, rising above the tops of the long grass, hovering for a moment, then streaking into the burnished sky, pirouetting as they drifted to the earth, all the while filling the warm air with a golden music that Tynan could capture in his pipes only as a muddy trickle compared to the waves of liquid gold that rolled from hill to hill under the late summer sun.

"Larks and sheep go together," his grandfather said, the larks rising and falling on nests built on earth warmed by the resting sheep and the grass that grew beneath them, keeping watch over the meadows where nothing quenched their fire. Swirling up at the approach of the wolf, the lion, the bear: the alarm they sounded as their song rose to a shrill high note had saved many sheep and their shepherds.

Tynan rested that day on a hillside slope overlooking the farm. Cap sat by him, their only dog now, but a good one. Herding was in his blood, and he herded everything in sight: sheep, cattle, and even had rounded up children in the market square, not letting them go until Tynan had whistled him off, half the village standing round laughing. Cap was as tough as old leather, eager to please, and approaching his prime.

Together they looked out over the waving green grass—it was long and full that year—and the small white dots of the sheep spread out around and below. The buzzing of the insects, warm sun, and cool earth were lulling him to sleep when he heard his cousin Ab calling.

"Hi, Tynan! Tynan! Where are you! You're wanted back at the house."

Tynan scrambled to his feet. "The house?"

"Yep—and right quick too. Looks like there's some folk here from the army rode in this morning that wants to see you."

"Hmm . . . the army. Hope there's no bad news coming," Tynan said, handing his staff to Ab. "Watch them close—they seem half-mad today, more like spring than summer, wandering off, trying to eat the poison weed, or throwing themselves willy-nilly into ditches—I'll be back as quick as I can. Stay, Cap!"

He turned and trotted down a well-worn path that wound through the grass across steep fellsides toward the stone farmhouse below. As he neared, he saw three large horses tethered outside the front door and, slowing to a walk, he went past them staring, as their enormous bulk moved back and forth, shifting their weight from hoof to hoof. These weren't farm ponies or even full-grown plow horses, but true war horses, with blue and silver trappings and gear lashed to their saddles. He went inside and down the hall to the kitchen.

Grandfather was standing beside the kitchen table, an unrolled parchment in his hand, his eyes staring out unseeing. Grandmother was at the window, her back to them, slowly rolling and unrolling a dish cloth. His stepfather was there as well, sitting in a dim corner by the fireplace, scowling and impassive.

And at the table, eating and talking quietly, were two warriors—it was the only word that fit them—each dressed in full armor, helmets set on the floor beside them, wearing blue and silver mantles.

As he entered, they pushed back from the table, turned, and looked at him. "Is this the piper?" one of them said.

"It is," said his grandfather. Then to Tynan, "Son, these men have come from Caerleon with an order to take you there for a short time."

"Caerleon? When . . . what of the sheep?"

"Oh, you won't need to worry about the sheep; your lazy ways won't be missed much around here," his stepfather said.

Tynan looked at him, but his grandfather spoke.

"That'll be enough of that, Ebner, if you please." Then he turned back to Tynan. "As soon as you can gather your things—and make sure you bring along your festival pipes."

"My pipes?"

"Yes," put in one of the messengers. "It is needed for an—er—ceremonial purpose, and it was made known to us that you are skilled at piping."

Tynan looked at his grandfather, who shook his head. "Go ahead and get your things—you should be back in a few days."

"That's what you said about the others," his grandmother said not turning from the window. "And they haven't a single one of them come back again."

"Yet they may—yet they may," said his grandfather. "Go on now, Tynan."

Tynan went to his small room at the very back of the farmhouse, closed the door behind him, sat on his cot and tried to catch his breath. His head was spinning round—things were happening fast. The room tilted, slewing back and forth, and he closed his eyes putting his head between his knees holding on tightly. After a few minutes the rush in his mind steadied, and he looked up and across the room at a large oaken trunk. It was time-worn and deeply scarred, large chunks of wood riven away. The surface was blackened, burned in places, bound with heavy bronze straps, and closed with a clasp shaped as a shield, a clasp that looked as if it had been broken by a heavy blow.

It was his father's—My *real* father, he thought—as he went to it and swung open the battered lid. The woody smell that seemed stowed in the trunk along with all his other things brushed his face gently. It was peaceful in that trunk, quiet and undisturbed, the one place that Tynan kept in perfect order, everything neatly folded and carefully placed.

To one side were two woolen shirts, a pair of cotton breeches, and a thin cloak made of brown homespun waxed to ward off the rain. On the other side, wrapped in a separate cloth, were his father's short sword and belt. Tynan couldn't remember his father clearly now; but these and the medallion stamped with the winged horse of Caledon that the king himself had sent his mother after the battle were reminders of him, comforting in their way. He rechecked their wrappings and left them in their proper places.

His festival pipes were there as well—hand-hewn for the Westcombe Games and gatherings in the towns and villages around. Tynan had honed the seven tubes that formed the pipes—each made from a different kind of wood—to a fine-grained thickness, then bound them with copper wire that strengthened the notes and gave varieties of pitch when he played. In each of the tubes was a wooden reed that had been grown far away where it was warmer than in Caledon, then dried in the sun for two full years before being inserted carefully into the mouthpiece that was attached to the end of each tube.

The whole of the pipes together, when properly played, captured—it was said—the winds of Aeol that blew across the high fields of the heavens. He had won local competitions and once had played his pipes as he waited for his stepfather to come out of the feed store, being so immersed in the music and paying no attention to the folks in the square that when he looked up he found a large crowd standing round the wagon, silent and hushed, with some of the men having even removed their caps as they stood listening. "Why are you disturbing the market day?" his stepfather had snapped at him as he came out of the store and loaded the cart with bags. "And you all laggards—be about your business!"

Tynan placed the pipes carefully in a wooden case and slipped the whole into his pack, weathered green by rain and wind, which he had taken down from a hook on the wall, taking only as well the homespun cloak, then carefully closed the trunk, lashed his pack closed, slung it over his shoulder, and left the room.

The two messengers stood as he came back to the kitchen. "Thank you for your hospitality," they said and bowed slightly to his grandparents. "We'll wait outside for the boy."

"Ask Ab to hold my staff for me until I get back," Tynan said to his grandfather. "I loaned it to him in the sheep fields today."

His grandfather nodded, his eyes glistening. He put his arm around Tynan's shoulders. His grandmother didn't say a word but held him long before letting him go and turning back to the kitchen window.

Tynan shouldered his pack and went out to the waiting riders.

"I'm Lieutenant Ross and this is Sergeant Major Smith," said the tall trooper. "Do you know how to ride?" he asked, as he buckled on his helmet.

Tynan eyed the towering horses, ears flicking back and forth. "Only small beasts—ponies and such—nothing you'd even call a horse next to these."

The two laughed. "No matter! We'll help you on and tie the reins. Old Cinder will follow the others and do his best to keep you from falling off."

"Cinder?"

"All of our horses are named battle-friends and that's his field name. It'll help if you look straight over his head between his ears. Hold the reins but don't move them. Tuck your elbows in close to your sides and keep a light firm grip on the saddle with your legs."

At this, they lifted him onto a thin leather pad girded to the smallest horse of the three, then leapt upon their own horses in a single spring, and gathering the reins, galloped off the farm without a backward glance.

They immediately turned and rode southeast, keeping up a tremendous pace for the first few hours, then reining back to a brisk canter as they saved their horses' strength for the journey, taking only short rests, pushing on with great urgency toward Caerleon, riding far into the gloaming dark before stopping for a short bivouac, the stars revolving above them silently as the night rolled away.

The next day, they started off early and rode a little easier "to spare the beasts," Lieutenant Ross said, and would walk short stretches beside their mounts, allowing the horses to graze and drink.

"Is anything known of this road?" Tynan asked during one of these breaks.

"Only that it has been there a long time," Ross said. "And is somehow connected to the Drover's Road that passes your grandfather's farm, maybe even built by the same ancient people. Out beyond your way is sort of the Edge of the Wild. The writ of the king doesn't extend as far as it should, so the maps there are vague and trouble often breaks out, either from the Mataens of the North—they are an evil wayward people—or squabbles about grazing rights and boundary-stone settings that get out of hand among our own folk."

As they rode, Tynan saw that several small streams flowed down each side of the vale; and he savored the rich flowering of the country. The road itself was lined with water-meadows and small pools with reed beds that rattled softly in the gentle airs, shaded over by ash and birch, running at times through wet pastures with oak and chestnuts skirting the fringes. The bracken, heather, and gorse of the fields were kept trimmed by the cattle he saw foraging along the roadsides, and farther out were meadows proper; sparsely covered by alder, willow, and poplar.

They splashed through many shallow fords, sandy and strewn with small gravel, then turned nearly due east, cantering parallel to what became an ever-broadening river. Small knolls, outcroppings of chalk, and granite faces bulked into the road as it wound around their feet. Some of these knolls were topped with small villages and some with a watchtower, but most were empty save for ancient groves and wind on the hilltop. On the road were farmers and their herds or the occasional cart loaded with hay and produce trundling on to the next market town.

They rode on, pushing down the road through the late afternoon. "The sky and the air are going bad," Smith said as they stopped to make a small meal.

"Bad? What do you mean?" Ross said.

"Well, they feel bad at any rate: foul and wrong."

Tynan looked up. The sky was a bleary shade of red and the air that stumbled oddly about them carried a strange smell.

"Don't like the look of that," Ross said, walking to the edge of their campsite studying the airs, his face toward the sky.

"'Red sky's a warning,' my old uncle would say," Smith said. "More often than not he'd put his rain slicker on then and there, without a cloud in the sky, and we'd all laugh; but he'd be the dry one later on. 'Yep' he'd say, 'Thought it would turn out to be a wet one.'"

"He taught you well," laughed Ross. "We best be up and on our own way. The sooner we get to the Crossroads, the better. We'll keep an eye on the upper airs and our slickers near to hand."

They continued along the road, which rolled up and down steeply. A haze rose from the trees, grass, and hills around them. Overhead the sky was fading to a reddish brown, growing indistinct. Dark cats claw clouds appeared overhead, running from the west, and a gloom drew down upon them; towering clouds shot through with green and bluish-tinged lightning lowered as the rain gusted and spattered.

Ross called a halt and took out a map, studying it carefully. "We need to find shelter and the only place near is the ruins of Carnifex."

"Carnifex. That place comes with a bad name attached, a name infested with ghosts and worse than ghost-like spirit things," Smith said.

"That I don't know," Ross answered. "Some of our patrols have stayed there and reported nothing of that sort."

Tynan shivered as the drenching rain swept in.

"Well, if that's the place, then that's the place," Smith said. "I don't like it but if it's got to be then we best get there as quick as we can."

An hour's ride in the steady rain brought them to a narrow grass-covered track branching off from the main road that curved up to their left, passing through a heavily forested slope where the trees tossed and sighed, then on out upon a small clearing where Carnifex stood.

Stones were set there in two concentric rings, one inside the other with a low stone platform set in the exact center. The stones themselves were fifteen feet high, seven or eight feet wide, four feet thick, and set with a crosspiece like the lintel of a doorway—a doorway onto an expanse of emptiness.

Nothing about the place or its history was known for certain; it all was a mass of rumor and conjecture. What was true was that they found it enclosed by low drystone walls which gave some shelter from the rain and wind. There was no roof however, and the rain poured down.

"Let's set up as far from that as we can," Smith said, pointing to the low platform. Placed purposely, it seemed, in the precise center of the group of stones, the platform was a rudely cut squarish shape, and of a different sort than the statues and figures. "It looks like something that escaped from a cemetery."

The wind gusted and swirled as the rain fell in great sheets, running down the stones. But the place gave some shelter from the raw weather and, more importantly, they could light a fire. They found some neatly placed stacks of wood and soon had a roaring blaze going. The stone glowed golden in the light of the flames.

"What do you make of these carvings?" asked Tynan as they worked to cook a meal. The broad stone face behind them was covered with strange markings, some were like pictures or images; others looked like oddly-cut letters of some long-forgotten script.

"It's hard to say," said Ross, twisting around and looking up at them. "Some barbaric chatter or spell or other. But they aren't all evil-looking; some are quite skillfully done."

"May it be that the stories about this place are just stories, but what's the point of such a huge pile being put up in the middle of nowhere?" Tynan said.

"Don't know what this place really was used for; and hope I never do! Meantime let's keep that fire going no matter what the hour," Smith said.

After a small supper, Tynan wrapped himself in a rough horse blanket stretched out on the ground next to their fire with his back to one of the stones and, as Ross and Smith talked horses, tack, weapons, and maneuvers, he stared into the crackling light and slowly fell into a deep sleep, feeling the ground below him moving as if he still sat upon Cinder.

Quite unexpectedly he seemed to drift away, and in the dim chill gloom of a very late night, he found himself riding alone toward a darkened vale.

The way ahead rose before him, a lightless void between the darknesses of the high hills, shrouded and brooding. He cantered along a glimmering path that faded as it wound ahead into the darkness, his horse's hooves muffled beat on the sandy soil all that broke the heavy stillness. Looming shadows wrapped in silence grew up before him as he rode, while a pale thin moon was sinking below the far western rim of the world.

He halted just inside the mouth of the valley, his horse stamping and sidestepping nervously. "Peace, peace," he said, patting the horse's neck. The horse snorted, bobbing and shaking his head, his bridle jingling in the silence.

Sliding from the saddle he knelt on one knee, left hand palm-down upon the damp earth, then exhaled deeply, and waited. Time passed; then faintly—very faintly—like the shadow on the border of a distant murmur, far away but real—rhythmic, persistent, and heavy, he felt the earth tremble, rolling from the east. They always come from the east, he thought. He knelt there unmoving for a time until there could be no doubt, then slowly stood and turned to his horse, pausing a moment, standing there silently, then remounted and rode forward into the dark.

The vale was filled with a great stillness, like an immense and ancient solitude, mutely vigilant. As he rode, whispers of tumult and disturbance began to echo dimly along the path of the rising sun. The moon sank at last behind the far distant rim of the earth; a predawn clamminess sat oppressively on him. At one place, a confused rush of small, panicked creatures—fox, rabbit, pheasant, and even tiny deer—rushed past heedless, fleeing as if before a wind-driven wildfire. Ahead, in the remote east, light began to creep its way up through an unnatural fume of haze and smoke that stained the sky a strange wash of ill-mixed colors. His horse tossed his head and Tynan with difficulty held him back.

Suddenly, the gray grassy floor sloped steeply up before him, rising sharply like the canted deck of a storm-pitched ship; smooth and coverless like a glacis before the walls of a defended city. Wide—exposed to shot, bolt, and dart flung down from an over-commanding height—the bare slope ran up to meet the sky where, edged against the rising day, stood a motionless figure. In one hand it grasped a wide banner bound to a long standard that streamed in a wind rising in the east; in the other was a battle-mace that flickered in the deep gloom: an enigmatic form upon the high ridge framed against the fire-flecked sky.

Tynan checked his pace, reining back hard as he reached the sharp upturn, staring at the figure above him. His horse reared and neighed, pawing the air. "Ride on, ride on," he shouted, though the wind now risen to a gale tore the words from his mouth and flung them useless into the void behind. He drew his sword as his horse sprang up the slope, and as he did, the figure above raised its arms and called out in a loud voice. Above him, shutting out the sky like an unnatural roof, a silent mass of dark birds appeared, racing like a reeking cloud bearing down, rushing on into the west. The tumult grew, and the slope quaked and still the figure stood above him looking down; the wind rose to a roaring howl as a brooding darkness welled up, inky black in the eastern sky.

Shining golden and alone against the sea-hill of darkness that stood poised above him, Tynan rode up. At that moment, the blackness was torn along one edge and a shaft of clean sunlight shown full upon him, his brightness dazzling, his sword a blade of flaming light whirling above his head, his horse burning gold, lighting the earth.

Only for an instant. Then the figure, framed as a black void as dark as a fall into nothing, turned and waved his rod forward. Behind him, the wave of night, which was now an army it seemed, wrapped in the massy gloom, a thicket of spears and shields and a host of mounted troopers, bowed at last to its own weight and swept forward, its malice bent solely on Tynan as the wind roared and whirled around him like a dark serpent coiling, twisting, circling, and pursuing him in the night.

And as the earth shook and the dark winds turned to enemies whirled around him, it started to rain.

"Tynan!" A voice called to him from beyond the rain. "Tynan!"

"What is it?" Tynan answered, shaking himself free of the blanket he had entangled himself in.

"It's time to be up and going; we must be at Caerleon no later than noon today," Ross said and turned to finish packing their gear.

After a quick breakfast of barley porridge, dried beef, and fruit, they rode forward as the sun shone brightly in the storm-washed sky and soon came upon a broad crossroads in the center of which was set a carved statue of a horse which loomed up in the midmorning light. Rearing up, its forelegs stretched to the sky pawing the air with mane and tail flowing as if in a great wind. The stone was dark, whether from the natural hue or weathered by time it was difficult for Tynan to say.

"Nearly a capriole!" Ross shouted, waving to the statue as they road past and took the northward turning, which climbed beside a loud cataract of water that hurried down to join the widening river below them on its journey to the Narrow Sea. They came out to the foot of a tall rocky hill, open to the sky, and looking up at the city, stopped there to put themselves in inspection order, as Ross called it. "Because we are going to the house of the king and will present ourselves to one of his household—perhaps even the Marshal himself."

They remounted and went on. The city rose before them, its walls growing out of the living rock, following the contours of the hill. They crossed a small bridge then climbed following the road as it turned across the bluestone-tinged escarpment disappearing around a far shoulder of the rocky outcropping. The city took Tynan's breath away, the towering curtain walls lined with armed men and hung with massive shields that shone golden blue in the declining sun, a broad glowing band that radiated light like an azure crown.

They rode echoing through the gates that stood open until they came to a stone building that looked like a large square house, built on a granite hillock. They dismounted at a small side door, which was guarded by two soldiers with long spears and shields.

"We've brought a piper for the Marshal," Ross said. One of the guardsmen saluted and went in through the door. Brisk footsteps were heard returning shortly, the door opened from within. An old, richly dressed man stood there.

"Well?" he said.

Ross and Smith stood rigidly to attention, saluting, right hands touching their left shoulders. "Sir. We have brought one of the pipers."

The man looked like no one Tynan had ever seen before, clothed head to foot in satin-like material of the darkest blue with a broad collar of gold. His sleeves were long and cut closely to fit his arms and he had wide cuffs of engraved leather on his wrists. He wore breeches styled like a soldiers', and boot-like sandals richly embossed with metal studs, fitted with hobnails that clacked on the floor. Over this all was a rich blue cloak mantled with dark fur and a leather sword belt inlaid with gleaming metal, its pommel encrusted with precious stones.

Tynan must have been staring at the man with his mouth open for the man said to the troopers, "Did you bring me a piper lacking sense? This one stands with his mouth gaping open and I shouldn't be surprised to see him drool presently."

"No sir," Ross said. "He is one of the pipers named in the orders and can speak as well as any, though the ride seems to have tired him."

"Where is he from?"

"Westcombe—he was the first we were able to find."

"Westcombe? Can anything good come out of that miserable sheep-infested mudhole?"

He stooped down and inspected Tynan closely for a few uncomfortable moments, his breath smelling strongly of onions and wine.

"All right. You—come in."

Tynan entered the house, and the old man swung the door shut on the two troopers still standing there. "Follow me," he said to Tynan, walking down the hall, then up a narrow side stairway, onto a small landing and stopped at a tiny wooden door, which he opened and gestured to Tynan. "Go in."

He found himself in a tiny room smaller than a cupboard, like a balcony or alcove, draped and curtained on all sides, fitted with a wooden bench. A highly carved lattice-work wood screen formed one wall.

"Sit," said the man. "You have your pipes?"

Tynan nodded and sat down.

"Now listen to me," the man continued. "You will soon hear voices and people coming into the room below. You are not to look out upon them, and you are forbidden to speak of or make mention of anything that passes here, under the strictest penalty—is that understood?"

Tynan nodded.

"Now play if you can."

"I can play. What would you like?"

"Play what you would play to sooth the sheep in the fields when they are jittery, to calm the stirrings of a nervous flock at night. Keep playing no matter what happens, no matter what you hear; and play until I come back for you. Remember again that you are sworn under the king's oath not to speak to anyone of anything that passes here. Is that understood?"

Tynan nodded again and drew his pipes from his pack.

"Very well," said the man, then shut and—rather disconcertingly to Tynan—locked the small door.

Tynan paused for breath, then began to play. For a few minutes, there was only his own music, then a door in the room below could be heard bursting open.

"Don't take me in there!" came a voice.

"Lord, it's the room of healing."

"Healing? Are you mad? That room is where *it* has always assailed me—bringing down wrath and torment on my head."

"It, my lord?"

"What lives in the music."

The voice broke off and others shouted. "Stop him!"

"Strap him to the chair!"

"Is there a piper?"

"If you are there, piper, play!"

Tynan played louder and the music spread out from his pipes, a soothing wave dropping slow, easing somewhat, it seemed, the violence and chaos below him.

The voice raved on. "Ha! I told you! The music is in this room. Why are you tormenting me? It's because of Quentin . . . isn't it? Yes, he thought he could betray me and not pay the penalty—but he did pay, did he not? In league with the Terasians. Yes. My own blood kin. Betrayed by my own sister's son. But I caught him. Ferreted him out and hanged him from the highest tower. Like all of you will be hanged—you're just not found out yet; your schemes hiding behind masks of—stop!—the music is driving my mind apart."

"Lord, your drink—it will help calm you."

"What? Where is he—I'll pin him to the wall!"

"Who, lord?"

"The piper! That music—it must be killed!"

Tynan started, faltering for a moment.

"See? Heh, heh—threaten it and it *will* go quiet. Destroy it better still and it will be silenced forever. No—go on! What is this devilry? What has become of Landon?"

"Gone, sir."

"Gone where? Is he killed?"

"Yes, lord—slain by your bodyguard."

"Landon? He was a good man—loyal and strong in war."

"Traitor, sir. So was said."

"Yes—traitor like all of you! Of course—got him before he got me. You're all in league together and would poison me if I didn't keep my spies after you."

Tynan played on, the notes reaching high above the ravings.

"Stop the playing! I'll have him torn apart. No—No. Keep on!"

"Yes, lord. The music will do all of us good," said another voice. "It draws down the good power of the high heavens upon us."

"Well, well!" came the first voice again, sly and low. "Well, well. That sounds very pious of you—yes, very much like old Bascom—he was always dithering on about some better place outside the walls of this world—beyond the pale, in the clouds, the far side of the mid-heavens or wherever he said it was—he was always blathering on about it wasn't he? But in the only world that matters he wouldn't go through with it. He said it was an *impious* act—his very words!—an affrontery to some deity of his or other. Well—I sent him across the final abyss to talk it over with that deity personally and now we've one less gabbling mouth on this side of the divide to endure."

The voice changed, but it was the same speaker. "You murdered a good man!"

"Bascom? Murdered? A good man? Anything for the kingdom. Fire and blood and iron and sword—this kingdom will be established on earth. A paradise it will be, I tell you! He had not the right to cross me. . . . Stop that music . . . the words are unbearable."

There came the sound of a scuffle. "He's seized my spear!"

"No!"

"Not one of you can do it, can you?"

Tynan heard a loud, fierce hum and the wooden latticework above him was shattered. He threw himself down in the tiny compartment, showered with fragments of wood, tearing down the velvet hangings as he rolled to the floor. A long bronze spearhead had buried itself in the plaster wall, its six-foot shaft rattling with the force of the strike. Tynan lay there covered in debris, too dazed to move or think.

"That's done it—I knew by my right arm and by the power of my will, the awful speech would be silenced by *me*, the lawful lord of this place."

"Play, piper!" came another shout. Tynan dragged his pipes toward him and took up the tune again, sitting on the floor under the windowsill, while below the voice subsided into low muttering.

For a long space of time there was a complete silence in which no one spoke and the room below was filled only with the presence of the music.

"What was that?" came the voice at last. "What was that? What were we talking about? Ah—what about that western border? We need stop those Mataens from marauding across when they like, burning farms and killing folk. What's Gerald been doing with all the men and money we've been sending him? And the North Tower—it could collapse any day—get more workmen on it!"

And the council—for so it sounded now—went on. Tynan kept playing softly until the scraping of chairs and the sounds of feet and the slamming of the door below signaled the end of the council. He stopped and sagged back against the wall, sweating and shaking.

Soon after, the door to his tiny chamber was unlocked and flew open; the old man stood there again.

"Come!" he said. Tynan stood and followed him down to the same door he had first entered the house. He had no idea how long he had been there.

The man turned and gripped him tightly on the shoulder. "Well played. Remember again on pain of imprisonment or worse that you are not to utter a word of these things to anyone. Is that clear?"

Tynan mumbled and nodded.

"He's back in his right mind for now," the man said. "But the episodes are getting worse . . ." Here he stopped short, as if he thought he had been speaking to himself, unaware that what he was saying was out loud, then remembered Tynan was there. He glanced at Tynan sidelong and then appeared to smile, though it looked to Tynan like more of a withered grimace, as if some new thought had occurred to him.

"Half a moment . . . half a moment. . . . What have I been thinking of . . . ? Yes, that may be it. . . . Hmm, you see, um, young man, your playing has soothed him more than anything else we've tried—all the doctors, phony healers, magicians that have been herded in—completely useless! But you . . . we may need to keep you here with us a little longer than we meant. Have you ever thought of being in the army?"

"A little. My father was in the Foot Volunteers."

"That so? Very good. We'll see what can be done. Wait here on the doorstep and someone will come to fetch you presently."

He closed the door and Tynan was left outside on the doorstep between the guards who neither moved nor spoke, staring fixedly ahead. The sun was going down and the city was fading into shadows. "What day is it?" he said aloud. Who knew? Lights were coming on and dinner smells were wafting in the street.

He sat down on the step, his pack and his pipes beside him. A great weariness came over him. Soon, though, the door opened again and a girl about his own age stood there holding a tray.

"What a grubby boy," she said. "These are for you. Do you know how to use a fork?"

Tynan struggled to his feet again. "A fork? Of course."

"It's a wonder." She handed him the tray and was gone, slamming the door behind her.

"Thank you," he said, for the tray held a plate of simple beef, potatoes, a vegetable Tynan didn't recognize, a small loaf of brown bread, and a flagon of water. Whether or not his hunger played a part, he always looked back on this as one of the best meals of his life. Now *that* was a meal, he'd think, and always compared anything that claimed to be good with the simple food he had sitting at the king's side door on the first day of his coming to Caerleon.

Tynan sat back down on the doorstep and eagerly ate—for some reason feeling compelled to take extra care not to chew with his mouth open and use his fork properly—then drank down the water. He rested there, content for the moment just to do nothing, when the door opened behind him again, and Lieutenant Ross came out on the doorstep.

"Hello, Tynan! All well with the—ah—patient?"

"Yes, sir, it looks to be."

"Good! The kingdom secure for another day and all that?"

"Yes, sir."

"Right, then," Ross said. "Let's get going."

"Back to Westcombe?" Tynan said as he gathered his things.

Ross looked at him for a moment, then at a sheaf of papers he had in his hand. "Well—no. As a matter of fact, we're ordered to the recruiting office," he said and held up the papers, looking brightly at Tynan. "You have been nominated to join the Academy—by the Marshal himself!"

"Join the what?"

"The Academy—it's a new school that's being formed. You'll learn thinking and horse soldiering. It's a great honor to be chosen by the Marshal—he is second only to the king in the land. Follow me!" And Ross started off at a slow trot.

Tynan stood there unmoving.

Ross turned to him and waved his arm. "Come on!" Tynan shrugged, picked up his pack, and jogged after him.

They threaded their way through the city, which Tynan saw was laid out in well-cut stone yet still with wooden buildings, huts, and even had places where long grass and untended bushes still grew among the pavement stones of the City of the Seven Gates—that was what the name meant, but only four of the gates were completed and had actual gates that could be opened or closed; the others were mere barriers guarded by troops set amid the stones of construction. The Academy itself was outside the city, reached by going through the Horse Gate and winding up a roughly paved road to another smaller fortified enclosure.

Here they were met with a gate heavily reinforced by metal of some sort and—Tynan learned later—a double gate opening built using the most up-to-date military engineering of the time.

A challenge came from above the gate. Ross answered and the gate swung open. Once inside, they went down a wide central aisle lined on either side with rough stone barracks and proceeded along a narrow way about halfway in. They turned into a large building, climbed the stairs quickly, and entered a small office. Ross handed the papers to an officer sitting at a small table, who flipped through them and looked up.

"Ah, Tynan is it? At ease—very good—now this report from the Marshal says that not only are you a piper—placing . . . er . . . fourth it seems—at a county fair competition last year, but that you once collected fifty silver talents for bringing in the skin of a catamount or stonetiger that had been terrorizing your home district?"

Suddenly, Ross and the recruiting officer were no longer there; and he knew a lamb was gone. There was no mistake—Tynan had counted every sheep as it passed under his staff coming into the sheepfold; and then recounted. There was one missing, and besides the ewe next to him was baaing incessantly facing out toward the growing darkness. They had hurried the flock into the Medway Pens as the sun went down in fire.

"There's a lamb missing!" He shouted to his stepfather.

"Just noticed it did you? You idjit. It's been gone half a day and what of it?"

The ewe went on bleating and trying to push past them. "You knew? You left it out there?" Tynan said, grabbing the man's arm as he turned away.

His stepfather spun, slapping Tynan hard to the ground. "Mind your lip, fumble foot! Any more talk like that and you'll get worse. What's one lamb more or less? And besides it'll keep that blasted catamount from coming in after the rest tonight. See they're properly penned." Then he trudged away toward the other keeps laughing and drinking around a large watch fire.

Tynan lay stunned, feeling the blood trickle from the cut on his lip. For the hundredth time he asked himself why his mother had married Ebner after his father had died. He had heard rumors of family rights and family duty, among other reasons. At first things had seemed well, but Ebner was a drinker, who had ruined his mother's life and was well along the way to ruining his with it.

Out of the darkness, a shape appeared carrying a shepherd's lantern. It was Gaven, the keeper of the Pens. Gaven paused, watching Ebner walk away, seeming in debate with himself, then looked down at Tynan and helped him up.

"I saw what happened. Pay no attention to Ebner; one day he'll receive what's coming to him in full measure."

"Maybe," Tynan said, wiping his lip and spitting out the blood. "But no matter what he says, I'm going to take Cap and Sweep out to find that lamb—I can't abide thinking of it out there." He turned to Gaven. "Will you keep an eye on the others—just to make sure they stay in the pen?"

Gaven looked worried. "That catamount is a bad one—it's said it's a man-killer who attacks shepherds then tears apart their flocks—goes after the keep first, mind you, rather than going after the flock—it's unnatural. You'll likely get yourself and your dogs killed trying to track it down but . . . all right, I'll watch them; but I'll feel better about you if you will take these with you in case you come upon the beast." He reached into his shepherd's pouch and drew out what looked like three small, weighted arrows, examined them carefully in the lantern light, then handed them to Tynan.

"What are they?" Tynan asked.

"Kyros darts. They work just like slingbullets. Fit the weighted end into a slingpouch and sling it, just like a stone or bullet—same motion, same pace."

"I've heard of them," Tynan answered, weighing them in his hand, feeling their balance, then slipping them into his own pouch that also held five or six slingstones.

Tynan turned. "Cap! Sweep! Come up and follow on."

They left the Pens and retraced their way through the oncoming night onto a wide, flat land of close-cropped grass, stunted trees, and wide-scattered rocky outcroppings.

"Cap! Sweep! See sheep! See sheep!" Tynan called, and the dogs loped ahead, following the Drover's Road. About four miles onto the plain, both dogs bent to the ground, fanning out in widening circles as they hunted. Then Cap lifted his nose straight in the air, barked once loudly, and set off east toward a black hummock of stone that rose as they approached it, the grass running to its base. Sweep went after him, Tynan trotting behind. The stone massif looked to be an impassable wall, but they found a narrow defile and passed through following a rocky channel that was went straight on and upward toward a rock-wrapped basin.

The dogs threaded their way up through the glistening stones winding into the gloaming dark sky, the walls of stone overlooking the path. Coming upon a wide dell, both dogs stopped ears forward, stiff legged, bristling, and growling low, Cap pointing with his nose, front paw bent.

Tynan's gaze followed the dog's pointing and he saw a dark cleft high up one side of the dale. He tightened his rucksack, lashing his staff to it, then turned to the dogs. With a signal, they lay down, eyes fixed on the cave. Tynan struggled up onto the first rounded boulder and made his way, angling up toward the cave's entrance.

He slithered and scrambled up slowly toward the yawning mouth, pausing for a moment, crouched on a ledge just below the opening, listening intently. Not a sound was coming from the cave; but flowing out in a noxious billow like the compounded evil of many years of decay was a putrid stench that choked him. He took a strip of cloth and covered his nose and mouth, then sitting there eased out his sling, strapping one end to his wrist, drawing a smooth stone from the leather pouch, placing it in the cloth centerpiece, and looping the other end around his finger. He picked up a rock from the ground beside him with his other hand, paused a moment, then threw it hard into the cave entrance. It shattered with a loud crack. He waited, straining for any noise but not a sound came from the cave. He eased himself up and peered in.

The cave mouth was a blank wall of darkness. Then the moon rose, and the recesses of the den showed a tumbled mass of torn and broken forms, the remains of the huntings of the beast in its wanderings. He entered slowly, feeling his way, not bearing to think about what he was touching, and crouched, listening intently, when he heard faint sounds from the far recesses of the cave. Working toward the sound he drew out from his pack a shepherd's lamp, small and heavy, with moveable flaps that directed the light through heavy glass to block the wind from blowing out the oil-soaked wick, and in its light, he saw the lamb—a huddled mass of torn fleece and wounds—but alive. Tynan took out a flask and poured oil on the wounds and bandaged it as best he was able, giving the lamb small sips from his waterskin.

He looked down on the huddled ball of wool—torn and bleeding and smeared with mud and grime. Hardly recognizable as even an animal—more an abandoned grimy rag with gashes and tears—but miraculously there was the smallest movement of the sides; the lamb was breathing though ever so weakly and tremulously as if poised on the border between life and death. He whistled up the dogs then took the lamb gently, dressing and bandaging the wound as best he could. As the dogs looked on, he wrapped the lamb in a cotton shawl.

"Let's get going," he said when Cap sprang to his feet growling low.

Cap's growling increased. Tynan heard a low scrambling sound then in the moonlight saw illuminated a beast whose bulk nearly filled the cave mouth as it came crouching slowly over the rim. Tynan froze, slowly moving his hand toward the bag that held his sling and the stones, and his hand closed over one of Gaven's darts.

The beast turned its head from side to side as if unsure of the smells it had found in its den. Its eyesight was said to be weak, and it hunted mainly by sound and scent. But once it had the scent of its prey, that prey was hunted down relentlessly; and it rarely failed to kill when it was locked onto a scent. Its tail twitched and its ears flipped back and forth as it scanned the cave—then it lifted up its head catching a whisper of the scent of the intruders, and Tynan saw its eyes widen suddenly then focus on him and spring forward. Tynan in a flash swept up the sling with the dart loaded and flung it, striking the beast in the shoulder. Staggering, it uttered a howl of pain that shattered the cave.

He fitted a second dart into the pocket of the sling. It was well-balanced, carved and grooved and tapered to a sharp point. He took a step toward the beast and with a full motion launched the dart. It struck the beast and it roared, screaming in pain, shaking the cave, its long teeth snapping and tearing as the dart plunged in its side, then it spun toward Tynan as he loaded the third dart into the sling—and with an ear-splitting howl leapt. In that moment Cap rushed the beast and was struck with a powerful swipe of the cat's paw, and flung to the far wall, laying still.

Sweep charged from the other side, rolling under the beast as it stumbled across the dog's body, crushing him. Then it let go another earth-shaking roar, its red mouth opening wide, its long teeth dripping with blood and saliva, and Tynan flung the dart through the open mouth.

The dart buried itself deeply in the roof of the cat's mouth, lodging itself just below the brain. Tynan took a step forward, loaded a stone and slung it at a full windup that would have brought down a deer at fifty yards. The blow struck the catamount straight between its eyes, sinking through. The cat staggered back on its hind legs, clawing the air, then turned slowly and toppled out of the cave, crashing down the side of the rock face to the floor of the dell below.

Tynan hurried over to Sweep and knelt. The dog lay broken and bloody, moving weakly, then, as he watched, Sweep stopped moving and was still. Tynan felt the body go limp and then there was nothing. He took out his shepherd's cloak and covered the dog; a dog that had been a good worker on the farm and a comfort besides.

He heard whimpering from the far wall where Cap lay broken and bloody, shaking with pain. Tynan bandaged him and applied oil. The dog was clawed deeply over one shoulder and side by the cat's paw. Tynan gently massaged it but could feel no broken bones.

"You're lucky, Cap! Those scars should be just enough to brag about later on and show you're a real war dog. But shouldn't be too bad to live with."

He spent the rest of day clearing the cave out, burying the remains of the beast after he had skinned it with the rest of the carnage of the cave. When he had swept and cleaned the cave, he built a small fire at the mouth and sat there chewing on dried beef, watching over the lamb and Cap—his two patients that would both be mending slowly.

It was nearly a week before Cap and the lamb were healthy enough to be moved. In that time, Tynan found from the remains that the beast had been hunting here for a long time and might have been the ghost hunter that had prowled and terrified the region for five years or more. The grisly piles of remains and scattered debris attested to its reign of terror.

The beast's hide lashed to a handsled that he pulled along behind him, Tynan walked slowly back into the Medway Pens, Cap limping along beside. Many keeps were still there, and his stepfather silently stood waiting as he approached.

"Where're you been?" his stepfather shouted at him. "There's chores to be got done and others that have been doing them for you."

"That's enough out of you, Ebner!" said Gaven, who came walking up. "Are you a complete fool? Why do I even need to ask? He's brought the lamb back and killed the catamount!"

"But at what cost? Gone a week and every day someone needed to cover his chores; and a search party sent out twice coming back empty-handed."

"He's brought the skin of that cat on the sled—that settles it. And there's a fifty-talent bounty on it that will be paid."

"Fifty talents?" Tynan said weakly.

"Yes, sir!" Gaven said clapping him on the shoulder. "And well-earned from the look of it. That cat must have weighed well-on two hundred stone."

"Son? Son? Was that a stonetiger or a catamount?"

Tynan suddenly focused and saw the officer poised with a pen over the sheaf of papers.

"Yes sir—sorry sir. It was a catamount. Many thought it a stonetiger, but a catamount is worse. It took one of our lambs and we had to go after it. We tracked the beast to its den and got the lamb back. We lost one of our best dogs, though, which was hard to bear."

"Yes, that would be. Where're you say you were from?"

"Westcombe."

The officer looked startled. "Westcombe? Didn't know there was anything there but a collection of thatched huts. . . . Hmmm—er, sorry, no disrespect intended—a man can't help where he is born can he? *But he can make a difference of the life he lives and how he dies. Well now.*"

Here he stopped and cleared his throat. "We're looking for men for the Academy. It's tough to get in and not an easy life once you're there but many say it's worth it—a chance to make something of yourself, better yourself, and help your country. Also it looks like you're a council appointee, so the king himself will likely have an interest in what happens to you and would have your best interests at heart in thinking the Academy would be good for you; and you would be good for the Academy, which would of course coincide with his best interests for the kingdom, so it seems the Academy would be good for you. But we're not like the blasted Mataens or even the accursed Terasians that take men that don't want to serve and use them like slaves—*no.* Volunteers are the way—those that believe in their country and way of life and will fight for it if they need to. It's a risk that you might not get enough men to fill out the battleline; but the men you get are men who are really dedicated."

The recruiting officer paused here as if waiting for a reply. Tynan hadn't quite followed the exact line of reasoning but said, "My father was in the Fifth Volunteer."

"The Fifth Volunteer! They were wiped out to a man at Monroe Pass—but they gave my corps time to come up and stop those Mataen devils getting onto the valley road and doing who knows what kind of mayhem. Many say that battle saved the king—and maybe the country."

"Yes, sir. My father . . ."

At this the recruiting officer looked uncomfortable but wrote something on the page before he answered. "I'm sorry about your father—he was part of a good unit. What was his name?"

"Eason . . . my father's name was Eason."

"Very good." The officer made another note in his file then signed Tynan's paperwork and handed it to Ross. "Carry on and good luck."

"That went very well!' Ross said as they left the command post. "This induction business can be a shock, but it goes fast and then we'll get you to the unit."

A shock it was—a barber shaved Tynan's head to match Ross's— nearly no hair and a shiny scalp. A medical specialist thumped his knee joints with a special hammer, had him jump over a chair from a standing position, cough several times, then drink a foul-tasting liquid—"it will keep sickness off you" he was told, as the medic signed and handed the growing sheaf of papers back to Ross. The quartermaster cataloged Tynan's personal belongings and stored them in a plain wooden box that was locked, engraved with his name, and added to a growing stack stored on pallets.

Then he was issued a mountain of new gear, including a uniform for summer, winter, and physical training as well as sandals and a leather belt, all of which fit into a large duffel bag that he carried back to the barrack building. Ross didn't help him—"every man needs to handle his own equipment"—then Ross showed him how to "stow" the gear correctly in the large wall locker in a barracks room, then trotted to find the rest of the unit, who were heading to the parade ground.

They hurried down the broad avenue between the barracks. As they went, they could hear orders being shouted. It was nearly dark, and fires had been built around a large dirt parade ground. Several groups of cadets were forming into companies. Ross led Tynan to one of the groups and called out. "Sergeant Webbe! New cadet recruit reporting."

"New recruit? Highly irregular and not proper. What's all this lateness about?" shouted a soldier who came walking toward them angrily. Then "Sir—sorry sir!" when he saw Ross' rank, snapping to attention and saluting.

"At ease, Sergeant. The Marshal sent me with a new cadet, and we've now just come from the induction center."

"Right, then! We'll take it from here, sir!"

"Carry on!" Ross said, then handed Webbe the growing stack of Tynan's paperwork, spun on his heel, and marched off.

"New man, eh? Let's have a look at you," Webbe said.

Tynan felt all eyes on him as he stepped up and tried to stand somewhat at attention before the sergeant.

"What's your name?"

"Tynan, sir."

"How have you come here?"

"Sent for by the Marshal, sir."

"The Marshal! How so?"

"He had me come to play my pipes for—er, a sick man."

"Well, that's something! What else can you do? Fight? Shoot?"

"Not much, sir."

"Not much?" The formation laughed and Webbe rounded on them. "That will be enough of that! Looks like discipline is slipping around here, isn't it? And we can't have that, can we? We'll have to tighten it up and this twenty-mile field march is the right way to start."

He turned back to Tynan. "All right! Cadet Not Much, into the cadet squad with you—last line in the back—we've got this pleasant march through the countryside planned in *your* honor to welcome you to the Academy, so hurry up and let's be quick about it!"

"Webbe went easy on you. I've seen him shred others to mincemeat for far less than being new or late to formation," said the cadet next to him as Tynan hurried to join the formation. "He'll likely make up for it later, feeling he has overlooked something in your training."

"Silence in the ranks, there! Any more talking and mark my words, you'll be cleaning the latrine with your tongue!"

CHAPTER 2

An Armed Academy

Tynan was jolted from his bunk next morning by a blaring trumpet and loud shouting. For a few minutes he had no idea where he was, then the soreness in every corner of his body brought back last night's march and events of the days before. He leapt from his bunk and landed on a cadet coming out of the lower bunk. Two others promptly fell on them from the stacked bunks across the tiny room.

"Sorry! I'm Marc," said the cadet as they struggled to untangle and sort out their uniforms.

"Tynan."

"Devon," said a thin dark-haired cadet from the other side of the room.

"Kiefer," said the fourth, who towered head and shoulders above the others. The four hurriedly dressed and ran out to the parade ground.

They were marched into what looked like a very large barn or storehouse, stacked as far as they could see in the dim light with various types of military dress, uniforms, and equipment: all dark blue with dark brown leather straps and belts.

"More gear?" Tynan said.

"Yes, indeed, Cadet Not Much—*more* gear! The king will make sure you're equipped for every situation and every season you're asked to get through.

"Now, all of you, stand cap bill to hat brim of the man in front of you—close it up! We need everyone to move as fast as you can through the lines—don't ask questions! Just tell them your shoe size, tunic size,

24

and so on. If you don't know it, they'll guess and they're pretty good at guessing but not perfect. They'll give you the right size as they see it, and it will be altered—*by you*—to fit later on."

Two hours later Tynan staggered out under a small mountain of equipment, thinking dubiously about the very small locker into which all that stuff was to be stowed. And not only stowed but pressed and folded and labeled and starched with sharp creases; edges and corners all in a standard pattern.

"So you know how to put it on when reveille sounds and you've got to dress quickly in the complete dark or an enemy comes upon you, surprising you with an attack on the camp and you must spring to arms and mount your horse in the midst of confusion, noise, and shouting without an officer to tell you what to do; and then rally to a preset point near the camp; fully armed, mounted on your horse, and in the correct battle order," Webbe observed.

They marched back to the stone barracks, really a dormitory with several smaller rooms branching off around a common room. He was issued a small silver shield, the size of a badge that could be worn on the shoulder or front of his uniform, silver with a galloping horse engraved upon it, winged with lightning bolts crossing behind as a sort of background. Then was ordered to put down his gear in the room he started from. The tiny, cramped space was filled by the two double bunks, two tall narrow lockers, two wooden tables, two wooden chairs, and two oil lamps, and with Marc, Devon, and Kiefer unloading a similar mountain of equipment, it looked impossibly crowded.

"Don't stand there gawking—hurry up!" shouted one of the senior cadets. "Stow your equipment in that locker and fall out in PT clothes in front of the barracks in ten minutes." Then he spun on his heel to march out.

"PT?" asked Tynan.

"Physical training, cadet!" The senior cadet spun back. "What else do you think PT means? You'll find out in a hurry that around here PT doesn't mean *play time*—like some playground game of walk-the-wheel or hopscotch. It's all about taking charge of your body and your mind to make sure you can do your duty. Is that clear?" the senior cadet shouted.

"Yes sir—thank you sir!"

Marc was rapidly stuffing his equipment into his locker.

"This hustle and frantic action will take a little getting used to," Tynan said as he did the same.

Marc laughed. "My father, his father, and four generations before them went to the old army school and somehow survived it, so there has got to be at least a chance for us to get through this new one."

"Very good!" Tynan said. "But my head's spinning round at the moment.

Waiting for them outside were Sergeant Webbe and six very large senior cadets, standing silently on the parade ground as the squad tried to assemble. On a small rostrum a flawlessly uniformed officer stood, gazing at them, his eyes moving slowly and purposefully, looking directly at each one of them in turn. He was ramrod straight wearing a perfectly pressed uniform of a blue tunic, leather breeches, tall hob-nailed sandals dark brown supported by leather leggings, a riding cane, and was wearing an incredibly polished silver breastplate and helmet that flashed brightly in the morning sun—so brightly Tynan could not look directly at it.

"At ease!" commanded the officer. "I'm Lieutenant Colonel Cage and I command this training unit. Welcome to the Academy. Most of you have heard of it and now you'll have a chance to earn a place in it. Each of you have come here by a different road. Forget about all of that once and for all! Here, you have no past, no rank, no family, no breeding, no privilege, no property, no name.

"All you have is yourself, your cadre, and your god if you believe in one. The Creed—chiseled in marble with bronze letters cut four inches deep—is what we go by here. This is what it says and this is what we will make you:

I will be the strong:	*I must protect the weak.*
I will have the choice:	*I must choose the right.*
I will face the hardship:	*I must endure.*
I will have many enemies:	*I must never give way before them.*
I will be tested:	*I must be steadfast.*
I will be questioned:	*I must be faithful.*

"The Academy will help you learn *by heart* what each and every word means at the proper time. Sergeant Webbe!"

Webbe, chiseled muscle glistening with oil and stripped down for work with a leather cap, a dark blue single tunic, and heavy leather field sandals, marched up. "Yes, sir."

"The new cadets are yours to command."

"Thank you, sir."

Webbe pivoted on his heel and faced them. "Now listen up! Some of you didn't do so well on the march last night and we need to shape up fast! To help us along, all of us are going to do a few exercises with the cadet guides here. Look at them! They've been here three months and there's not an ounce of fat on their bodies or in their minds. They all started out like you when they got here: basically uninspiring blobs of weakness and indecision. They'll help you on the way to becoming actual men starting today.

"*Then* we're going to send you out on a little run. Don't worry! The Academy just wants to know you can do it. This will be good for you: you'll need a basic level of fitness to keep up with your cadre and the training pace. If we see any shortcomings, you can be sure we will help you correct them, as the training regime is designed to assist you to be the best you can be.

"By our thinking, you're one half the person you can be—some of you even less! At the end of all this—*if* you make it—you will be closer to ninety percent of your potential as a cadet or more. Why not complete one hundred percent fulfillment some of you would-be math geniuses are asking? Because no one's ever achieved one hundred percent: that's why! Some have tried, but the effort killed them, and would certainly kill the likes of you—but oh, oh, oh—what a *very* good death it would be!"

Though Webbe laughed, Tynan was sure he was completely serious—there was not a flicker of humor on his face.

"All clear? Any questions?" Sergeant Webbe clearly didn't expect anyone to speak, but someone from the end of the line spoke up.

"Sir—how will we know if we have made it?"

"You'll be told in clear terms. Just like everything else at the Academy: clear and easy to understand instructions are the way it all works. Which you'll find out about if you are one of the few who do make it. Take a good look at the cadet on your right—then take a good look at the cadet on your left: two of you won't be here at the end. Some can't handle the physical or mental pressure, some don't like to be uncomfortable, and some are just not cut out for it. But don't feel a failure if the Academy isn't for you. It just means that life has something else planned for you. But if you make it . . . well that'll be the start of a life worth having lived!

"For today's exercises, a cadet guide will say either 'go' or 'no-go' when you cross the finish line at the end of the run. If a 'go' you'll form up next to that blue gate; if a 'no-go' next to that black one. Further instructions will be given once every cadet is sorted out. Any more questions? No? Good!"

The next two hours were filled with exercises: push-ups, sit-ups, and pull-ups mainly that were repeated until the cadets were groaning in pain and collapsing, all the while the cadet guides shouting at them to "push harder" or "give me two more repetitions" or "we're not going to let you give up on yourself"—this last Tynan found strangely funny—the place seemed to be all about personal responsibility. Then they rested for a few minutes and were allowed a small drink of water.

The sun was now past midday, hot and slanting. "Everybody up and everybody on the line!" shouted Webbe. "Double-quick! Are you tired? Why are you moving so slow?"

The whole unit lined up on a chalk-drawn line on the ground. "Now listen up! This run is just like the long-distance final at the Caledonian Games: twenty standard miles on a clearly marked course that you will follow out into the country and back into this parade ground. You must complete the run before this sun dial shadow crosses here—basically four and a half hours. Now set—go!"

They started out shuffling together in a mass group. Tynan had chased sheep over the fells since he could walk and quickly adjusted his pace to match his breathing. Soon he was in rhythm and lost in that curious floating mental state that enveloped him when he had to run delivering messages or lunch to the farm workmen. It was hot and sweat rolled down.

About twelve miles out and they had been going for nearly two hours, when a cadet in front of him stumbled and pitched headlong to the ground.

Tynan stopped, bent down, and turned the cadet over—he was ghostly pale with blood trickling from his scalp; his right ankle twisted and bent in an unnatural angle, swelling darkly, and blood flowing from an ugly break in the skin. Other cadets ran by, paying him no heed—then Marc came up.

"What's happened?"

"He's fallen and looks like his ankle is broken."

"Better leave him," said another cadet who slowed down for a moment. "If you don't finish under the time, you'll be sent off."

"Can't very well just leave him like this can we? He looks bad," said Marc.

The cadet shrugged his shoulders. "Suit yourself—it'll be a no-go for sure." And jogged away with a passing group.

Kiefer and Devon came up and stopped. "That ankle looks ugly! Surely, he can't walk on it."

"We'll need to make a litter and carry him," Marc said.

They fanned out among the trees lining the trail, broke off two limbs, and bound smaller branches crosswise as a makeshift stretcher. As they lifted the cadet, he groaned for water. Tynan searched beside the trail and, finding a small stream, filled his cap and hurried back, trickling some into the cadet's mouth.

The four each took a corner of the litter and in a measured trot went down the path. There were no other runners coming by now and they couldn't speak for the weight and the heat.

The sun was declining into the west, casting long shadows across the trail in front of them as they rounded back toward the campus still with nearly seven miles ahead of them.

After some time, they stopped for a moment to adjust their grips. The man on the stretcher groaned again.

Marc looked at him. "We need to get him straight to the infirmary." As he spoke, they heard the footfalls of someone running from behind them on the path and turning saw one of the PT medics coming up fast.

They sprang to attention. "At ease, at ease," the medic said as he ran up, knelt by the litter and unslung a bag from his shoulder. He checked the injured cadet, gave him a few sips of a liquid that seemed to calm him, rewrapped the bandaged ankle, then stood.

"News came back that someone was injured," said the medic.

"You ran all the way?" Devon said.

"It pays to stay fit," he answered. "Now, we need to get him quickly to the infirmary. You four have done the work this far—can you carry on the last few miles?"

"Yes, sir," Kiefer said. "I'll make sure these small ones carry on." He smiled as he said it and they lifted the litter again, trotting on toward the campus.

Finally, they made their way back to the Academy campus. The medic led them to a columned building that bordered the parade ground. Tynan felt every step as a straining effort as they bore the injured cadet across the paved courtyard, up a wide flight of stairs, and into a large entry way of a wide hall. Going in, they set the injured man down on the marble floor. The floor shone and the whole hall glowed with light reflected from the immaculately clean and polished marble.

Two orderlies came running, tending both wounds with balm and bandages. Marc explained what happened and stepped back, letting the medical personnel do their work. Tynan noticed a small group of medical students standing behind the asclepiad doctors observing and taking notes. They were looking back at Tynan and his friends.

"Are you new cadets?" one said.

It was the voice of a girl.

"Yes, ma'am," Marc replied.

"Plebes only, by the look of you," said another of the students.

"First Trividium," said Kiefer.

"Of course—you all look like babies," she said.

"Plebes!" said the matron professor, who attended the students, as she came up the corridor toward them. "Take yourselves out, please— we've all we need for now. Initially, it appears that the cadet has suffered a concussion, a compound fracture of the right ankle, and severe heat exhaustion. Let your sergeant major know we will send a report over later today. And you four: please stop chitter-chattering and pay attention to what is happening over here. This is an important treatment to learn."

"Yes ma'am," Marc answered. "And ma'am is there possibly water in the house?"

"If you go through to the cookroom, they'll give you some water— back that way," she said, pointing.

The four made their way down the long wide hall. It was faced with marble and highly polished, as was the rest of the infirmary. The cool cleanness of the place made a pleasant contrast to the heat and grime outside its doors: a place for healing and rest, Tynan felt.

As they went, Tynan caught a glimpse of a side hall, smaller and quieter. A door was open midway down the hall where a blue light shown out, bathing the hallway floor.

"I'll catch up with you guys—just want to check down here a minute," he said and turned aside toward the open door.

"Don't be too long," Marc said. "We'll need to get back as quick as we can."

"Right—will just be a minute."

Tynan went down the hall and turned into the doorway. A door, richly carved with sailing ships, apples, lions, and other beasts, hewn in heavy wood highly polished, stood open. Clear light streamed out; and

Tynan found he was looking at a chamber, large and vaulted, the walls soaring high with artistically turned glass, worked through with polished gold, interwoven upon a blue field.

In the center of the room, which seemed a solemn happy place, was a richly burnished figure wrought in gleaming metal, laid out as if asleep on a bed of marble. At its head, rising some thirty feet above the floor, was an ornate edifice chronicling, it seemed, the life and feats of a man: a sword, a ship, and several shields hung there. The chamber was oriented east-west, with high windows built to catch the setting sun as it sank below the rim of the world; and light flowed in igniting a flame of blue and gold, turning the image on the raised marble platform into a molten blue-green fire that set the room aglow.

There was also a living man there as well, kneeling before a small alcove. "May it be," the man said and stood, turning to Tynan a face that seemed old and young at the same time, calm and rested, yet alert.

"Ah! A cadet are you?" he said, coming out of deep thought and seeing Tynan standing in the open doorway.

"Yes, sir," Tynan answered.

"Turned aside to see this place?"

"Yes—it's beautiful."

"One of the most beautiful rooms in the kingdom and one of the oldest. At times, the Doctor seems to stir from his bed, to arise, and go out to complete his journey home," said the man, gesturing to the figure. "Though great as our healing arts may be, we shall all be as he is one day, whether small or great as the world sees us."

"Who was he?"

"I'll read an entry of his journal to you." The man turned to a heavily bound volume standing on a pedestal, turned a few pages, and began to read:

In the fifth month after finally leaving the destroyed city behind, when nearly in sight of our home's welcome shores, we were assaulted by fierce and contrary winds, which stirred the deeps to a relentless boil. Our ship was cast about by mammoth seas for many days. No stars shone, or sun or moon was seen, the water was streaked by evil gray foam. On the fifteenth day, we threw the ship's tackle overboard with our own hands and prayed for deliverance. And so being driven thus by raging wind and seas, on what we reckoned to be the eighteenth day, our vessels were shattered upon the rocks of a strange land, suffering great loss of

life and cargo, with the most grievous loss of all being our logs of
navigation and wayfinding, so were cast upon an alien shore with
no hope of returning to our home or lives, and that after ten years
of desperate war.

He looked up at Tynan. "It goes on to detail the founding of my order by two survivors of that wreck. The man you see was one of the survivors, and by his work this place of healing was built and has been nurtured and sustained for over five hundred years, rescuing the lost and providing guides to those who do not know the way."

The moon was rising now, its light gleaming through the colored window glass, appearing as a numinous sphere arising from a depth of clean blue ocean; as if poised at the very margin of the world, where one could stand and see the sun, moon, and stars before they lifted themselves over the wide blue horizon of the immortal sea. And the moon as it continued to rise looked to be an ascent of a queenly orb through royal blue waters, rising steadily higher against the windowed wall. In the figure's hands was held a crowned staff with a vine that twisted round it; and as the moonlight reached it, the crown flamed into living gold, and sent a shaft of golden light fully onto the bronze figure lying at the foot of the memorial. The reflection of that light suffused the whole room silver-gold.

"Tynan! Let's go—double quick to the finish line!" shouted Marc from out in the hallway.

"Yes—time for us to be going as well," said the man. "Abelard: heel boy!" A great golden dog rose from where it lay leashed to the rail of the alcove and calmly came to the man's side. "Good lad!"

"That's a beautiful dog and obeys as well, like some of the sheepdogs where I'm from," Tynan said.

"You're fond of dogs?" replied the man. "That's good! Abelard here helps the minds and calms the spirits of some of those seeking healing in this place, so most days he follows with me on my rounds."

With that, Tynan, the man, and the dog left the chamber, which continued to glow blue, silver, and gold.

The cadets ran as they saw the finish line before them. The troop—a much smaller group Tynan noticed—was formed up and silent. Webbe and the other cadet guides stood grimly before the corps of cadets.

They crossed the line, and it was nearly dark. There was no possible way for them to have made it under the required time.

Webbe towered above them, looking down. They were shaking from the exertion. "It's obvious you four didn't finish on time."

"Yes sir," they said in unison. Tynan's heart sunk to his feet.

"But you may have saved that cadet's life, which is worth something."

They remained silent, standing stiffly at attention, staring off into the distance above Webbe.

"It's what all in this Academy *must* do—never leave a fallen comrade behind."

"Yes, sir," they replied.

"Therefore, you are a 'go'! Now fall in by the blue gate with the rest of them!"

"You are not common soldiers!" Webbe shouted. "You are—or *will* be the best of the best—soldiers of intelligence, of manners, of politeness, of education. The country looks to you! The king looks to you! The Academy looks to you and . . . ahem . . . ahem . . . ! Mind the company, wheel right!" They were marching straight at a blank wall, as Webbe had got caught up in the excitement of his own speech and were just able to turn in-column. "Head of column to the left! Guide right! Quick march, now!"

CHAPTER 3

On Courtesy

"ALL RIGHT EVERYBODY—LISTEN UP!" Sergeant Webbe was especially nasty that morning: five extra miles of running and everybody shoveled out the latrines; then they cleaned them so "a sensitive soul could eat off the porcelain" and polished all leather until it shown black and brown and red, glistening and nearly reflecting Tynan's face in the work.

"Listen up!" he shouted again. They all snapped to rigid attention, eyes focused miles away.

"All right—parade rest!" The cadets swung to a wide stance, hands clasped behind their backs.

"We want to talk to you about the dining hall, as some of you may find the food not completely to your liking, and while you may not get everything to eat that you ever dreamed of, you'll not starve, either.

"For breakfast, you'll get good coffee with a sufficient quantity of milk and sugar—coffee in the morning is for soldiers and you'll be soldiers—or else! Fresh bread with butter—and eggs: the fruit of the fowl!—and smoked beef or ham or cold meat with radishes, cucumbers, and tomatoes to hide—er . . . *enhance*—the flavor of the meat when in season. And sometimes, porridge with dried fruit. Porridge is the best breakfast food ever made and will help you get used to eating on the march.

"For the midday meal, plenty of fresh water—the elixir of the gods!—to drink. Drink as much of it as you can—it'll help you stay on your feet. Fresh meat: beef, pork, veal, or mutton—well roasted, not raw—with good bread. Potatoes and beets, onions, turnips, cabbage or carrots: all the vegetables your mother ever wanted you to eat and more than you ever thought existed on this good earth. When in season, dried beans soaked in hot broth may be served, but not to exceed once in every six days to keep everybody's digestion in control. And there will *always* be proper sauce or gravy for the meat.

"For supper, tea of good quality with milk and sugar; fresh bread and butter. Then beef, chicken, or pork with a mix of more vegetables. In addition, the steward may choose to serve, once a week, pie for dinner and pudding for supper. Those delicacies are served when and if you have earned them by your attitude and hard work.

"So, no complaining! If it so happens that complaining is heard from *this* cohort—I could care less about *other* cohorts: who knows what unmannerly dolts they are made of?—but *this* cohort will not complain and *will* learn to express gratitude.

"So far; so clear? Good! Now, when entering the dining hall, you will remove your field cap and raise it up to slap the top of the door frame above you while calling out heartily the name of the Ruler of the Feast: 'Policrates'! After slipping your field cap into your belt at your lower back, you will march by files to your table—maintaining the utmost order and complete silence—and seat yourself at the table in the position of attention with your head bowed over your meal and eyes closed to complete one minute exactly of meditative silence. Perfect order and precise manners must be observed at all times at the table with no talking except when spoken to by the table master, a senior cadet who will note any deficiencies in utensil skill or official decorum and endeavor to assist in remedying them. When the meal is finished, you will rise at the same time from the table at the command of the table master, re-form files, and march out, again slapping your field caps on the upper doorjamb and shouting, 'Thank you, Ruler of the Feast'!"

"Now. There are many battlefields in this life that you must make yourself ready to face. Some battlefields are prepared for on the training grounds; some in the library and classroom—a real battle against your own ignorance—and some in the gymnasium; all to make you as ready as possible for the actual fight in the field against an enemy.

"Today you're going to learn about a new fight that you must train for and think about as seriously as any other, as someday you will be faced not with a hedge of spears but an array of forks, knives, and spoons—don't laugh!—not a wall of shields but a neat stack of plates, saucers and bowls; not a field of grass but a table of maneuver just as important and in its own way just as deadly as any field of war you can care to name. I said don't laugh!

"Many a good soldier's career has ended abruptly because he spilled the wine on the general—or worse, the general's wife—or jammed an elbow into his tablemates side or—and this really happened—tried to swallow an uncommonly large, ill-cut chunk of beefsteak, choked and nearly died at the table before, I must add, he had spewed the contents of a first class meal all over five of his nearest neighbors—it was beyond horrifying—*and* earned himself the nickname 'Spew' that stayed with him all his days, undermined his time in the service, and impeded his chances for promotion. So, that unfortunate soul lost his dinner, his career, and his honor all in one moment, not to mention his troop and his own brother officers forever called him by a ridiculous nickname to the end of his days. The dangers are real!"

As the cadets laughed, Tynan was suddenly back at his grandparents' farm. Warm light shown there. Sausage was frying and popping in a large skillet, cups and plates rattled together. He came out onto the wide stone-flagged kitchen floor framed overhead with dark oak beams, well-lit with clean-burning oil lamps set in wall niches and stands. A stone fireplace was there as well; large enough that when Tynan was younger, he had been able to walk into it without stooping.

"Hi! There he is now!" said his grandmother. "Lend a hand in setting the table, will you, Tynan? It's no holiday, you know."

"Aye, no holiday indeed." Tynan said to himself, slinging his pack into a corner and lifting a stack of plates. "When is it ever a holiday around here? Nothing but chores and sheep and work, day in and day out."

Tynan's older sister was setting out platters of bacon, eggs, and potatoes. His cousin Ab was placing the silverware. A large pitcher of cream, a dish of yellow butter, and a stone porringer of oat brose sat upon the time-scarred table. Over the fire, a great black kettle of cider was just coming to brew. Tynan set out the plates, threw himself into a chair, and served himself a large helping of scrambled eggs.

"Well, glad to see you made it," said his stepfather sitting down across from him.

"I had a bad night's sleep is all—nothing wrong with that is there?" Tynan said through a mouthful.

"Nothing wrong except this," said his grandfather, who limped into the kitchen leaning heavily on a staff that served him as a cane. "That you know you need to wait until everyone is seated and served before starting to eat, and—as always—please don't talk with your mouth full, as it can be unpleasing to the sight and damaging to the appetite of others."

"Sorry, Grandfather," said Tynan, putting down his fork.

"How is your leg today, Joss?" said his grandmother.

Joss eased into a chair, propping his leg up on a stool. He was past his seventieth year, still strong and sharp of mind. He reached over and took her hand. "I'll be fine Becca—just a small dent is all."

"A small dent? You pitched into the drain culvert with that cart on top of you. You're lucky to be sitting here in one piece."

His grandfather looked at her and laughed softly. "Likely as not . . . likely as not. Now. All ready?" Then for a moment it was silent in the farmhouse kitchen and the fire crackled on the grate. "Good," he said. "We may begin."

After a few minutes of steady eating, he said, "Well, Tynan, first time over the Rim. How do you feel about it?"

His stepfather broke in. "I still think we should hire Barley to take the flock over. With you stove up and can't go, and Tynan here but a lad, we stand to take a big loss, and those sheep are the future of this place."

Tynan stopped in mid-bite. "I've been with the flocks for two years now and haven't lost a single one."

"You're just a sprig," his stepfather retorted. "First time over the Rim and with the Stowe Market coming on besides, moss rangers will be thick as fleas. I wouldn't wonder if you turned tail at the first sideways look."

Tynan started to speak, but his grandfather held up his hand. "Ebner, you know we can't afford Barley or anyone else. Tynan and Ab here will keep those sheep safe as can be." He stopped and looked directly at Tynan, pausing, then turned back to Ebner.

"Remember that rogue catamount that snatched Bwlch himself and made off with him on the drive up to the Medway Pens? Well, Tynan bearded that cat in its own den, put a slingstone between its eyes it couldn't deal with, collected the bounty, and there's its skin as a rug under our feet before the fire to this day. And that beast had an argument mind you not with words but claws and teeth. Regardless, Tynan got Bwlch back and now Bwlch's our bellwether ram, leading all the flocks and winning shows left and right."

"Maybe," said his stepfather, "and maybe Tynan was just lucky and a good teller of tales."

"That'll be enough of that kind of talk if you please," said his grandfather. "Anyway, what happened to Tynan shows what he can do; and with you needing to get up the road with the big flocks and the other three away with the new army, there's nothing for it."

"New army?" said his stepfather. "That's a fine joke. They're training with mop handles for swords and old buckets for helmets. The only thing they can beat with that gear is a dusty rug."

"That so?" said his grandfather. "Your own brother was killed at Monroe Pass to make an army like that possible—something to start with anyway, so please show some respect at what might be."

Tynan said nothing, looking down at his plate.

"Well—what happened to Eason was bad," continued his stepfather. "But that still doesn't make Tynan the one to take the flock over the Rim."

His grandfather stood and hobbled to the fireplace and reached into the darkened corner by the hearth. "I've been waiting for the right time to give this to you and now is as seemly as any." He returned with a long package wrapped in cloth and handed it to Tynan.

Tynan took it from him and unwrapped it slowly. It was a polished staff that gleamed warmly in the light. It fit well in his hand, was shod with an iron tip, and had a graven ram's horn for a crook, its shaft deeply filigreed with bronze.

"Thank you, grandfather; it's more than I could have asked for."

"May it bear you well, like the one that's borne me along for some sixty years with not a split nor flaw. It's cut from high forest black walnut and a little tall for you now, though I expect you'll grow to match it soon enough."

"I'll do well by you, grandfather," said Tynan.

His stepfather guffawed and turned away. "Enough of this gas. I'm off. Three days from now I'll look for you coming onto the Rim—don't be late or there'll be the devil to pay for the money we'll lose." With that he stumped out of the house and was gone.

"Well, it goes without saying that that boy can be as sour as an old grape," his grandfather said, then turned back to the table. He pulled his cup toward him. "Becca, how's that cider doing?" She brought the kettle over and poured out a steaming mug. They looked at each other for a moment.

"You're right about Tynan and Ab. They're good boys and will be fine," she said. "But you get them to take care, all the same. I've sent three sons to this new king and sacrificed a fourth to the one before him. I've lost too much and can't bear to lose more."

He nodded. "So have I—so have I. But who can say what we can or can't do? We can only hope for the best and take the things that are sent our way. Now, Tynan, Ab," he continued. "Come over and have a look at this map."

Tynan came around the table and looked down on the figured parchment his grandfather was unfolding. It was age-cracked and torn in several places, but the sketched figures and lettering were clear. The old colors must have been brilliant when the map was first drawn, thought Tynan, and they shone in the kitchen light as some kind of translucent glow from an ancient time that had long since faded away.

"You'll need to be mindful of this stretch that winds up to the Old Rim Gate. It's narrow, steep-sided, and falls away sharply into the valley on the east. Many a battle and many an ambush happened right there back before the Border Guard. Keep watching the ridges and high slopes above you—that's where any bad ones will be."

"They always try to take the high ground," Tynan said.

His grandfather nodded and pointed at another place on the map. "Stay alert when you come up over the Rim right here. The road leads through a narrow cutting—a prime spot for moss troopers to pounce if there ever was one, then it's fairly level with broad fields to the Pens." His grandfather sighed a little and folded the map away. "I'd go with you if I could." Then he smiled. "But you boys will do fine if you keep your eyes open and your wits about you."

"We will, Grandfather," Tynan said. "We will."

Tynan and Ab finished eating, then cleaned up and walked out through the morning.

Sergeant Webbe had kept on talking. "And there are other forms and courtesies which must be observed as it is beyond doubt that, contrary to good sense, there will be at some of the events you must attend members of the female-side of the human population, that you will be required to know how to properly behave with. It's the way it is and we must accommodate for it accordingly."

"Do you mean girls, sir?"

"Yes—I mean girls, you idiot—do you think I meant geese?"

"No sir."

"Then keep quiet and at least make people think you're intelligent! More on this later, and I know the rest of you I hope are smarter than this cadet here. And I am absolutely expecting that this cohort will bring further honor to the Academy with its decorum and bearing throughout this . . . hmmm . . . curricula. Or you'll be scrubbing the floor with your toothbrushes—so remember that and keep sharp.

"At the Academy we always give you the chance to practice or improve in real-life or as close to real-life scenarios as we can. Mainly to keep you from embarrassing yourselves or your unit. At least everyone will know that you *should* know better, even if you choose to play the fool or the hog, because you have been trained to know better and it's your own fault if you forget or weren't paying attention, so we've arranged to have a little help from the senior cadet Gold Shield. They'll help you learn and remember."

They went inside to the dining hall, slapping their field caps and saluting Policrates's name and filed to their tables. Tynan's table master was Cadet Major Maggerle, and Maggerle lost no time adding his stinging commentary to the loud noise.

"Cadet! Cadet! Stand to attention and salute when you answer me."

"Yes sir—sorry sir," Tynan said as he sprang from his chair.

"Cadet—that's a dessert spoon not a soup spoon! Don't you know that? Or are you from some backwater swill-house of a village? A soup spoon is bigger and rounder and used for sipping. No—don't pull it toward you; you can spill on yourself if you do that!—sweep it away from you gently . . . gently now—don't hold it like a wrench—delicate, delicate like a painter's brush and for heaven's sake don't slurp the soup like the hogs in the pens slurp the slop back home! Small sips taken quietly, gently is the way—dessert spoons are narrow for simplifying the eating of cake and other dainties—don't laugh!—you'll be thanking the Academy up and down after that first formal dinner where you're not flung out of the room as some kind of country bumpkin that drifted in from the fields with mud on your boots and grime under your fingernails—and by the way, wash your hands and scrape the junk out from under your fingernails—it'll keep you healthy. Do you know what kind of sickness lurks in that muck?

"Now—what do you do or say when you enter a room and are greeted by the host or hostess?"

"Sir, ma'am I am very pleased to be here and thank you for your warm hospitality."

"Very good. And how do you greet a lady?"

"With a slight bow, removing my hat if I have one on and seeing to any needs as far as escort or coverage in bad weather—cloak or jacket or help into a carriage or tram—an assist out of narrow places or if there is danger from ruffians or mere impudents, to stop their mouths and to set upon them with the flat of my sword or even its point if they come armed to try to overwhelm me by numbers or stratagem."

"Correct—and they *will* try, so they can brag about it to their filthy friends. But you must overcome them.

"And what of the dance? Not some vulgar swirling about in a barn somewhere, but a real dance with a first-rate orchestra and formal dinner?"

"I must be willing to entertain any and all requests and not for a moment allow any one of my assigned charges to be left alone or ignored but to see to it that they are attended to and be particular to allow them to dance as much as they would like."

"And what of conversation?"

"It must be like words seasoned with salt—savory, interesting, and varied—not dull or commonplace or the discussing the price of corn or other banalities but with wit—which is not to say jokes or deplorable barracks or bathroom humor—but the wit that delights and uplifts the mind and the spirit through diversion and refreshment."

"And what of drinks and dinner?"

"Not to drink more than two cups of strong drink or mixed wine— it's the third cup that bites like an asp and turns men into garrulous fools. As with soup, sip slowly and tastefully—do not drink enough to over-loosen you tongue, for you must remember you are on duty and must always be aware of spies and untoward advances aimed at wringing information from you that can be used against us in the field of battle or in some sensitive negotiation or diplomatic mission—many of which have been lost or failed of their promise through thoughtless speech or behavior in a social setting."

The lessons continued all through every meal and every situation, until Tynan could be asked about them in his sleep and likely be able to provide a phrase suitable to just about any social occasion.

CHAPTER 4

The Stacks

ONE MORNING EIGHT WEEKS into their training, Tynan, Marc, and a detachment of others were marched to a wide courtyard before an imposing building and halted. On the marble steps stood a small, rounded man.

"Stand at ease!" Webbe commanded. "Professor Siwell and his staff here at this school will teach you things needed for writing, reading, and other tasks. Most importantly, they will make you smarter, which all of you need in detail. Obey them like you obey me and you'll be glad of it!"

Siwell stood quietly before them. "Thank you, Sergeant Webbe. You may return for them in time for the evening meal."

"Carry on!" said Webbe who saluted and marched away.

The silence deepened and settled over them. "Please follow me," Siwell said and began to walk up the stairs. The cadets stood, however, not speaking or moving.

Siwell stopped and looked back. "Oh, yes—my apologies—I had quite forgotten. What is the command? 'Fall out' I believe it to be. Yes, then if you would be so kind as to please 'fall in'—rather strange turns of phrases are they not?—behind me." This last was said with a wave of the hand. The cadets immediately broke formation, walked up behind him into the building, and followed Siwell into a large wood-paneled lecture hall.

"Please take a seat," Siwell said, and they alertly sat down.

"You are the first of a new way," he continued from the lectern. "A new academy, a new fighting force. Before we have taught only the skills, strategy, and tactics of war, which were good in their time and so helped us to throw off a yoke of great oppression. But now in this school, we also want to teach you how to think.

"When you are in these classrooms, you may speak your mind, ask questions, learn to see through the surfaces to the depths. They can both be true and there may be many sides to a question, but we will show you *how* to see. Outside the walls of this building, you are under orders and bound by oath to the king and his lords. However, there will be many times when you must decide on your own what to do—no time to hear an answer or direction back from headquarters—you must decide, and act, and abide the results.

"In those times what you have learned here of language, logic, music, philosophy, and even literature may be what saves you, as the things that have nothing to do with arms, men, and formations suddenly shed light on what you must do in that precise moment. Come victory or defeat, you may find your actions written about afterwards in the textbooks for those who follow in this Academy after you, as they see not merely the mechanics to copy, but the spirit to seize, and the method to model themselves after as to how you won that day."

Just then, Siwell stopped speaking and, looking over their heads, smiled. Tynan turned and saw the doors had opened and a man entered the room. Four guardsmen entered with him and ranged themselves across the back wall as he took a seat in the middle rows. The cadets moved to stand, but he waved them to stay seated.

"Please, don't mind my unmannerly intrusion. What are we reading today, Professor?"

"Welcome, Gerald," Siwell replied. "Today we are meeting *Of Lightning Tethered* for the first time."

"Of course—one of the best!" Gerald said.

Siwell unrolled a scroll and began to read aloud:

> *Poised, at rest; light-balanced seems*
> *On perch or leathern glove.*
> *Hunting searching tracking eyes;*
> *Obsidian glittered gleams.*
>
> *A resting bolt; light with wings*
> *An arrow on a string*
> *A called command at trumpet sound*
> *Into the sky it springs.*

A feathered glister; stroke to bring
Javelin from the sky
A flash of light; a bolt of blue
It makes the air to ring.

Poised, light-balanced, stands a choice;
Corded to the shelf.
Bound in hide, wrapped in clay, rolled in ancient reed:
A wounding word. A healing voice.

For those who heed the call
Of lightning tethered.

Tynan looked sidelong at Gerald. A vague rumor held that he was embarrassed about not being able read or write more than making his personal mark, but others said he could, and simply regretted not having enough time to study—the wars and orders of the king kept him constantly on the march—that he would slip away to the school whenever he had a few spare minutes merely because he enjoyed it.

As Siwell read on, Gerald's face was wrapped in deep attention, eyes half-closed, nodding at certain places, and smiling. Just then, another guardsman came into the study hall and whispered to Gerald. A brief look of disappointment crossed Gerald's face, then he stood up.

"Thank you, Professor! And all of you here: listen to him!" and then Gerald left the hall, his guards filing out silently behind him.

Siwell watched him go, then said, "Some say this work speaks of things long-dead, gone before their time; others that it's a prophecy of things to come. What say you?"

Marc spoke up. "It also may speak of all books and all minds of all time—that their fate is bounded by years and constrained by their own fear."

"Very good! There is concrete specific detail here. But is the image of the falcon something like internal strife or foreign invasion? Or the actual fact of what happened: a nameless fatal blow that struck down the people in such a way they could not recover nor rise again? So if the place were named and visited, what has been written here would be seen by our eyes?"

"It may be a double-warning," Devon said. "A historical event that happened to them—whoever they were—and what could happen to others if we hear not the warning against pride and the high-sounding ignorance spoken against the gods. Destruction may come upon us as it came upon them, not in time of their weakness, but at the peak of their power."

"Hmmm . . . that idea is . . ." began Siwell, then a small side door opened, and a young man entered.

"Ah, Linaes! Very good. We'll continue this discussion at a later time," Siwell said as he rolled up the scroll. "Now if you all please follow along with Linaes, he will show you around the Stacks and get you used to some of its workings."

Linaes bowed slightly. "Thank you, Professor." He waved for the cadets to follow him, began talking right away, and walked out quickly the way he had come.

"You may not know much about libraries—some of you no doubt come from villages that didn't have a written word of any kind except tavern signs, let alone scrolls, parchments, or codexes that you could get close enough to read.

"Beneath our feet is one of the greatest libraries in the western world. Scholars and researchers come from every land to immerse themselves in the tunnels and caverns stacked and piled with scrolls, parchments, and even some very ancient stone tablets, tablets cut in cuneiform letters and reaching back to the very early days of the Old Kingdom. You'll also find references to the Battle of Rollan Bay and other topics that you'll need to research for exams and field exercises for your time at the Academy.

"The Stacks are here to show us of the power of thinking—the ability to see things as they are and to see things as they might be. It's a region in which to read, to think, to dream, and to explore lands not yet known. It's also a sanctuary, an oasis in a desert of moral, intellectual, and ethical chaos. It's a battlefield, a retreat, a well of enjoyment, a refreshment to the soul—all in one place. The Stacks are meant as a repository of memory, a catalyst of action, a place of record and remembrance. A book, a line spoken in the context and unique aesthetic of a specific room, in specific light, on a specific day can guide a person's entire existence and inform their life to its very end. Keep yourself open to it and it can be a friend to you always.

"Just the same, it can be confusing! But follow the letters carved above the passages and niches—you'll find the subject. Find the subject and you'll probably find the work. If not, start back with the first letter of the authors' name. If all else fails, there are helpers in each level who can point you in the generally right direction and can find things for you if you are willing to wait a long while; but you'll save yourself time if you learn the ways of the Stacks yourself.

"And by all means steer clear of the Warden, whom we'll need to speak with today, as we are to view the Annals. He's a tough, old, hard-bitten, and some would say frustrated philosopher of the old-fashioned stoic or even cynic variety—Zeno, Aristo, Crates, and the like—and will sooner swallow poison than let someone he doesn't know or trust near to one of his cherished manuscripts. Stay alert when you come near to his high desk. He'll inspect you like a research specimen and will likely demand letters of proof that you are legitimate students, not some creeping thing wanting only to pilfer a scroll and sell it in some back alley to collectors for an amphora of wine or a few pieces of silver. His attitude toward students and younger folk in general clearly shows he thinks them capable of that and other pernicious crimes against the library and its holdings; and he *will* have your signature—preferably using your own blood as ink—before he'll let you pass him by."

They went with Linaes through the doors into the main hall of the Stacks. The ceiling arched forty feet above their heads, the heavy beams hung with banners, flags, pennons, shields, lances, and other trophies, emblems, and remembrances of battles long ago. High above all in the dim recesses of the hall's highest arch was hung a tapestry, sky-blue with gold woven in the form of the winged horse of Caledon, amid a field of fourteen stars. When the hall was fully lit and a fire burned brightly in the central hearth, the horse shimmered and gently swayed in the soaring upper airs of the high-vaulted room, shining like a golden sun in the blue heavens.

They crossed the flagstone floor to a heavy oaken door and passed through a long corridor that ended in another strong door, this one banded and embellished with wrought iron forming the image of a great tree. Beside the door at a tall desk sat the Warden, who looked to Tynan to be an ancient, withered person of vast unspecified age. They stood there below his rostrum silently for a few moments until Linaes cleared his throat and said, "Pardon us, sir."

The Warden slowly raised his head and looked sidelong warily at them. After several long uncomfortable moments of strained silence, he spoke. "Linaes. You at least I know. The others are less familiar. Not often at your books are you? Hoping to get by on your good looks and natural wit, not that you seem to me to possess an uncommonly large quantity of even those hollow qualities, eh?"

"Ah—they're new students, sir," put in Linaes. "It's hopeful they will become more known to you."

"Doubtful! These all at first profess a need for knowledge, truth and so forth, mostly I'd say in a ploy to gain admittance to the school; then are soon given over to games and hunting and symposia. Just minstrels and the singing of ballads; and jongleurs; jokers who are strong men at drinks and jests, never to have a written word set before their eyes or to attempt to link more than three thoughts in sequence again after they leave this place."

Nothing was said and the group shuffled uncomfortably. "Never mind!" the Warden continued. "You may be able to get on in this world somehow. Linaes, will you swear for yourself and these others with you that upon your person you have no sharp tools nor the means or intent to start a fire?" The fires that had destroyed Alexandria's great library centuries before had irradicably impressed the minds of those who loved books too deeply to risk repeating the tragedy in their own land for the sake of real light, let alone heat.

"I do swear," said Linaes. "And will speak for these, that they too will observe the prohibitions of flame and blade."

"Very well. And what materials do you intend to use or borrow?" said the Warden, with his pen poised over a thick book.

"The Annals of Caledon."

The Warden looked up. "How so?"

"Siwell has sent us to view them, as this will become a customary part of a new students' introduction to the Academy. It is a most serious need of these new Cadets to see and feel and touch what they may one day give their lives to protect, so while it is a great request, there is a greater reason for it. Regardless, Siwell desires these and others like them to be shown the Annals; and has asked me to take them to them."

The Warden nodded. "A very wise idea. I shall need to issue this key to you; and when you come to the place where the Annals are lodged, present it to one of the stewards you will find there and sign the logbook as required by law."

Then the Warden moved slowly and, in an age-worn manner, climbed down stiffly from his high stool, groaning a little; then suddenly stopped, fixing the group with a bright, curious look.

"Never seen anyone old, have you? You're all standing there staring as if you're looking at some oddity in a zoo or something that just dragged itself in from the wild."

"Pardon them again, sir," said Linaes. "They are new to the Academy and some come from benighted towns where respect and honor of the aged does not have room to exist."

"Time does irreparable harm, even leaving out for a moment the accidents of life," the Warden replied. "'*Time and chance will overtake us all,*' if you agree with the gloomy sage who says that and many more things like it. But remember that pessimism is just another philosophical construct, an ordering of what we see and experience toward a predisposed notion based on our personality or temperament or the philosophical tastes or bents merely fashionable for the day or reflecting the searing tests of our world; and so will in due time, whether that time be short or long, be discounted and discarded, as new voices emerge and new views come to the fore."

They stared back at him unspeaking, as if they were unable to take in a word he said or if he had spoken to them in a foreign tongue. "Yes, sir," was all one cadet managed to utter.

The Warden laughed. "Well, maybe you'll learn somewhat better while you're here. Your heroes of the games and the hunt and the drinking table will all find themselves slower, weaker, and less capable before their third decade is barely half gone—and you as well, mind you, you as well: think not that time will pass over you without leaving its mark—but the mob masses will simply worship someone else and forget that the age-long shadows are creeping up on them as well. They just don't know it yet, because the weaknesses come up on regular folk slowly as there's not acute demand to perform or lift or jump or run fast for more than a few minutes, so most people are encircled and taken down unaware. Only the final blow makes any impression on them and most depart this life with a quizzical expression forever etched on their unintelligent, uncomprehending faces.

"But don't let me or others like me alarm you—oh no! Because of course the infirmities and terrors of age—let alone death—will never overtake you. No! You'll be the only one in the whole history of humankind that goes on fresh, hearty, and hale decade after decade, neither fading nor weakening. Hah!"

He shuffled and sighed, huffing slightly; then stopped, trembling, and with great effort straightened himself upright. "Father Time does keep on giving his gifts, though," he said under his breath. "Welcome or unwelcome.

"I've been Warden since your fathers' fathers were suckling babes, which is a fair stretch of years by any reckoning and can still recite *The Voyage* from memory." He must have thought that was a devastating comment, as he paused expecting some reply, but when no one spoke, he shrugged and went on.

"The joints creak, the bones ache, the feet shuffle; the hands tremble, the mind and tongue stumble on the simplest of thoughts. The smallest effort—walking across the room, getting up from that chair as you saw—becomes difficult, nearly insurmountable. It's all written in the ancient treatise *Why Aging*, the questions of why the mere passing of time, the adding up of the years causes such damage to our bodies and minds. Of course, '*everyone wants to live long—no one wants to get old*' as Tertullus said in his day. It's a trouble that besets everyone born on the earth, and some think it's there to remind and forewarn of the final coming separation of body and soul that comes with the irrevocable dissolution which is death. Not much pleasing or comforting in these words, eh? Certainly not! Except maybe the consolation that we are not alone in it; that it comes upon us all, later or sooner without exception; and maybe the life we live between now and then can be less of a regret over wasted time."

The silence from the group was profound. "Sir, perhaps there may be a later time to consider these weighty thoughts that you are speaking for our benefit. I'm sure the cadets would welcome a chance to ask questions and hear more when they are more accustomed to thinking along the lines you are demonstrating?" Linaes said.

"Even more doubtful. Regardless, go in then, and be about your duty," continued the Warden. "Use only these lanterns and always bear these skins of water." He handed them three heavy glass structures. The glass, though clear, was extremely thick and within a single candle burned. By some craft, though, the light shed by these was bright and cheery.

"And above all," said the Warden as he turned to unlock the heavy door and paused to look at them. "Remember Alexandria."

"We will remember," they replied solemnly and passed through while the Warden locked the door behind them.

Tynan immediately felt transported to another world. The walls of books and parchments; not haphazard piles but arranged more like the ordered battle array of some universal profound army—the arsenal of ideas, the armory of concepts, the magazine of the mind—all here for the reading and reflection and marshalling of the thoughts and grand ideas that in some way moved the world as they moved the minds of men. A deep scribal well of knowledge, wisdom, and understanding; enough to make one wise and lose the unlettered simpleton-like diction and speech which had hounded Tynan's steps all his life and now at last could be dealt with and put to rest once and for all. He hoped he would find all this and more.

Reaching a table, Linaes took a scroll at random from a leather bucket and carefully unrolled it. The ink was faded but readable. When he reached the portion he was seeking, he placed a leather sand-filled paperweight on the page and held the wooden roller that marked the end. The parchment was old but not as old as the rooms filled with clay tablets inscribed in a tongue known to few but had been the fount for all the languages that followed and chronicled the early days of the kingdom and were said—some of them at least—to have been brought to Caledon even before its founding and spoke of the wandering of our ancestors after the fall of Mycenae.

Looking over Linaes's shoulder, Tynan was lifted out of himself as the words arranged themselves on the page before him. The thinker who had penned the words had a lively mind and even livelier wit, even catching his readers sometimes with a joke that seemed a fully dead serious argument only to burst upon the page with a gale of laughter; Tynan had to be on guard against laughing out loud.

> *Fear not to hold your own opinions and thoughts against all challengers—the weapons of this warfare are a steady pulse and cool words though the fire that may be burning inside and the issue one of physical or spiritual life and death.*
>
> *Never admit defeat in public discourse except when the future of a single mind or the whole of the people is at risk due to an error of your own but consider carefully the arguments of your adversaries in the silence of your own study and if there is merit, do not resist a change of mind or opinion as this is the way of true learning and even wisdom.*
>
> *Reserve any public admission of an error in judgement or opinion for a more apt time.*

"This is a brief sample of what is stored here, as well as serves as good advice—for that day or any day," Linaes said to the cadets as he closed the scroll. "Let's be moving on."

Within the sprawling chambers of vast size, rows of codex-bound books, scrolls, and manuscripts passed well beyond the reach of their lanterns'

light. There were several people there, some at work at tables, some searching the stacks; all equipped with a lantern and skin of water. Some of these nodded as they passed; most were too absorbed even to look up.

Linaes knew every winding path by each stack, each formidable wall of leather-bound volumes was well-traveled country to him. The knowledge in these dim chambers was a sweet ocean spreading all around and through Tynan. He saw the shelves of books and guessed that other caverns, tunnels, and chambers were bored deeply into the living rock below, holding vast treasuries of ancient wisdom housed below the main tower.

"The caverns are ventilated and heated to preserve the fragile parchments and vellum books from the damages of mold and damp air. A small hostel too is here, to shelter scholars from Caledon and other countries," Linaes said; and they went further in and further down.

As they went on, Tynan noticed or rather felt was an immense ocean of songs without words or speech without words sounding through the immense indoor space, for the Stacks was a building much bigger on the inside than it looked from the outside. Or rather like a mountain glade with a presence within it—so it seemed—in the silence that literally spoke volumes. He felt it as an almost palpable thing, an immense hush permeated with the tang of ink, papyrus, leather, and beneath it all, the centuries-old carved stone of what he later learned were caverns and tunnels and corridors and even vast chambers filled to every nook and cranny with books, scrolls, writings, and quartos—as if the stone heart of the rock had been replaced with the living blood of living words that catalogued and represented the major languages, thoughts, and ideas of the world at the time, stretching back to even the most primitive stones etched and scribed with letters and symbols not now decipherable but connecting on a human level the need to write it down and pass it on to the generations to come, that there were people who lived and thought, and the deeds they did and the things that came upon them in their time, lodged amid the silence and the dim rustle of scholars and pages among the dim towering immensity of the Stacks.

A quite pleasant drowsiness came over him, as images stirred, rose, and swirled around him hovering on the edge of wakefulness and sleep in a vision-like state of alertness. His most living and vibrant thoughts appeared and took shape. He felt the urge to write them down, attempting to capture the power and golden warmth and full-blooded life of the quickly flickering images; some would remain, some faded nearly as soon as seen, and it seemed a constant hunt for the linking thought or continuity of images that would sometimes arrange themselves as a story-like construction or a string of words that suddenly coalesced as a thought.

It *was* cold there—no heat or fire or flame of any kind was allowed in the stack area, so it was common to see professors and students putting on furred cloaks when they entered, though windows set high in the walls of the upper levels allowed much natural light, showing a glorious spring or summer day outside. Fortunately, the Great Reading Room had a bare trace of what could be called heat. The room was a study and reading wing that was reached through immense iron-bound, heat-resistant double doors that enabled him to sit at length; and there it was he began to taste and see that knowledge was what he wanted more than anything else and that between the scrolls and the learned men who taught them he felt his mind opening to what was possible as well as to what was beautiful.

The east wall windows nearly covered half the ceiling space which was sheathed in paper-thin polished crystal that fed the light which bathed the vast reading room for most of the day, the windows facing east and below them three levels of pigeon-holes filled with scrolls each placed in a carefully catalogued cubby-hole, set within a cabinet set back into a carven stone niche. And around the reading room there was a raised stone platform shaped like three steps, used for the lectures.

"This is a living house of scholars," Linaes continued. "Professors from many Caledonian cities and towns make the long journey here to study the priceless collection of scrolls, which were constantly added to by purchase, trade, and continuous copying by a cohort of scribes and students as part of their curricula. To copy out by hand some of the great works and pass them on to preserve knowledge against ignorance, to set a light shining in what could be a devastating darkness, is very worthy labor.

"Most times of the year—even midsummer on occasion—you'll see the Warden and his assistants in here, fighting a constant struggle against mold and decay that gradually but relentlessly eats into the works, reducing them at length to mere piles of useless material. But the fight is worth it. This place has become the heartbeat for us, a symbol of our aspirations and independence of spirit set against the dim slavery of mind and body, soul and spirit, as tyrants pressed ahead with their pretensions to rule.

"The alcoves you see along the outside walls are an ideal place to read and write and think, with a bookcase set perpendicular to the wall before and behind with a small window in each cell and a desk to write and read upon. Various other niches hold statues and carvings of Caledonian figures in literature, history, military as well as small wall paintings

depicting scenes both historic and mythic, while sections of the floor itself
are intricate patterns of set stone and carved wood."

Tynan had had no more than a village school education, often interrupted by the needs of the farm, harvest, sheep shearing, and market
days, but what he tasted had left him with an appetite for something
more: an interest, a curiosity about the larger world. And here before him
was not just a world but a universe of knowledge, a vast land where he
could plunge in as deeply and fully as he desired, following the ideas of
his teachers, each book a door opening to a fresh world; even in the turning of a page could be the remaking of a world. He found himself at times
so lost completely in the thoughts as he sat in the alcoves that the library
attendants would be shaking his shoulder to let him know the Stacks was
closing up for the day and he would be almost surprised to find that he
was at the Academy rather than aboard ship with Cynald, rounding some
distant unknown headland, or following Euclid through a cosmos made
of geometric shapes that combined and recombined in the deep places or
the baths of the northern stars.

It was some time before they at last reached the lowest and oldest part
of the catacomb of books. Set a little apart in a stone chamber of ancient
work, they came upon a plain-looking cabinet, some five feet high and
four feet wide. Its wood was somewhat strange, blackened by great age,
yet glossy and smooth, as wood that has been specially treated for the sea.
And so the old tales claimed: that this cabinet had been fashioned from
the ancient bow wood of Cynald's own ship, shattered upon the Caledonian shore. Here, they found what they were seeking: several scrolls
written in the hand of Terence, the scribe of Cynald, who rode with him
to his wars and composed the histories that gave a voice to the high hard
events of those days.

As the Warden had said, two soldiers stood there, fully armed
with spear, shield, and sword, their armor shining in the glow of heavily
glassed lanterns. They didn't move or speak as the group approached.

"Greetings," Linaes said. "We have come to view the books, the ring,
and other tokens of the time of Cynald contained in the Annals."

"Greetings. Do you have the key?" replied one.

Linaes took the key the Warden had provided and handed it to the
guard, who studied it briefly, then turned and unlocked the heavy door

behind him. The door swung open, the guard stepped in, taking another key from his tunic, and unlocked the cabinet that stood within, then stepped aside for Linaes. "May the days of Cynald soon return," said the guard.

"Indeed—may it be so in our time," replied Linaes.

Inside the cabinet were things some claimed as proof that Cynald, the ancient and legendary founder of the land, lived and walked in time and on earth. Their lanterns illuminated a small gray wooden box, the five books of the Royal Record, and a shield, nearly cloven in two by the force of great blows, its surface battered, dented, and scarred.

Linaes handed his lantern to a cadet and carefully lifted the box from its place to a small side table. Whether what the box and the ring it contained had actually belonged to Cynald or not was a topic long debated. Regardless, they were all aware of the great meaning it held for their land. A messenger would give his life to protect it; the one who received its summons would die to obey. They stood absolutely still as Linaes swung open the top. Within was the ring of Cynald; a simple band of gold set with an engravature of an azure lion of Caledon. Its authority was unquestioned as the call of the king to all the land in times of extreme need. For the king to summon it meant great things were expected or guessed by him.

Linaes then selected one of the books as well and held it up for them all to see, then placed it on the table, opened the book, and read a few lines:

> And so it was in the fourteenth year of the founding of the land of Caledon that a ship was sent to explore the seas to the west. It returned some eight months later with news that it had encountered a large island after sailing twenty-six days and had set a small party ashore but met no one. Beyond this island was only a trackless wasteland of salt sea.

"There is much to be learned in these records," Linaes said as he closed the book and returned them. "Things that all in this Academy are prepared to defend, even to the giving of their own life's blood. Two fair copies can be borrowed and read; and would very much repay the effort expended to do so. For now, we'll continue on to see some of the rest of the place."

It was when they reached the Sun Room that Tynan felt he was confronted with a modern marvel. Linaes paused for a moment before the door. "It may be quite bright in this room, so prepare your eyes. Behold the light." And then he pushed it open and entered, the cadets filing in after him. The light was dazzling; Tynan had a hard time maintaining his balance, let alone taking in what was above and around him. The sun slanted in large windows cut in large panes, diamond in form, reflecting the light and aiming some of the warmth of the sun into the interior. Silvered mirrors, polished and buffed, received the light, channeling it here and there through the library like a huge system of flowing torches.

"The Sun Room employs a technique borrowed from the miners," Linaes said. "They use mirrors to shed light hundreds of feet below the surface of the earth, shining what seems to be a great light into the very heart of deep subterranean darkness, dispelling it for a time. The tracing of the path of the sun through the sky makes it a race against all the sundials of Caledon to get the work done, either the work of the digging of ore, either metals or what the scholars bring up—one from the bowels of the earth; one from the depths of the Stacks—precious ore in raw form to be hammered and sifted and smelted and formed to the coin of the realm or the ideas of the professors and the thoughts of the philosophers.

"It can seem a magic room of the bronze-moved silver mirrors there; a meeting of heaven and earth; a profound synchronization of the music of the spheres and the echoes that reverberated in the minds and souls of those who lived beneath them.

"One of your earliest tasks as new cadets will be to work the levers and turn the handle cranks that guide the movement of the mirrors set in this heliosphere under the central dome to all the areas of the Stacks, the mirrors following the sun in its trek across the heavens. Here you'll spend many days as you learn the motions of the heavens and follow them catching their radiance in the silvered reflections."

Tynan learned to love the Stacks, spending so much time in them that the Warden and his assistants grew to know him well enough to wave them through when he approached the door.

"Just remember to use the lantern and the water; and return the material to its proper shelf before you leave," the Warden or his assistants would say.

He had a favorite alcove to read and study, a corner nook surrounded on three sides by tall bookcases lined with massive leather volumes, some of them chained to the shelf—such was their value—with a small bench and writing desk beneath a large arched window whose sill opened out onto a green quadrangle, small and grass-covered, one of the few view-points in the library, the majority of which was delved deep in the rock below the keep with tunnels, corridors, and paths that wound extensively though the cliff. In the spring, small fruit trees planted against the walls of the quadrangle that caught the most sunlight blossomed a spectacular burst of blue, purple, pink, and red blossoms, followed by apples, plums, and cherries all gathered for the Academy kitchens; cultivated and studied by the botanists and arborists of the court.

Tynan would read and write and think as the day rolled away, sometimes dropping into a deep meditative frame of mind as he strove to decode the early Caledonian poets, philosophers, and sages. The sweet aroma of the place is what belonged to his keenest memories, and sometimes later in life he would open a book or unroll a parchment and the wonderful smell of the library at the Academy would be there and in an instant he would be cast back in memory to the first days when he drank knowledge like strong nectar.

The Stacks were open twenty-four hours and at night hot drinks were served in the Grand Reading Room with small sandwiches—sometimes Tynan dozed off in the muffled silence, his thoughts and near-waking dreams mingling into fantastic visions of apparent glory and insight.

The Grand Reading Room had many tables and lanterns spread across a vast semicircular space with three tiers of high bookshelves around it, the uppermost reached by wooden ladders and small catwalk paths. The catacombs below housed the most ancient works and served as storage of remembrances of past events writers, statesmen, and generals.

Tynan found that he could enter a new world through a book. In its pages, he was transported to places he'd never been and into the lives of people he would never know and even at times into the realm of the spirit, high-flown and breathing the sweet air of thoughts and ideas that elevated him in a nearly physical way, lifting him up and flying toward the sun. It was a sanctuary, a gateway to other lives, other worlds, a portal to knowledge and a pathway to wisdom. And it was quiet, the quiet and cool of studied reflection, the pursuit of knowledge, wisdom, and even higher things.

Tynan found he even liked the smell of the place itself: a warm mix of damp mold, old leather, and fresh-mown hay drying in the field. He later attributed the hay smell to that fact that many of the scrolls were written on papyrus and, despite all efforts to keep them dry, would absorb moisture, seeming in an effort to return to their days growing alongside an Aegyptian river—maybe even the Nile, one scholar had proposed—and the fragrance was somehow pleasing.

There was no escaping the cold though. He'd need to put on a wool sweater as well as borrow one of the fur-lined cloaks that hung on hooks beside the Warden's rostrum to stay even tolerably warm. On most days— except in high summer—he could see his breath smoking before him, and he had to pace in his small study carrel to keep warm. The insulated feel though had its own reward: he felt a wrapping warmth shielding him from the outside world and helping him to see more clearly the flow of thoughts and images stirred up by his reading.

At last, Linaes led them to a central hall, a rotunda of sorts. "There are seven corridors that radiate out from here. See, their names are carved above the entryway: Mathematics, Arts, Astronomy, Music, Rhetoric, and so on. Each of these halls is a way lined with books and scrolls according to the topic, with study chancels, rooms, and niches designed to be places for further thinking."

Tynan wondered at the craftsmanship of the frescoes, carvings, and tapestries hung along the way, scenes of Caledon's past lining the hall of each subject. Life-size statues stood at intervals—professors, kings, leaders—a history wrought in stone figures. Rows of shelves dark gray-brown with wire-screened doors protected the books and let air circulate around them—'to ward off the ill effects of the damp' said Linaes—running three levels high along all the hallways into the distance. Tynan felt these corridors would be important to his life, the path ahead into the future of what might be.

"What do you think of it now? As we said, it can be confusing!" Linaes said. "The place can seem to be a regular warren of twisting passages and corridors, but the Grand Reading Room is a helpful landmark of sorts and always open, so if you stray, find your way there. As a reminder, for now, learn to follow the letters and you'll find the subject. Find the subject and you'll probably find the work. If not, start back with the letter and follow the author's name. As a last resort, the helpers like myself at each level can point you in the generally right direction—but you'll save yourself much time if you learn the ways of the Stacks on your own."

No one answered and Linaes continued. "I think we've covered enough and more than enough ground for one day—the experience can sometimes be overwhelming at first and takes some getting used to. Let's return to Siwell and he will instruct you as to how to proceed on the journey before you."

CHAPTER 5

On Running with Horses

THE HORSEMEN GALLOPED SINGLE file into the training arena. The riders were all cadets and absolutely silent, each horse galloping in step and in time at the same cadence with each other, so the entire effect was one of magnificent beauty and power. The cadets all wore full armor and carried throwing darts and small buckler-type shields. They pivoted left in front of the grandstand—not paying attention to any of the watching cadets who filled the stone benches—riding within inches of each other without touching, then galloping at top speed around one circuit, then a second circuit.

A single hand signal went up from the leader and they wheeled in line, galloping line-abreast straight at the cadets. At a second signal they drew their javelins simultaneously. Three strides from the grandstand, they raised their javelins; then one after another flung them at posts arrayed in armor as foot soldiers, each javelin striking the post one after the other, following a pattern middle, high, low, equidistant from each other.

Now the squadron galloped counterclockwise, drew their second javelin, and rode straight through a series of jumps over barricades, speared a ring hanging from a cross bar, then flung them at another set of targets arrayed as mounted horsemen, which were transfixed with sixteen javelins at the end. They wheeled in line again at a hand signal, drew their swords with points levelled ahead and the riders bending low—nearly prone—over their horses' necks, then they charged full gallop again at the grandstands, halting within inches of the wall, every point level with each other so it appeared as a line of bronze fire flickering in the sun. Without a command, they resheathed their swords, bowed on their horses, then pivoted left and trotted silently out of the arena by the gate they had entered.

As the dust settled slowly and Tynan gazed at the target stanchions, bristling with javelins, a lone horseman rode in and reined up in front of the silent cadets.

"What you have just witnessed is what you can and will be," said the officer. "Tomorrow you will start your own journey to being a horseman. Dismissed!"

The next day, a crowd of cadets had gathered in the arena filling the stone benches, laughing and talking. Tynan recognized a few as riders from the performance the day before—glowing with satisfaction—and staring out on Tynan and his unit with an odd, disconcertingly eager look of anticipation.

The horsemaster rode in and reined to a halt. "This exercise will require all four of you working together to catch and bring under control four horses, one for each man of the cadre. Those beasts are as wild as they come and most have a definite predisposition against humans—especially it seems they don't like the way people smell—so prepare yourselves to encounter a handful of lightning and earthquake on four hooves."

Kiefer grasped the training line and stood to one side of the pen's gate. Devon held the saddle; his job was to sling it over the horse's back and cinch it down. Marc had been nominated as the first rider, being the most skilled and least heavy of the cadre. Tynan was there to help Kiefer hold on for dear life; the colts they had drawn were massive, strong, and aggressive, having already earlier that morning sent one of the grooms to the infirmary and were now systematically—and happily, Tynan couldn't help but think—kicking the wooden interior wall of the pen to splinters.

The horse sergeant grinned strangely as he checked their stations. "You all take care around these 'uns. They look mean and spiteful, so be extra specially careful or you'll be digging yourselves out of the arena floor minus a few essential body parts."

"All ready?" shouted the horsemaster, who then blew a whistle and the arena corral hands slipped the gate loops and the gates flung open. The horses were out of the pen like an arrow shot from a bow, knocking Devon down and would have dragged Kiefer across the ring if Tynan hadn't jumped on the rope and together they were able to hold one of them barely in check.

The horse lashed a kick that flashed by Tynan's ear.

"Be careful! These animals are wild and green. Any approach from a strange angle may get your head stove in and them horses will think they're doing you a favor, protecting themselves and the herd," the horsemaster shouted as he rode by.

All around them chaos had ensued. Cadets were being dragged, stomped, bucked off, and trampled while the people in the stands were laughing uncontrollably, pointing, and hooting. At one point, Tynan was whiplashed against the side of the arena right below some of the loudest hecklers and as his head rung, and he spit sand out of his mouth, getting up on his hands and knees he looked up into the crowd and saw a girl who sat still, one of the few not taking part in the mirth of the festivities, in the midst of the revelry one who seemed to be looking out at the horses with compassion.

Tynan scrambled up, snatching the rope as Kiefer was kicked over the top of him, crushing him back into the muck that the arena floor was fast becoming. Marc had somehow grasped a horse by its mane and Devon slipped on a bridle, then quickly slung the saddle across its back, and cinched the belly band snug. Marc swung up and gripped the reins, holding them close-drawn. Tynan thought the horse must have been tiring by now, but the feel of the weight of something alien on its back sent it off into new furies, snapping the training rope and bucking high as it charged around the arena.

Tynan and Kiefer lay exhausted in the dirt and watched as Marc gradually got the beast under control, slowing to a walk, then stopping altogether and with an expert touch guiding the horse across to a hitching post and tying it up. After they had secured three more horses and guided them into stall boxes, they stood—a tattered, dirty, and bloody group, attempting to appear somewhat orderly—and waited for the horsemaster to inspect and allow them to lead the horses out of the arena to the stables.

Tynan was cleaning up in the stables and looking sidelong at his horse, whose power and high spirits had flung Tynan to the ground many times that day—hardly any improvement on the wild mustang he'd help wrangle across the line—as well as covered them both in the grime of the arena.

"It's horrible the way those horsemasters try to train them with whip rope and spur—it makes slaves not partners."

Tynan turned and looked at the voice. Leaning against a pillar of the stable stood a girl; the girl he'd seen in the spectator's box earlier that day who was obviously not enjoying the proceedings.

"You don't look like you've ever ridden?" she continued.

"Other than my dad's old cart horse, I've never ridden before."

"Cart horse? That isn't riding; that's being carried along like a bit of baggage. You're a scratch job and no mistake, but who knows: you look tolerably smart and have a brighter eye than most."

"Can you do better? Some say our cavalry and the horses that are part of it are the best in the world today."

"The best for what?"

"Well, fighting, patrolling, and such things."

"That's nonsense. We only say it because there is nothing to compare them to. Why shouldn't there be some land beyond the encircling sea that has better? The worst thing would be to find out too late that we haven't the best, wouldn't it? Losing some pivotal battle because we were outclassed in the crucial field?"

"Hmm. If you put it that way, of course. But how does anyone know for certain which side has the best riders and horses? A country can't be the best at everything, can it?" Tynan replied.

"Perhaps. But I've heard of riders in the East that have a single mind and will with the horse. I half-believe the tales because I've tried some of the training methods I've heard by rumor on my own and they help."

Her eyes flashed as she spoke, and she looked down on Tynan, taller than he at their age. "But I can see you're like the rest—just an unthinking drudge who'll march lockstep to whatever they're told; and the home-side is always the best and always right."

Tynan shrugged. "Don't let me stand in the way of Caledon's only genius horse trainer," he said and stepped back bowing slightly and waving her toward Phaeton, as his horse was named.

She looked him straight in the eye, then moved toward the horse. The horse skittered and shied away from her, bobbing its head to avoid the bridle.

"Always come slowly from where they can see you; they're afraid of anyone or anything they don't know," she said in a low voice. "Never approach a horse from the right or left rear, as they can't see well in those directions and easily take fright; and as you know, their slashing hooves can do you a lot of damage if they happen to connect."

"Who are you?" Tynan asked as she slowly approached the horse, continuing to talk quietly to it.

"Can't you see me? I'm Lydia—and you obviously need help with this horse. One can see in an instant he doesn't like you or trust you."

"What makes you say that? How would you know anything?"

"Do you want help or not?"

"If you can show me something that helps, I'd be grateful. I can't get him to do anything."

"Of course you can't," Lydia said as she moved to a position ninety degrees and about five feet from the horse's head. "You're like the others who think the only way is to dominate and bludgeon the poor beast into submission. That ridiculous display in the arena with the mustangs proves time and again that the horsemasters are mindlessly brutal. They won't listen or learn any other way and have needlessly ruined many good horses. My father is the worst of them: all bluster, and boots, and thumbs."

Tynan's horse noticed her and rotated its ears quizzically in her direction.

"Here, boy, nothing to fear," Lydia said and held out a closed fist. The beast sniffed it for a moment, then she turned her hand over and uncurled her fingers until her hand was flat, stretched out palm up; and there was a cube of sugar. "Go ahead, it's yours," she said quietly to the horse who snuffled it up, crunching the sugar loudly, and let her pat its nose. Then she moved a little closer, showing the horse the bridle. "Take a look at it—nothing to fear from it at all." The horse sniffed it briefly and let Lydia lay the bridle gently on the side of its neck. Soon in this same way Phaeton was bridled and the saddle was slid on, Lydia moving all the while slowly and quietly.

"Horses fear everything. As big as they are, they are the prey of other animals, so they stick together fiercely in a herd and will lash out or flee panicked at anything they think of as a predator or threat. But once they're trained and used to something, they are fearless; and once they recognize you're the lead horse, they'll follow any command and go anywhere you ask them to go: across a river, through a burning building, off a cliff—if you're with them and if you praise them afterwards.

"To do it, you *must* become the leader of a herd of two. In the wild, the lead horse comes to the water first with herd spread out behind—he checks for dangers, predators, drinks a few sips to ensure the water is safe

and good, then backs off to stand guard while the rest of the herd drinks
its fill. Then and only then does the leader return to drink for themself."

As she spoke, Marc, Kiefer, and Devon had stopped what they were
doing and gathered round Tynan.

"Who's that?" whispered Devon. "She's magnificent." The other
three looked at him strangely. "Er, I mean the horse . . . the horse is
magnificent."

"That horse is a *he*," Kiefer snorted.

"Of course. I meant she's magnificent with the horse; it's like it's under her spell."

"That so? Who's under whose spell, I'd be wondering?" Kiefer said.

"I don't know who she is," Tynan said. "She calls herself Lydia, and
showed up after the wild horse race, saying she knew how to handle
horses better than the horsemasters."

"She's the daughter of the Marshal," Marc said. "He'd be furious if
he knew she were here, especially if he knew she was talking to the likes
of us."

"The Marshal? I've met him . . . he's a formidable man." Tynan said.

"You've met him?" Marc said. "How did you manage that?"

"He's, uh, had me play my pipes for him a few times since I've been
here."

"Take care that you don't mention anything about Lydia being here
if you come near him again. He'd likely have you cleaning out the pig
styes or even living in them permanently if he ever caught you—or any of
us"—this last to Devon and Kiefer as well—"talking or even looking too
directly at his daughter."

"No need to worry; she's only here for the horses," Tynan replied.

"You blockheads," Lydia interrupted. "Were you paying any attention at all? Probably not; just hobnobbing ignorantly among yourselves,
no doubt. Remember—horses are *intelligent*. Treat them like your own
kin and they'll be more than kin to you.

"Fortunately for you, the horsemasters are at least smart enough
not trust any of you with any of these. At first, you'll get assigned to a
training-horse so you'll be less likely to be killed outright by your own
foolishness. Then, *after* you have proved you know a small something
about horses, you'll start training with this one and the others."

"What will we do meanwhile?" Devon asked, taking a step closer.

"You'll learn to do what the horse handlers do. They labor and care
for the horse, to give it the strength and courage to go into a battle: able

to run full out, bumping hard, stopping and turning on a dime, 'heart as big as the sky' heads high, ears forward, and coats glistening.

"Horses never say no once they trust you, so it's up to you to care for them, help them to rest, help them to find a good pace; first you and then the horse handler, polishing their chiseled muscle to a power inspired by passion, courage, and a fervent love of action. Horses are one of the earth's most glorious creatures and need to be treated so."

Lydia finished speaking and looked around at them. "Well, what are you standing around for? Please brush them down and get their feed—do you think they can do it themselves?"

The horse trainers entered the covered riding hall, leading strings of four horses, each bridled and saddled with a light leather saddle no thicker than a thin pad. They walked together to the center then turned facing Tynan and his cohort, who were all standing rigidly at attention, saluting the officer.

The horses they led were all high-spirited, raised in the semi-wild fells and open grasslands of the West, of hardy stock—fearless and tireless—able to canter at great speed and gallop with almost racing-horse speed over distance of less than a hundred meters. Most of them were brown or dark brown, a few black; not the largest horse, but pound-for-pound competitive over most ground and in most circumstances. The Caledonians raised some of the best horses heard of in the West, but no one had ever seen those rumored to live in the eastern regions—bred slim and high-strung for speed and delicate beauty.

"All right," the training sergeant said. "You may know nothing about horses and their ways. In fact we expect that you know nothing and indeed the less you know or think you know the better. Take a good look at them. They and their brothers will be your main care and concern all the days you are in this man's army. If you care for them, they will care for you. They can become your inseparable partner and may someday even save your life. But if you neglect or mistreat them, they will be a bane to your existence and one day when you need them most, they will fail you and leave you standing in the path of death or destruction with no way out.

"They must trust you first: everything depends on that one thing. When you have earned their trust, anything is possible—without the trust it will be a constant struggle to overcome resistances, a tug-of-war that often ends with a flat refusal, even laying down or worse, going into what could only be described as a deep depressions, which is sometimes even fatal to the horse."

Tynan looked at the horse opposite to him, the third in the string to match his own position in the cohort, a dark brown almost black stallion, calm yet bobbing its head and sometimes prancing energetically on its lead. The name engraved on the brass ear plug was Dart.

"Horses can be dodgy creatures," the sergeant went on. "Skittish and liable to kick out or bolt if they get nervous. Fight or flight is their normal way, and mostly flight if they have a choice, so get them used to things slowly; new things easy-like—nothing too fast and no more than one lesson a day. One new thing a day and not too much of that, or it'll make 'em dispirited and downtrodden feeling. Nothing worse for a horse than overwork; they just give up the ghost. But if you take them gentle step-by-step, one day they'll be able to charge full-tilt through a hedge of spears or a wall of fire, and come back eager for more.

"These now are training mounts—old veterans who have been in wars and under saddle for years. They'll help you learn the military commands and ways of horses, and will be like your battle partners that will train with you from this day on. You'll learn how to care for them, giving them more time and attention than you give yourself, and together learn how to ride, fight, patrol, recon, parade, guard the commanders, and track moss troopers. But mind! They're not above giving you a nip or hard knock from time to time to get *their* point across, so stay alert.

"Always come slowly from where they can see you and remember they're afraid of anyone or anything they don't know. Never approach a horse from the right or left rear flank. They can't see well in those directions and easily take fright; and their hooves can do you a lot of damage if they happen to connect.

"Now, take a handful of mane with your left hand and swing your right leg up strong now! Don't hesitate. Take the reins in both hands and sit up onto to saddle—smoothly now—don't touch its sides when you come over its back, then sit firmly."

Suddenly Tynan found himself sitting up on the horse's back. The horse shifted its weight from hoof to hoof patiently. Its ears flicked forward and back.

"Good! Now slip the reins between your fingers of your right hand and let your legs hang down loosely, toes pointed slightly outwards. Pat the horse gently as you do—reward him, make him feel good about doing what you tell him to do. Then, very lightly touch your heels to the horse's side—*very* lightly."

Dart started off at a slow walk. As Lydia predicted, Tynan did feel like a piece of ill-strapped baggage, holding on awkwardly, jostling up and down, bobbing from side to side, barely able to hold on, leaning on the horse's neck, grabbing its mane. The horse didn't like this at all and nipped Tynan on the arm. Dart was an aged cavalry charger that had been in wars and had the scars to show for it. He was used to new riders, but it took him less than a minute to show Tynan that he was the product of old battles.

They walked once slowly around the ring, then trotted around for a few minutes, then rested. The group would train every day for the next ten weeks, working together one or two hours, gradually moving from a walk to a trot to a canter to a fast canter then full gallop, all done with weapons, without weapons; then over broken hilly terrain among ridges, through streams—even learning to swim rivers, with Tynan fully armed holding the saddle with one hand and swimming alongside with the horse between him and the current, springing out of the water as they scrambled up the far bank.

An hour later the riding master called a halt. "Enough for one day. You all did well to stay onboard this long. Now dismount and lead them into the stables. Each stall is numbered to match the number on the horse—the stable master will show you how to rub them down, water, and feed them and see they're properly stabled. Treat them well and they'll treat you well; treat them poorly and they'll fear and hate you and will likely desert you in your greatest time of need in some battlefield or in a remote place a long walk from anywhere.

"Other countries beat and drag their horses to obey—and those horses are smart and remember things, seizing the first moment to throw or abandon their masters and escape before their spirit is completely broken. If it happens that their spirit is shattered and beaten down due to neglect or rough handling, you can be sure they will be no good and so our opponents defeat themselves and come to grief. They don't understand the horse, so they ruin them, converting them to cart or pack animals only and rely on the infantry—infantry which is very good, by the way; their regiments are the arguably the best in the world, but our combined arms—horse, foot, peltasts, siege artillery, and navy together—are the finest fighting force at present on earth—at least the earth we know of.

Let's work to keep it that way! You train *with* the horse and he'll want to be your very best friend in any hardship or condition."

Several weeks later, Tynan, Marc, Devon, and Kiefer led their new horses into the training ring. "I must say those training horses have a mind about them and knows what's on foot," Tynan was saying as they walked in. "They understand trumpet calls, lean the right way, and in a battle would be a big help in keeping me from being kicked off by some Terasian trooper."

The horses suddenly skittered and shied away, bobbing and lifting their heads to avoid the bridle, and began to trot in a circle. Tynan tugged on the lead and Phaeton pulled hard, dragging Tynan a step.

The next ten minutes were a frenzy of scuffling horses with the cadets shouting and stumbling after stray mounts, trying to coax or strong-arm them back by any means possible. It took some time but Tynan was finally able to wrangle his horse to a standstill.

"No!" said Lydia, who was watching over the training ring wall. "Is muscle-power all you can think of? They're just not used to the place. Remember that the lead horse will make sure all is safe for the others, then drink or eat himself last of all, alert for predators, protecting their herd.

"You *must* be the lead horse. Stand tall and face one direction. He'll see you're not intimidated or following him—you're taller, bigger than he is, so shorten the rope for him to notice you are wanting him to do something else. *You* must lead." Sure enough, the horses slowed down, coming at last to a slow walk, then halted. Phaeton tossed his head eyeing Tynan, one ear cocked toward him.

"Steady on," said Lydia. "Steady on. Wait for him to turn and face you." The words were hardly spoken when the horse did just that, both ears forward, looking at Tynan. "Now, give a gentle tug on the lead." Tynan did and the horse took a step toward him. "Keep a slight tension on the lead—he'll know what you mean." The horse took two more hesitant steps, snorting and unsure. "Now reach out your hand, closed fist down, and let him smell it."

Step by step, Tynan and Phaeton trained together and learned each other's ways. Phaeton, however, was not above bucking Tynan off from time to time or trying to bolt off in an unexpected direction.

"When you fall, learn to fall loosely, even floppy," Lydia said. "Tensing up causes you to be really hurt—be like a rag doll, a limp cloth, a wet noodle—you'll get bruised and scraped a little but nothing serious. Roll yourself into a ball if you can and you'll bounce harmlessly.

"Keep your focus and physical cues in harmony, concentrating on what you're doing, where you're going. The horse will sense your focus and respond with the quickest, most efficient way to do it. Remember that your horse will remember—better and more clearly than you and longer than you. Some things he will never forget, so be consistent."

"For the past ten weeks, you have been trained by a horse—from now on you will train with a horse, the horse that you wrangled together on the first day in the ring," said the horsemaster. "No question in my mind or in the records of this Academy that this is the most serious phase of your training and the partnership with your horse, a partnership with the most important fellow soldier on the field of battle. These which are gentle creatures now will learn to charge fearlessly into a defended line of infantry, become fierce warriors—fiercer than you can imagine, nearly bloodthirsty and enthusiastic competitors for one reason and one reason only: they will put their ultimate trust in you, and whatever you ask them to do, they will do wholeheartedly, because you have taught them to overcome their in-born fear which is to run or seek the safety of the herd.

"They theoretically will become something more than just a horse; and will in effect worship you as their god, the leader of a herd of two. They will become extensions of your mind, your will, your energy, and be more than happy to rush to death at your command." He paused and the quiet neighing and shuffling of the young horse's feet was all that Tynan heard. "But you must earn their trust and maintain it. You are the leader, but if they feel fear or hesitation, they will reject you or resist you, and in battle that would likely be fatal to you both. Be worthy of their trust! Treat them well: tend to their needs before your own; make sure their stall is clean, make sure they have the best fodder you can afford, use only the best tack and saddlery. Train and work with them every day and they will—mark my words—they will save your life someday. Treat them poorly, neglect or abuse them, and they won't be there when you need them most.

"Their strength and inner spirit are far deeper and stronger than you can imagine. And they are more intelligent and capable than you could begin to appreciate. It's said some of the wild southern tribes worship them as a type of divine being and prize the ones they've captured nearly above their own kin. The great ones are born and trained as we protect them along their way to their destiny, when they—with you astride them, maybe—carry the line or break the shield wall or ride nonstop for three days to deliver the message with the lives of men, kings, and countries at stake.

"They will respond with precision and grace: a thousand pound fellow warrior then can turn on a moment's command and move without fear into the thick of battle. The weapons you wield are seen as extensions of you and will not harm them; and they learn to fiercely hate the colors, smells, and looks of the enemy, everything and everyone who is not you. Now, let's continue."

Before long, they were comfortable with trotting, cantering, and even short gallops, with equipment and weapons, or without, riding figure eights and learning to jump over low barriers on command. The care and training of both horse and rider took up full days at a time, riding indoors in the covered riding ground, outdoors across all sorts of terrain—flat, hills, broken landscape, forests, rocky ground.

They traversed steep slopes, crossed narrow ridges, walked along sheer drops, always working under the instruction of the horse master, becoming one in mind and will, though Tynan was the leader of the two-horse herd, so that his will became the will of Phaeton, as he spoke to him and as he rubbed and oiled the horse's dark gray coat to a bright shine for innumerable inspections.

Phaeton had a fiery personality that would make itself known, especially in the intra-cohort games they played, one cohort against another in which a small, wooden ball was struck with a long wooden mallet through upright posts at either end of a wide grass playing field, four horsemen to a side, a game that had been handed down for centuries and some said came for the distant East when great kings played it with their courtiers to train for the rush and cut of high-speed combat on horseback.

The winners of the local tournaments played each other in the Great Tournament that was staged each year at the graduation of the Academy classes. At the Lodging of the Colors, in which the class was awarded its own coat of arms, banner, and regimental name in a ceremony of great pomp, the class would parade before the king himself and place them in the Hall of the Colors, where all horse guard companies from time immemorial in Caledon arrayed their colors and built monuments and memorials to their great men and of the battles in which they had served.

The hall where they trained was a very serious—even somber—place but one that reflected the glory of the army, and Tynan felt instilled in him the feeling of being part of something larger, of being a participant in the crucial events of his time, continuing the tradition and values of their country, which were worth preserving in the world at that time and would be, at least in his generation, the freedom to speak, to have a say in the government of the land, to rise in the culture due to merit, to have a part in how the land developed, what was put into law, and what was written in the books. Not every country or land was so constituted—many were ruled by despotic kings or worse, tyrants who used the people and the land for their own personal gains and glory and viewed others as fuel for their ambitions. At least in Caledon, the worst of these abuses were curbed by the Archons of the Assembly, though of course nothing was flawless, and abuses occurred, and kings were overthrown through barely lawful—some would say unlawful—proceedings.

Regardless, Tynan and Phaeton melded together in the next months while passing through a blurred whirlwind of marching, running, orders, details, equipment, and formations. Training with spear, sword, bow, and shield—first with heavy wooden copies then blunted bronze weapons of actual weight and size. Learning to know each other, taking better care of each other than they did of themselves; a slow acquaintance gradually built on learned mutual trust until horse and rider were bonded as nearly one being, able to ride through a wall of fire and—indeed—were tested on this very obstacle in a field exercise, coming through singed and slightly smoke-damaged but able to form up and press home the attack.

CHAPTER 6

The Rise of Spring

MARC CAME INTO THE stable carrying a bag of oats and dropped it near the horses' stone feeding trough.

"Well," he said. "We've been ordered to stand watch at the Rise of Spring ceremony tomorrow."

"Rise of Spring? What's that all about?" Tynan said as he tightened the girth and checked the quarter strap on his horse's saddle.

"It's a tradition that's supposed to be a kind of forecasting of the future. All the wise folk will be there, taking notes, hobnobbing, and generally predicting the end of the world."

"Bad luck for you," said Kiefer. Tynan looked across the stable aisle at him. "That kind of thing is a pile of cantrip from my point of view."

"Cantrip it may be, but it's bad luck for you as well," returned Marc. "You're to be there and when you see Devon, let him know."

"Let Devon know what?" Devon himself walked by yawning and looking around bleary-eyed.

"We've got to stand guard at the Rise of Spring ceremony tomorrow—at sunrise no less!" Kiefer said.

"Sunrise?" said Devon, looking shocked. "I'm not sure I've ever been up that early; and honestly, standing about contemplating the sky at that hour sounds like a dreary time."

"Dreary it will be, but we've got to be there before the sun rises tomorrow," said Marc, who led his horse out of its stall and into the sunshine while the other three finished getting ready, then followed him.

Tynan had been looking forward to today's training ride. It was the kind he enjoyed, as it was a variation on a follow-the-leader game he'd played back home. Each of them would in turn take the lead of the squad and whatever the leader did—jumping obstacles, zig-zagging through trees, figure-eights—the rest had to mimic at the leader's pace while maintaining the proper military interval. Failure to do so meant extra duty for all and coming in last during the final race back to the stables meant mucking out the stalls for a week, so that afternoon Tynan planned to hold nothing back on the last stretch.

They rode for three hours together weaving in and out of formation, cutting back and forth skillfully. After a halt and a brief rest, the four of them arranged themselves in line for the final dash back to the stalls and at Marc's signal, spurred their horses toward the curious blue-tinged walls of the compact Academy fortress, which looked that day like far mountains seen through a dim haze.

Over the smooth green ride that paralleled the main road to the Academy they raced, forming a tightly bunched group that hammered the ground. As they turned along the final sweeping turn, Tynan urged Phaeton on, giving him his head and letting him take the bit in his teeth, and started pulling away from the others.

Without warning two small children stood up from a sandpit not ten feet ahead, directly in the path of the furiously galloping horse. Phaeton stopped in a step and plunged away in an abrupt right turn. Tynan could not maintain his seat as the horse swerved and whirled; and was flung high above the astonished upturned faces of the children, crashing to earth in some longer grass. He lay there gasping and choking, his breath knocked from his body.

An old woman who was minding the children pounced on him at once. "You big oaf! You and your mighty horses rushing about. Can't be of any good to anybody. And these but two bits of girls. For shame! Play your high games somewhere else and stop bothering the common folk. Why . . . it's a miracle anyone here lives to see their tenth year!" Her two charges giggled from behind her field dress, as her words were being punctuated by swatting Tynan on his chest with a bundle of cut flowers.

Sitting on their horses nearby, his friends laughed loudly. "Leave off beating him, woman!" called Kiefer. "Don't you know that he may someday be a guardsman?"

"Guardsman or no, he should watch where he's driving that great lumbering beast. All the same," her eyes suddenly glistening. "I thank you that you turned from my Reda."

"You're very welcome," gasped Tynan.

One of the children, a young girl not six years old ran up and leaned over him. "Sir, I'm glad that you didn't hurt my flower," as she showed him a field lily, yellow and freshly picked. She turned to go, then turned back again. "Since you saved it, you may have it," and placed the lily gently in his hand.

"Reda," Tynan said weakly. "Thank you."

Reda ran toward the town with her small friend, herded along by the old woman's voice. "Don't go running onto the road! Watch those horse carts!"

Marc and the others rode up. "What a spectacular fall! Thank heavens the ground was there to receive you!"

"Yes, thank heaven," groaned Tynan as he raised himself onto his elbows. "How is Phaeton?"

Devon was tracing the horse's legs with his hands. "Seems sound. Nothing broken or torn. He's not limping nor cringing."

"For that I'm glad," said Tynan. "Though I think I shall be regretting this fall for the next few days. Help me up, will you? I'm not certain I can manage on my own." They helped him slowly to his feet, shaky and bruised.

"I hope this is not a taste of the year to come," said Marc as they remounted and started at a slow walk back.

"You mean the Rise of Spring? It didn't seem there was much to it—just an official gathering of some sort," Tynan said.

"I guess we'll see tomorrow won't we? It never pays to have a completely closed mind about those sorts of things, as one never knows when it may touch upon something real."

The next morning they rose, met Devon and Kiefer for an early breakfast, then marched out into the semi-gray darkness. A light mist hung suspended between stone and sky. High above them, the Blue Keep itself loomed darkly in the southwest corner of the compound, where they would stand on its platform above the murk, with a clear view east.

As they climbed the many stone stairs that early morning, Tynan thought about what he had learned of this place near which the sea swept in against a dark stony coast and green moor grass grew to sheer drops, softening the edges of the blue-black glistening sandstone. Fierce winds flung sea foam vaulting over the high cliffs, driving torn clouds into the eastern mountains, scouring stale thinking from mind and soul.

It was near here long before—or so the old histories claimed—that Cynald had made landfall, driven by a fierce gale and the ruin of the world before the Old Kingdom. Here, he had planted his banner and built this tower, founding the land of Caledon.

In this tower Cynald had placed his cloven shield, his signet ring, and the records of the royal house, the annals of the ancient long-generations before him; then he led his people to the more pleasant lowlands to build there his capital city and to settle the earliest of the Caledonian people.

Then a day came when he sailed away into the West, and he never came back again. Thus, for Tynan and many others Cynald had become a jumble of vague ideas and fragments of dim memory, the story of his times better a tale told to amuse small children by a fire burned low on a windy night than a history to be wagered on by Academy scholars.

Other lords of more certain history had risen in his place and strengthened the keep, adding a strong curtain wall, a spacious main hall, and stone stables all built of the same curious blue rock of this edge of the island. Each king had taken the endowment and supported a garrison here to stand watch from its rocky exposed height, and the keep had become the keystone stronghold of a chain of watchtowers along the borders, towers that watched the horizons.

At last, they came out onto the uppermost platform, and they were in time: the sun had not yet risen. Siwell was late, but the clerk who watched over the proceedings and had kept records of many spring-risings past was there as well as Cage and a few others, all of whom peered steadily into the gloom as if to see into the uttermost east. The battlements of the keep were damp and cold. Below, a sea of fog rolled and swirled about the foot of the walls, cloaking the green moor. From the watch platform five hundred feet above the bailey floor they looked out over a soft gray carpet to the margin of the world, and the sky unfurling beyond was a growing spectacle of red, orange, and blue.

"Well," said Cage. "How comes the spring?"

"As far as it goes, it seems well," replied the clerk. "But the morning has not been truly born. Still, it looks to be a normal birth of a lively year."

"A spring to remember, do you suppose?" continued Cage.

"The seasons are all memorable in their unique way," said the clerk.

"You are quite right," said a voice behind them. Tynan turned and saw Siwell, breathing hard and bent over with both hands on his knees for some time, sweating heavily despite the chill.

"Siwell!" said Cage. "You would do well to spend a bit more time training your body to work better under effort. It might save your life someday and will certainly save you the embarrassment of such moments."

It took a minute or so for Siwell to catch his breath. When he did, he ignored Cage's remark completely and continued. "The years are themselves each new, and a page in the growing tale of time." He paused and looked doubtfully east. "But how unrolls the scroll of heaven this day?"

Tynan looked himself and he felt a deep unease growing, for the sky in the east was now flowing bloodred, the sun itself obscured as if by smoke behind a huge black wrack of rising clouds. A wind from the east streamed steady, thin, and icy cold, driving the clouds before it. He shivered and felt a sudden menace as the tumultuous clouds borne by the wind rose, darkly brooding. Many on the platform looked unwell, others uncertain, and no one looked pleased.

"My!" said Siwell. "This rise bodes little good. From this tower, I have seen the coming of nearly thirty springs. None were so ill-favored."

"Perhaps no good will come of it," said Cage as he turned from the gathering gloom, wrapping his cloak closer about him. "I maintain that history, fair or foul, is written by the words and actions of men, and they carry the future with them."

"Colonel Cage," said Siwell, "Have I labored over your military self these past ten years for less than nothing? Is not the learning nor observations nor speech of the wise of value to you? If so, then please do not speak lightly of things you do not understand; if not, then for the sake of others, it would seem better to keep silence and in doing so exhibit at very least the appearance of the wise."

Cage laughed. It was a clear and cloudless laugh. "Oh my! Not a lesson so soon after breakfast!"

"A rider," said Marc suddenly, and looked away from the east, north across the wide mist-hung moor.

"You have a watchman's ears," said Siwell. "I cannot hear a sound but the wind off the hills."

"Yes. A horseman riding hard is but three stadia from us," Gerald said, leaning out over the battlement, peering hard into the thick gloom.

Soon they all could hear the heavy thud of hooves on the grass then, springing from the rolling shrouds came a rider, heavily armed and bearing a standard which Tynan didn't recognize. The rider quickly drew near the mass of the Academy and clattered through the gate into the courtyard below. He did not dismount nor call out.

Tynan left the battlements and hurried down to where others were gathering. The horseman sat still, silent as stone. His mail and helmet shone wet and dripping, his cloak weather-stained and muddy. Only his horse's rough breathing and stamping hooves betrayed any life. Gerald, last of all, came down into the group.

"Welcome. What word do you bring us?" Gerald asked.

"Hail, lord," said the messenger, his eyes fixed straight ahead. "My message: a Terasian vessel has been intercepted passing into Jarlhof Strait and is being escorted to Aston Quay. The passage towers are now ordered at watch night and day. Kendric has raised the local levy and has sent to meet this ship. Dunross Pass has been closed and garrisoned. He asks that you join him at Aston Quay as soon as you are able."

It was completely silent in the courtyard. Tynan looked around at the faces of those there. They were grim and pale, some fearful. The mist poured uncannily over the walls and through the open gate, filling the courtyard with an eerie pall, dimming sun and sky even more. A shroud seemed to be drawing over them.

But Gerald said to the messenger, "Thank you. Please report back to Kendric that we will prepare to leave immediately." Without dismounting, the messenger saluted, turned his horse, and rode away into the mists to deliver the reply.

Then Gerald turned to the others. "You men of books, return to your books. Perhaps you will find something we need to know for these times. Colonel Cage, it's likely we should double the watch, bar the gates, and light the beacon fire. And all of you, gather your gear and sharpen your swords. We will leave tomorrow at noon to see what this ship of Teras brings and whether it be sailed by men or by monsters. And we know that Teras is populated by mere men—therein lies much hope."

At his words, the mists seemed to lift somewhat and retreat beyond the walls of the keep, and the sun shone through bright and strong. The men shook themselves then went to their tasks eagerly, those of books no less than those to sword. All save Siwell, who stood alone, unmoving and looking down, hands clasped behind his back.

"Old friend," said Gerald. "Did I not say men of books, to your books?"

"You did . . yes, you did," said Siwell, looking up but not at Gerald. "And it is close to the mark, if not in it, to say I am little good with horse and hauberk, still less with bow and blade. Yet . . ." He paused and looked at Gerald. "And yet . . . it may be of worth to have recorded and written down what may pass in these days. For though my sword blows are weak, my pen strokes are less so."

"Has it not been said that one man's book of leisure is another man's field of battle?" replied Gerald. "Isn't one battlefield enough for you?"

"Well, hmmm, yes . . . there is that possibility," Siwell said, shifting uncomfortably and looking down again.

Gerald looked at him steadily. "Can your pen be a blade and your book a shield on a day hedged in by a thicket of spears?"

"Perhaps not, perhaps not," answered Siwell. Then he looked up smiling as if he had just solved a particularly difficult question. "However . . . *however*, if I am led by a captain whose mind I know as thoroughly as my own and can lend such advice or recall such history as I am able, it may be that I can aid all, including myself, from arriving at such a disagreeable end."

Gerald laughed. "Very well argued, my friend! If you will, please bring the Annals from the Stacks and be ready to leave with us tomorrow. I would welcome your company on the road for a time, though it might not be so far as such a desperate day."

CHAPTER 7

The Coming of Teras

THE KING SAT ON his throne slouching, his head nodding forward, bobbing slightly, hanging down as he muttered to himself. In his hand a cup hung loosely—a cup that looked as if it would be worth the price of a great portion of the kingdom, made of gold or precious metal, studded with jewels and the carved winged horse of Caledon—some of its contents had leaked out, dripping to form a small puddle on the floor.

A king's servant had come to Tynan's barrack room late in the afternoon following the events at the Rise of Spring. As he went over the Academy bridge, low, dark clouds strangely paired with unusual heat made for an oppressive afternoon; and he wasn't really surprised to be summoned, as the fits that beleaguered the king seemed to come most strongly with the onset of dark news.

From a side door of the throne room, Tynan looked silently from the king to the Marshal.

"It's as bad as it's ever been," the Marshal said quietly.

"Eh? What's that mumbling about over there? Plotting, plotting as ever are you?" Policrates staggered to his feet, tried to draw a dagger from his belt, caught his foot on the corner of the stone pedestal, and fell headlong on the polished floor, the knife skittering across the stones, spinning into a far corner. Two of the Royal Guard hurried to help him up—the king was gashed across forehead and nose.

"Get Marten," the Marshal said to an orderly. "And you—piper—stop standing there gawking and play; that's what you're here for."

"What has happened to me and why is there blood running down my face?" Policrates said, as he tried to wipe it away.

"Ah, you stumbled on an uneven pavement stone, lord. We've sent for Marten and will have the stonemasons repair the stone."

Policrates stood, dabbing his head with a cloth. "That boy. He looks like a cadet."

"He's part of the new academy's First Cohort," the Marshal replied.

"Ah—very good. How do you like it, son?"

Tynan had unconsciously stood to a ramrod-straight position of attention. "Yes sir, thank you, sir. It's quite challenging but I do like it."

"Can you play those pipes you've brought with you?

Tynan looked down. The pipes had slipped from his rucksack and lay there on the floor. "Yes, sir. Rather decently, sir."

"Rather decently?" laughed the king. "Well let me hear you then. Pipes are a sort of serious hobby for me and I'm rather fond of hearing them well-played."

Tynan played for about twenty minutes as the king sat, enraptured in the music, with a slight smile on his face, while being bandaged by Marten, who had arrived unnoticed.

"Yes," said the king clapping his hands. "That *is* music. Now I must go, but we'll hear you again. See to it, will you, Marshal?"

"Yes lord, we'll have him come again."

"What is your name, piper?"

"Tynan of Westcombe, sir."

"Aye, Tynan. Your playing is soothing to my mind."

"My pleasure, sir, my pleasure indeed."

The king walked out, strong and fully recovered now, shouting for someone to bring him a plate of venison and mead to drink.

Marten came over as Tynan was packing to go. "The king is bandaged—a nasty fall but really just some slight bruises and surface scratches."

"That's well," Tynan said. "It looked much more serious."

"His balance fails him when one of his fits is on him."

"Can anything be done to set him right?"

Marten looked thoughtful. "Nothing that we know of at the moment. The treatment of his symptoms and restraining him from giving harm to himself or to others is the best we can do."

"Why does the music seem to help?"

"It's thought that maybe the notes themselves arrange something in the mind of the afflicted, bridging a gap left there in the making of the soul, and for a time at least restores the breach, though the restoration is only temporary, as a wound that never fully heals and leaves a scar too deep to cleanse, resurfacing—yet never fully leaving either a clean scar or healthy skin."

"I feel pity for him; a man with so much power to command yet beset with an affliction that may be the ruin of so much. It doesn't seem quite fair that the gods should give such a large share of good and of evil into the heart of a single man—so much good might be done!"

"Yes—a meaty question for Siwell! Ask him about it and then come round, and we shall talk again," Marten said.

"I will," Tynan replied, and they left the throne room, empty now except for two servants, scrubbing the blood from the floor, and a stonemason arriving with his bucket and tools, not sure of where on the pristinely smooth floor his skills were needed.

Tynan had learned a little of the ways of the palace. After going out, he turned down toward the kitchen and helped himself to a couple of apples, a small loaf of bread, and cheese from the larder and went out into a small side garden, secluded from the rest of the busy activity, and sat on a small stone bench, listening to the wind and birds, letting his thoughts drift for a few minutes. He savored the sweet fruit and tangy cheese aged in caves in the West of the country some two years, he was told, and developed a strong flavor before being trimmed and carved and packed in parchment and waxed paper and sent all over the country. Tynan wasn't sure about all of that—cheese moldering for two years in a cave didn't seem like it would suit well for something that was to be eaten—but he had to admit that the flavor was good.

The wind sighed in the trees, the branches just beginning to show the green of the oncoming spring, tossing and bobbing. Great clouds swept by overhead, mixed with long patches of blue sky, clean of anything save clear light. The grass was cool and flicked back and forth as the wind rippled through it, sweeping clear eddies and flows of air as they made their way on their paths to the four corners of the earth.

As he sat there, he heard a scratching scrambling sound from the far side of the wall and looking, saw two hands grip the wall top. Above them slowly lifted the face of a young boy, his blond tousled hair ruffling in the wind and alert gray eyes darting side to side. The boy swung up over the wall, one leg hanging down inside the garden, the other on the outward side, sitting there for a moment then swung down landing lightly on the garden soil. He turned and saw Tynan sitting there.

"Hah!" the boy said. "How come you to the king's own garden?"

"I was going to ask you the same question," Tynan replied. "Except that it now comes to my mind that one of the king's household has a reputation for climbing this way when he is shy of being too closely questioned over what he is about."

"If you speak a word, I'll have you thrashed about the grounds!"

Tynan laughed. "I'm sworn to silence on many things and will consider it part of my highest duty to keep silence on this matter. Would you like an apple?"

The boy smiled. "For certain; and I think I've seen you on a time here before. Are you one of the pipers?" He took the apple and sat down beside Tynan on the stone bench. The boy was about ten years old and looked around the garden as he chewed.

"I am," Tynan replied.

A few silent moments passed. "Was he bad today?" asked the boy.

"Yes—it was a bad day, but he does seem better for now."

The boy nodded. "It's well, and better still that my brother is old enough to stand in as king if anything must happen; so say all, 'tis no secret."

"Well. Let us hope it doesn't come to that," Tynan said as he stood to go. "I'd pass along the east service corridor if I were trying to go through the house unseen. Farewell!"

Gerald and a small band rode slowly out of the keep. The gate swung shut behind them with a dull heavy sound and Tynan heard the triple bars slide deep into the massive gate walls. They turned away into the gathering light and cantered southeast.

They rode on through the day, pacing hard over green fells, spattering across shallow streams, cantering through wooded glens, trotting steadily down great cathedral aisles of beech, oak, and pine, where the sun sent green shafts to the forest floor carpeted with fresh spring grass. Despite the evil that might be before them, the group was nearly giddy as the day warmed and filled with spring life. Kiefer sang a song of Cynald and the Battle of Rollan Gap. Tynan felt strong and light, his horse alert and eager, scenting the air of a new season.

Twilight was gone and the cool evening long-begun when they stopped and camped for a small meal of cold meat, hard cheese, thick bread, and water, then wrapped in their cloaks for such sleep as they could manage. Being uncertain of events, they lit no fire and stood watches through the long night.

As he stood his watch that night, Tynan gazed at the revolving stars of the deep-blue heavens thinking of all he knew of the character, history, and policy of Teras. The Terasians were cruel to those who opposed them: destroying entire peoples who set themselves against their rule, yet rewarding liberally those who submitted to them. So they came to people after people, a golden chain in one hand, a drawn sword in the other. For what purpose? All that Tynan had heard whispered of them by rumor and been taught of them at the Academy made him think they possessed great riches, far-flung lands, and many slaves. Why did they need more of each? Maybe it was the army: a created tiger must be ridden against others, or it will turn on its master and it was known that the army had elevated many Terasian emperors. Or did pride simply demand a steady sacrifice of blood, human beings, and territory to be heaped like stones beneath a royal seat, raising a king to immortality? Can a man in that way become a god? Tynan shook his head to clear his mind and listened to the wind as the nightwatch rolled away.

Long before the sun rose through thick mists over the green hills, they had traveled many leagues from their stopping place. The land through which they now passed leveled out, being pastures and fields, well-tended but for now empty; all the country-folk who would be working called away to face the nemesis from the eastern sea. In the distance, Tynan saw the Mountains of Ross rising low and formidable, black and jagged against the red sun. Beyond them, hidden for now, lay Aston Quay and the saltwater passage to the Narrow Sea.

They passed on, cutting directly east across open countryside, the sun gentle and warm above them throwing long shadows far behind. The country flowed away wide around them; the sky was fresh and blue. Across the high plateau that covered much of the southern half of Caledon, they made their way to a narrow pass, steep-sided and clothed in green. Large rocks jutted out from the heather which made for a tumbled look which then smoothed out to gentle green hills dotted with slowly moving sheep, chewing the new sweet grass, and wandering open paths tended by young shepherds.

As the day drew down to a misty gloom, they rode through low hills, then upwards amid tumbled outcroppings of rock, a narrow, well-worn path winding toward the northern shoulder of the mountains, always higher, until they passed into a steep stony gorge, then out and further up, curling away left then back round a rocky shoulder, then entering Dunross Pass, a high-walled track which was wide and maintained for carts or small wagons to pass each other traveling in opposite directions.

The pass was not unguarded. A wooden barrier with a barred gate-way had been hastily erected, set there to control passage through the pass to the city below. Several men with spears and round shields stood behind the gate blocking the way.

"Hold!" commanded a guard in a loud voice. "Hold. Name your-selves and the watchwords."

Despite the obvious royal banners, pennons, and other gear bla-zoned with the arms of the Caledonian house, Gerald answered. "Gerald, with those of my guard. We are in haste to see Kendric. The watchwords are unknown to us, as we are lately come from the Academy."

The guard peered hard through the glooming air. "It is well, my lord," and he flung open the gate. "You will find Kendric at the quay itself. The Marshal has come as well. It is said that the Terasian ship is nearly in sight of the town."

"The Marshal? Thank you," Gerald said, and they trotted through the gate. They passed a second barrier, a wooden wall that was higher and stronger than the first, facing east and the menace from the sea.

Beyond the last sentry, they came to an abrupt drop off, the path disappearing over the edge of a cliff, or so it looked, as it dropped precipi-tously down to the city.

Aston Quay itself, built solidly of stone, hugged the curving shore, a safe harbor and refuge from the storms that roared in the White Sea north of Caledon. Many had been saved by the high-walled fjords and the strong quay that reached far out into the bay.

They rode down the smooth, well-tended path to the city where they found Kendric and the Marshal on the pier sitting upon their horses with troops about them, their arms gleaming in the sun, with a small contingent of archers, spearmen, and footmen arranged behind.

All were looking east. A ship slid silently and slowly down the inlet from the sea, its oars dipping together into the water then out again, the cadence kept by a flute whose notes drifted and echoed in the high-walled passage. Nearly half of the four rows of oarlocks had unmoving oars and

Tynan wondered uneasily as to what that might mean. Clouds had swept up suddenly from the east, masking the sun, the water reflecting the slate gray sky and near black cliffsides.

The ship, once brightly colored, was dull and grayed, the mainsail shredded. The mast had snapped and been replaced with a spar lashed to the stump. The hull was held to by cables girding the keel below. Though shattered by storm, the ship still projected a massive bulk, its power in open water unquestioned anywhere east of the Euxine Sea.

On the foredeck, two orderly ranks of armed men stood looking out. Long spears were in their right hands; heavy square shields were strapped to their left arms. One, without shield or spear, shouted orders, then stood, his right arm raised palm-outward toward the Caledonians.

"Greetings, Gerald," said one of the riders. At the sound of his voice Tynan with a start recognized him as the old man who had met him at the door of the palace when he was first brought to Caerleon to play his pipes. Now, however, the Marshal was arrayed in the finest armor and sat easily upon one of the most magnificent horses Tynan had yet seen in the country.

"Greetings," said Gerald to the Marshal, then turned to the commander as he and his men drew up. "Kendric. Well met."

"Yes," Kendric said. "For this time and this purpose, it's well."

"And what may we say of these somewhat unwelcome guests?"

"By the looks of that ship," Kendric answered, "they have not come here by choice."

"They've been at sea a long time," Gerald said. "And that ship is built for war, not trade."

The Terasian ship skillfully stood into the stone quay, its mass dwarfing the two Caledonian barks that trailed it. From aboard the ship, the heavily armed marines stood silently. The flute had ceased. Only the lapping of water and the creaking of the battered hull ruffled the silence. Far overhead, a sea eagle wheeled. Above all, Tynan heard his own blood pounding in his ears.

"We will ride down to welcome our guests to determine if they require aid handling their ship and what the nature of their visit to us might be," Gerald said, and accompanied by Tynan, Marc, and another rider who bore the Caledonian standard, he cantered down the quay to where the towering ship had been moored, raised his right hand and called out. "Is there a commander aboard who can speak with us?"

A tall man in battle dress appeared on the high foredeck, looking down at them. "I am Septus." His voice was strong and rough in Tynan's ears.

"Indeed, General Septus," said Gerald, "and for your master you command all ships and armies west of Teras. Are we to expect more of your number shortly?"

"They will come when you do not expect them," said Septus. "And then all lands will serve the ruler of the Middle Seas."

Tynan felt, as he looked at the powerful Terasian ship, even damaged as it was, that Septus was making no idle threat.

Gerald didn't change his expression or tone of voice. "Of course. Likely as not that shall be seen to at the proper time; however, what then is your present errand to our small island?"

"We have no concerns here and come unwillingly," Septus replied. "We were driven by fierce winds to this waste place and request only what the law of the sea permits: timber and materials to repair our ship and stores for our journey back."

"Items which you must purchase," added Gerald. "A small clause in that worthy agreement often overlooked by Terasian armies, who do not always pay for what they acquire, according to reports."

"Don't believe everything spoken of in a ramshackle hut," Septus said. "And do not trifle. Will you supply our need—or not? If not, then perhaps some of the unflattering things told of this place may be truer than I took them to be."

"Of course, we will assist you as the law calls for," Gerald replied. "As payment you will deliver to our care all slaves yet alive on your vessel. Also—neither you nor any of your crew will be allowed to pass further than the dock at which you are moored, and onto the dock only as needed to mend your ship."

Septus paled but said, "Agreed. I will produce a docket for you to fill and will release the slaves when we are refitted."

Gerald looked steadily at the Terasian. "Our requirement is that you free the slaves to our care at once."

"They are needed for the work of repairing the ship," said the Terasian.

"We will send skilled shipwrights to you—free men—to ready your ship."

Septus stared back at Gerald, the Terasian's face a blotchy mass of white and purple. Then he turned and shouted, "Bring up the oar rabble at once! They are to be traded for our bread." He spat over the side of the ship. "Dogs!"

This last was spoken under his breath, but Gerald had excellent hearing. "It's thought that even the dogs of Caledon live better than the servants of Teras, who cannot feed even on the crumbs from their master's table."

"One day our master will be your master," said Septus. "Then you will be glad even for crumbs."

"As has been said," replied Gerald. "*Better to be a dog in some places than a nobleman in others.*"

Septus grew darker purple and turned to a Terasian marine. "What's the delay? Be quick! Bring up the filth, before this bogtrotter continues regaling me with homespun wisdom!"

"Aye, sir. They are come," said the marine.

The gangway was lowered to the dock and the first of the galley-slaves appeared, standing there at the deck rail. He was scarred from the beat of the oarmaster, covered with grime, sweat-soaked from the stale below decks with an iron collar on his neck and iron manacles on his waist, wrists, and ankles; but he gazed steadily away beyond all of them, unbowed, it seemed, to his captors or his chains.

"You may retain their shackles," Gerald said. "We have no use for them here."

Septus's face contorted. "Unbind them, fools!" Quickly the first man's irons were hammered off and he strode down. He did not look back nor show any fear, but walked directly to where Gerald sat upon his horse.

"Lord," he said. "Do you free us from Teras to yoke us for your purposes?"

To the man's astonishment, Gerald burst out laughing.

"No!" said Gerald, after he gained his breath. "No! Though your question is well-put considering your most recent employ and the way the world as it now stands does operate. You and I are brothers. Whatever thanks, obedience, or loyalty you may owe while you are with us, you owe to our king, for by his law you were unbound. In this place, men and women are constrained only by their unconquered fears and unstudied disbelief."

Then Gerald raised his voice, for other freed galley slaves had gathered behind the first. "All of you! Welcome! Unlawfully you were brought captive to our shores. Now live as free men!"

At this, many cheered, but some were silent and suspicious as wagons from the city rumbled up the quay. "These will bear you to lodgings and there you will be renewed, as it appears you have not eaten nor bathed well under the jurisdiction of your late masters," Gerald said.

"Sir," said Tynan. And he pointed to the top of the gangway. There, an old man stood, clutching a tattered rag bundle, staring at his feet.

"Be gone, you bag of bones!" Septus said. "Why do you stand there blocking the way with the repairs waiting?"—and struck him with a blow on the back. The old man crumpled like paper onto the gangway and rolled a little way down, not moving. Septus stepped after him, drawing his short sword.

"Stay your hand, General," Gerald said. "You will not take this life and will certainly lose yours if you do not immediately sheath your sword—our archers do not easily miss." Then he dismounted and walked up the gangway. As he did, Septus stepped back a pace and sheathed his sword.

Gerald gazed steadily at Septus for a moment, then turned from him and bent over the old man. "Grandfather, take my arm and we will leave this ship." The man's eyes shone brightly as he looked up and gripped Gerald's arm. He was too weak to stand, so Gerald lifted him and carried him down to a wagon.

The old man spoke. "Put me down, child." His voice was weak, his breath rattled in and out.

Gerald laid him gently down on the quay, rolling his riding cloak to pillow the man's head. It was some moments before the old man gathered the strength to speak.

"Are you the prince of this land?" he asked, his blue eyes watery but bright.

"I am not a prince, Grandfather, but there is a prince with us here," answered Gerald.

The old man laughed. "I believe I do have grandchildren," he said as he waved his hand vaguely toward the sea. "Out there."

"Perhaps you will again see them. You are now free to go where you will."

The man laughed again feebly. "Not in the body . . . not in the body. Nevertheless, I am content, save for one thing."

"What is that, my friend?" Gerald said.

"I have a gift to give you. It may be a great gift, one of the greatest ever brought to the West, if one but knows how to use it. Though it is mine to give, I made it not. It is from the distant East. And with it . . . with it . . . it may help you."

The old man reached slowly for the small bundle which he had held as he left the galley. His hands shook uncontrollably as he handed it to Gerald, who took it, placing it in his lap, feeling a small heavy weight beneath the wrappings.

"Look upon it," said the man.

Gerald pulled away the tattered cloth. There, shining dully in the late afternoon sun, was a triangular piece of shaped metal. A single loop was welded at the apex. He had no idea what he was looking at.

"You don't know what it's for!" laughed the man, "Neither did I . . . when I first saw it long ago in my travels. Yes! I was a great traveler before I was taken by the Terasians and chained to those oars for some thirty years. In all that time, though, I kept this near to me."

"But what is its use?" asked Gerald.

"It will help your riders. Horsemen use it."

"Horsemen?"

The old man grasped Gerald's arm fiercely, his face suddenly bright. "Use it!" Then he slipped back, sagging down again. He looked at Gerald, as from a great distance. "You have been kind to me. Kindness has been rare enough in my years."

Gerald smiled down on him. The old man turned his face to the sky, his eyes very distant and with a deep sigh his life of hardship slowly drained away, the scars and disfigurements of slavery and suffering smoothing to simple peace.

"Thank you, Grandfather," Gerald said, and turning to the others. "Did anyone know his name or country?"

"No," said one. "He was one of the few not from our land."

"Then we will bury him here according to the honors he would have among us as an elder, for we do not know the customs of his birthplace." Gerald said. "And we will place a marker: 'A life in chains ended here, free.'"

"And what of his gift?" asked Marc.

"We will retain it and look into its uses, following his instructions," said Gerald who handed it to Tynan.

Tynan wrapped it in its original tattered cloth and tucked it in his saddlebag, looking up at Septus. The Terasian general looked down unflinchingly, then walked back up to the ship shouting orders.

That night, Tynan found he could not sleep thinking of the old man, of Teras, and of the days that might be coming. He rose from his cot, left his tent and, wrapping his cloak about him, walked down to the shore of the bay. The quiet murmuring of the sea, the bright clear sky, the sigh of the wind all added to the depth of his thought. Tynan looked out across the dark water, stars mirrored on its surface. Aston Quay was dimly lit, and all was quiet there.

Without warning, loud cries rang out and the clash of metal on metal rose in a tumultuous clamor from the far end of the dock. A growing clangor shattered the stillness. Tynan ran toward the quay and as he ran, the clamor grew, men running heedless in all directions when Gerald suddenly appeared, leaping upon a platform, and shouted out, "Hold! Hold! Stand to order!" His voice stemmed the rising tide of men who began to gather themselves into cohesive battle groups. Far down the jetty, Tynan saw flames lighting the night sky. Marc, Kiefer, and Devon came running up and Marc handed Tynan his sword and belt.

"From the sound of things, thought you might need this," he said.

Tynan nodded, buckled it on, and called to Gerald. "What's happened?"

Gerald looked down from the platform. "The Terasian ship burns at the dock."

Tynan looked at the burning ship and saw that beyond along a further stretch of the pier, a small Caledonian vessel was just slipping away from its moorings.

A soldier came running out of the darkness. "What news, soldier?" said Gerald.

"The Terasians attacked unprovoked, slew the watch, and have taken one of our ships. They are fleeing down the strait to the sea."

"We must overtake them before they catch the outgoing tide," Gerald said.

Tynan saw a man step forward from the milling crowd. It was the tall galley slave who had been the first to be released from the Terasian ship earlier in the day. "I and my men shall row for you. The Terasians were more than thorough in their training and we are able to row quicker than all other crews of their navy."

"Very well!" said Gerald. They hurried down the dock, boarded a small harbor galley, cast off, and fanned out the oars sweeping them in double-quick time. Tynan felt the boat fairly lift out of the dark water with every stroke. Those not needed at the oars stood well forward on the deck and strained for sight of the ship ahead in the dark fjord.

As they rowed forward, Tynan saw that dawn was coming on and with the dawn would come the tide and a wind also, blowing out to sea. If they did not overtake the Terasians before the turn of the tide, the longer-keeled ship that the Terasians had pirated would stretch its lead and soon be far out to sea. It was a race of rowers.

Then a watchman in the rigging shouted out: "Ship dead ahead!"

"What distance?" shouted Gerald.

"Five hundred yards and we're gaining quickly."

"Quickly enough?" Gerald said, turning back to Tynan and the others. "The tide may change before we overtake them." He looked ahead, feeling the wind and peering closely at the passing water.

"Hallo! Our coastwatchers are closing in—one from each side," called the watchman. "The Terasians are having to come about."

Tynan saw the ship they were pursuing swing to the right, crossways, athwart the channel as the Caledonian coastwatch cutters warily kept their distance, maneuvering to stay between the Terasians and the open sea.

Unexpectedly, the Terasian shot forward rowing madly at the nearest Caledonian ship. The sudden move allowed them to close rapidly. The Caledonians backed oars frantically, but it was too late. The Terasians smashed into them, shattering oars and cleaving the ship nearly in two. Terasian soldiers vaulted the rails of the mangled ships, slashing down the sailors on the Caledonian deck, quickly overwhelming the outnumbered crew. Meanwhile, the remaining coastwatcher swept near, raking the Terasians with flight after flight of arrows. Many found a mark. As they passed, they sheared off one half of the Terasian oars, intending to haul around and ram them amidships.

"They are as desperate as a boar caught by the chase," said Gerald, then turned and gave quick orders. Several bowmen went smoothly up into the ship's rigging; a squadron of swordsmen knelt silently on the aft deck.

Now they were within fifty yards of the two ships that were locked together; the Caledonian coastwatcher was slowly taking on water and listing heavily. The surviving crew had been roped together at the wrists and herded onto the other ship. Several Terasian troopers were hacking at the upper bow, trying to cut away free of the foundering vessel. At that distance, Tynan could hear Septus shouting.

"Cut us free, fools! Do you want to sink in these waters to your death? Or be taken to sure execution—those other slime are almost on us!"

"Prepare to board," said Gerald.

Tynan, Marc, and the others drew their swords and crouched near the rail.

Gerald turned to look at the Terasians. Two soldiers guarded the surviving sailors; the rest—about thirty—were divided between trying to cut their ship free and gathering around Septus, facing the Caledonians. Not a man among them looked ready to throw down his weapon.

Gerald called out clearly: "Septus. You are guilty of both piracy and murder. Just it would be if you were slain without delay. However, surrender yourselves and release my crew. Then you will at least receive a thought of mercy in your sentence."

Septus laughed loudly. "You Caledonian pigs are consistent in your rustic humor. If you come even a single yard closer to me, every Caledonian on this ship will be slain. *My* demand is for that other ship to be immediately turned over to me and then for free passage out of this fjord to the sea. "

"Your opportunity has passed," said Gerald, then dropped his upraised arm. Tynan and his squad vaulted over the rail as the vessels ground together. Arrows sped across the waters separating the two ships, then a second, and a third volley. Deck-mounted crossbows raked the Terasians. Septus was struck twice, his armor deflecting several others bolts that ricocheted harmlessly away. To escape the arrow storm, he swung across to the slowly sinking coastwatcher and turned like a lion at bay. None of his men were left alive to follow him. Tynan and Marc cut free the living Caledonian sailors, who reboarded and stood away in the ship they had retaken, and slowly began rowing back to Aston Quay in hopes of salvaging the vessel.

Marc and Devon ran toward Septus, who pulled a leather pouch over his head and flung it far out into the channel, then drew himself to his full height and called out, "May the Emperor receive me in his eternal kingdom, as I died loyal to his name," then plunged his sword into his own body and threw himself into the dark water.

Marc dove over the side, swimming out to where the pouch had splashed in. After some minutes thrashing about he found it and swam back to the ship with the pouch clenched between his teeth.

The other vessel had sunk lower and was taking on water, so they took aboard the crew and rowed against the tide—which was by now flowing strongly out to sea—back to the quay.

"Well done!" Gerald said, as he leaped on the dock. "Well done, my friends!"

The man bowed slightly—Gerald's enthusiasm could be infectious—and answered. "As we said, the Terasians were thorough in their training, which was punctuated with the beat of the oarmaster's lash, and the drums of the row sergeant."

"Aye, but you and your men have paid them in full for their lessons," Gerald replied.

Tynan looked at the oarsman. It was the tall man, freed first earlier in the day and the one who had volunteered the rowing crew to pursue the Terasians.

"What are your names and country?" Gerald said.

"Tredegar, and these are mostly with me from the city of Warrec."

Gerald started to say something further but was interrupted by Tredegar. "But we are not important. What is important is that some here that know the Terasian speech heard them talking of a mission to Dara, which is why Septus was at sea and on that vessel when the storm that blew them here also scattered the fleet that was to blockade Dara and complete the overthrow of the city."

"Dara?" said Gerald. "That city has never fallen to any attack—land or sea."

"Things may have changed," said Tredegar. "From the sound of it, they are heavily besieged by Teras and may have fallen or will fall soon even without the help of a blockade."

"You must come with us later today. The documents from Septus's pouch will be translated into common speech and read out. Then your tale should be heard," Gerald said.

They gathered in the late afternoon in Gerald's tent where Siwell translated, then read the contents of a letter:

> *To Septus Quinius Gaulica: Greetings. The chief oracles have been read and the signs at the great feast are interpreted a vision that the subjugation of Aegis and the destruction of Dara have been ordained for the liberation of that country. You are ordered to aid*

from the sea the effort our land forces are putting forth now against
that rebel city. May your endeavors be swift and prosperous.
                Pliny Tertullian, Chamberlain

The package also held many other documents detailing a landing at Dara from the seaward side as well as directions for the organization of the country after its capture. Siwell lowered the scroll when he finished reading. Tredegar told of what had been overheard onboard the Terasian ship as well.

"Well," said Gerald after a few moments, leaning back in his chair. "How quickly they are in our waters! At the very least we must send a ship at once to Dara to see how things go with Aegis."

CHAPTER 8

Concerning the Fall of Dara

THE ONLY CALEDONIAN SHIP able to sail immediately was the *Sea Wind*, a small cruiser used mainly for training. Tynan's squad was assigned to go, and while the ship was being fitted out for the journey, he sat in his tent writing a letter to his grandparents—it seemed long since he had seen them—letting them know he was well and that he was going to be staying on at the capital for a while longer and would write again when his future was clearer. Clearer? he thought to himself. I really haven't been clear about anything since I got here. And now a ship?

Through the tent wall he heard the shouts and noises of the busy harbor. Before all this, he thought, I hadn't floated on anything bigger than a rowboat, and I think I like solid ground under my feet even more after that business with Septus and his crew. It seemed like one whirlwind coming through just after another had passed.

Nevertheless, two weeks after the death of Septus in the waters of Jarlhof Strait, the *Sea Wind* approached the coast near the city of Dara, and Tynan looked through a bronze glass across the still water. The entire harbor was afire. Ships burned at their moorings—even buildings and the wharf itself burned—but there were no soldiers nor fire brigades.

Gerald took the glass himself. "And there is more fire on the clifftop, where Dara's signal beacon burns," he said as he snapped the glass shut. "The city stands, then, but calls for help."

Beside Tynan stood Marc, Devon, and Kiefer. They all gazed at the red beacon that flared brightly atop the cliff upon which stood the city, then back at the raging fires that crackled and roared in the harbor.

"No one will be coming aboard from those docks," Gerald said. "But as the city's beacon is still lit, there may be some yet alive defending her that could use our assistance." He turned to the captain. "Would it be possible to sail down toward the beacon? There may be folk coming out on the beach there at the base of the sea cliff."

"Yes, sir. Back oars, if you please," said the captain.

"Aye, sir, back oars. Back oars!" shouted the deck officer. As the *Sea Wind* slowly backed out of the harbor, buildings collapsed in a rush of heat, stone and timber fusing together in an unnatural coalescence—but there was no sound or cry of living man.

Clear of the harbor mouth, the *Sea Wind* crept carefully south along the ink-black coast. The moon shone ghost-like from behind a thin gauze of clouds, casting a silver glow but little real light; their only point of reckoning was the signal fire of the city. Some half-mile of careful sailing brought them abeam of the beacon, and there, twinkling along the foot of a precipice, they saw a string of small flickering points of red lights, which seemed to float on the surface of the water.

"Stand in to those lights, soundings as we go," said the captain.

Suddenly, the clouds parted, and the moon shone down. The silver light lit up several ships, boats, and other vessels of many shapes and sizes. On the water small craft loaded with masses of people crowded the spaces among the taller ships, which creaked and groaned in the tranquil sea.

"These aren't Terasian, but they are from just about every other land besides," Devon said. "Men-of-war for certain, as well as a broad mix of everything else that can float."

The *Sea Wind* turned gently into the breeze and the chains roared as the anchors plunged into the luminous waters.

"Prepare to go ashore, Mr. Gerald," said the captain. "I would suspect that four cadet squads would fit well on the skiffs."

The craft were hoisted over the sides with boat slings and swung slowly onto the surface of the water. Tynan clambered backward down a ladder of rope-webbing, feeling the rough fiber digging into his palms, and with some difficulty boarded the small boat and cast away from the ship that towered above them. The sea slapped the side of the skiff as it moved among the many vessels at anchor. The moon stayed bright, riding high above the shadowy earth and the dim sea. A breeze from the open waters carried them forward through the surf toward the shore. Many small boats were alongside them or pushing off from shore laden with many people.

"Who are these?" Tynan asked as a mixed boat filled with men and women went past them.

"They look like refugees from the city," Marc said. "And there are as many more waiting on shore."

Tynan looked and saw a thickly packed, curiously quiet throng, sitting or standing in long lines near the water's edge, clambering into whatever vessel they were directed to, quickly and without panic.

"Ground us ashore, if you will, cadets!" said the tillerman in a low voice. Kiefer and another cadet jumped out, plunging waist-deep in the cold water, grasped the gunwale line and drew the boat in to the shore, the keel scraping along a gravelly shelf.

Gerald detailed the cadets of the other skiffs to help the children and women nearby into the boats to ferry back to the *Sea Wind*. Tynan and the others gathered around Gerald and crunched through the sand away from the shoreline. There was no panic among those who were on the beach, only a tense expectation, then vast relief when they at last climbed into a boat and were rowed away from the shore. The watch fires burned red in the night, their glow turning the surrounding sand the color of dark blood.

After some confused searching and near to middle night, the Caledonians found a tunnel mouth at the cliff foot where the lines of refugees seemed to be appearing from a sheer rock face. They entered and came to a rock-hewn stairway that sloped up steeply. All along the stairway, moving down toward the beach, a steady thread of people patiently waited in the dim-lit corridor.

Tynan looked at them in the flickering light cast by torches that sputtered and flared in rock niches. They were pale and drawn, eyes flitting back and forth, flinching at loud noises, some even throwing themselves on the ground, then standing back up and moving on, unembarrassed. Seeing this, Tynan thought that weeks of dodging hundred-pound stones cast by massive siege engines would make one conscious of sounds from the sky, quick on one's feet, and able to find instant cover at need. The Caledonians were the only ones moving up from the beach—all others were fleeing down and away from what seemed to be a collapsing city.

They followed Gerald out of the tunnel into a stone hall that opened high above, the gray carved ceiling arching to dim heights that fled into shadows, and hurried through, their footfalls echoing as they went into the city. On the streets, groups of soldiers and civilians were hastening in every direction.

"Where can Aegis be found?" Gerald called to a group hurrying by.

"Over that way," a man said, waving toward a crowded corner of the city. "In what's left of the east gatehouse."

"Aegis!" Gerald called as they walked in the direction of the man's wave.

"Gerald!" said Aegis as they approached. "How did you come to join our little . . . half a moment." He turned to a passing group of soldiers. "You there! You there! Help that woman with her bundle, will you please? Move on steady! Slowly now! Don't crowd! Haul that stretcher over and set him down easy."

"We have bad news," Gerald said, then told Aegis of Septus and the coming of the storm-battered Terasian ship to Aston Quay. "Galley slaves that were aboard that ship and a letter that was carried by Septus himself both say a fleet is on its way here to cut you off from supplies and help from the sea. It's only been delayed by storm, it seems, though we found your harbor afire."

"I expected something of the sort," Aegis said. "Yesterday, they landed a small force in the harbor. We were able to beat them off, but they sent in fireships that engulfed the wharf in flames."

Gerald nodded, then looked around. "To my eyes, this fight looks like it's already over. A blockade or no blockade wouldn't matter much."

"The Terasians are poised for the last push. They would be through already, except they maintain a fortunate superstition about fighting at night. Only after dark do we have any chance to bind our wounds, eat, or repair our walls, let alone sleep. The days have been one crisis after another. The defenses are nearly breached in three places. Food is gone a week. The water ran out two days ago. I'm afraid we're nearly done in."

"But why are all these civilians here?" asked Gerald. "Shouldn't they have been evacuated long ago?"

"We were taken off our guard," said Aegis. "Listening to the false assurances of our allies and the Terasians themselves. They built a force shielded beyond the Eildon Hills, bought off some of those who should have sided with us, and attacked without declaring war. Those who escaped the first onslaught barely reached the city. Many didn't make it."

"Are you completely finished then?" asked Gerald.

"Barring direct intervention of the gods, the city will fall," said Aegis. "Tomorrow perhaps. The next day at the latest. The aim now is to hold them off long enough to evacuate as many as possible."

"Well then," Gerald said. "We have arrived just in time. What is your plan?"

"Come with me," Aegis said. They followed him through the throng of Darans to a ruined gate, where men were pouring over heaps of paper; aides burned more in open fires. In the firelight, Tynan thought Aegis looked as tired and even more anxious than his people, but he gestured to a table.

"Please sit, and your men."

"Thank you," said Gerald as he took a seat on a broken crate. "As we feared, the fighting goes badly."

Aegis waved his hand around him, the pain deepening on his face. He gestured at the burning piles. "It's a pity," he said. "But as you see, events are not in our favor. They have us like a mole in a trap." As he spoke, an aide added an armload of parchments to the blaze. "We needed more men to hold them. And we had the men, though who would have predicted that Samuel would go over to them without a fight—and his fifteen regiments of foot soldiers. And Roger—ten thousand of the lands' best horsemen, now in the legions of Teras, riding as scouts and flying columns. For Teras—and a few bags of gold."

"And also a few promises of land and power, I'd imagine," said Gerald.

"Yes, I suppose you are right," answered Aegis, looking at him.

Well, your victory would be our victory," said Gerald. He smiled and put his hand on Aegis's shoulder. "You and your people rode together with us at Finigol. You cleaved that lance head off as it was about to do damage to the king and received a stout blow yourself for your troubles. We've long sought a way to put right our debt, and this may be the time."

"That was a fight to remember!" Aegis exclaimed. He grew serious again. "But what of *this* fight? The best we can do now is to hold them off for as long as possible, getting away as much as we can, that we may hope to fight better another day." Here he paused. "It is said that the first Terasian trooper over the wall will win one hundred talents of gold and that the spoils of the city are for the strongest takers."

Tynan gasped. One hundred talents of gold were the wealth of five kings and the riches of Dara were legendary.

"But to gain time," said Aegis, "We must sacrifice many good men tomorrow, or the Terasians will overrun us before we can evacuate enough to keep the slaughter from being irreparable. It will harm us for the worse later—every sword, bow, and spear struck down now when all hope is gone will make a gap much harder to fill later."

"What then do you propose?" asked Gerald.

Aegis bent over the tabletop and with a pen scratched out a rough outline of Dara's walls and the massive work of circumvallation that Teras had thrown up around the city. "Tonight, our sappers are digging trenches beyond the walls and filling them with bundles of damp branches and foliage. Alight, these bundles will make dense white smoke, which will shield the last of our horsemen, who will file out through this western sally port to charge their flank as their troopers rush on encumbered with siege ladders, battering rams, and other gear. In this court behind the main gate, myself and my household companions will draw up and at signal will break out upon them, hopefully delaying them long enough to finish the evacuation of the city."

"That," put in Gerald, "would be a victory itself over these brigands that when they break through, they find empty streets, deserted houses, and all the birds flown."

"It's the best we can hope for," Aegis said, leaning back.

"Good!" Gerald said. "Where can we be of the most help?"

"Why, you must return to your ship and depart at once!" Aegis said. "To stay would mean your deaths and a large blow to any future hope. I will not allow you to stay."

"But we won't allow ourselves to go," said Gerald. "As I was saying, this may be the time we are able to put right some of the debt owed to you. Regardless, it is a poor friend who is close by in the good times and conveniently far away when things are not so good; especially when every man counts and many of yours look weak, wounded, or worse."

"Well," said Aegis. "I won't say that we don't need the help. Most of my captains are hurt or fallen; and my men too young."

Gerald laughed. "Then we will fit in quite well as most of these with me are much too young. Of course, we will need horses, weapons, and any armor you can spare, then we will serve where you direct."

Now Tynan was in a battle he never asked for in a land he'd never seen. The dark foggy morning hid anything more than three feet away. The only sounds were of horses moving and breathing nearby. He felt numb and weakened by waves of fear that rippled across his stomach sapping the strength in his arms and legs. His mind buzzed and hummed, thoughts tripping over each other: pain, death, grievous wounds; being maimed or seeing a friend pierced through by an enemy spear. There was no use resisting the first rush. He had been trained to let them wash over him, letting the feared disasters expand and grow to their full nightmarish enormity: "First, listen to the counsel of your fears," as Webbe had said so often. To ignore them meant that they would grow in secret and rush out in the opening moments of the feared event, robbing one of strength just when they most needed it.

Rather, Tynan was taught to play out the power of the fear in his mind, so it could not sap his strength in the face of the real threat—to see and experience all the horror of the possible, to have "lived through it," and thus he would find the ground of calm and stability. Listen to the strident counsel of all your fears, live through them in your mind, then go on stronger, the fears having collapsed in vapor. Once this happened—again as Webbe had said—"never listen again to the counsel of your fears." It had proved a sound method so far, and this would likely be a supreme test.

Tynan stood and, like the horses around him, stamped his feet. It was damp and cold. He felt the cold leather reins of the brown gelding, whose ears were shifting forward and back, occasionally blowing and champing on the bit. It was a dark, false dawn. He could vaguely see Gerald, who stood not ten feet away, looking calm, standing very still, his hand on his horse's neck, looking up as if listening or waiting.

Tynan turned and busied himself tightening every buckle and strap, the borrowed Daran armor and harness not fitting quite properly. A long spear—unlike the javelins used in Caledon, lighter for throwing and quick work—was secured in a scabbard. Behind him in the file was Marc, his face pale and detached in the murky light; and beyond him were Kiefer and Devon.

Then came running feet and a messenger hurried past, saluted Gerald, and handed him a rolled page. He read it, handed it back to the messenger, then signaled to the gate guards to roll back the bars and swing open the heavy bronze door. Gerald led his horse through at a walk, and the others followed him out. Tynan tightened the girth one last time. He held the reins in his shield hand, and loosened his sword while steadying his horse with soft words. Then he was through the gate and immediately swung into the saddle, pulling back hard on the reins as the horse jumped and skittered. There was not a sound but the swish of hooves over grass. Thick smoke drifted across the field; the sappers had done their work well. Almost too well—the morning had raised a thick haze which, mixed with the smoke, obscured all but the barest outline of shadow.

Beside them, a detachment of archers slipped out to their right. The lead archer was a massive man who looked to Tynan that he had been "born with the yew in his hand." Across his shoulders he carried a double bow of size and length that Tynan had never seen. It was shaped of perfectly seasoned yew wood, filigreed with double-wound hammered bronze, braced with thongs of finest leather. No armor at five hundred yards could turn back a shaft from a normal bow held by a normal archer—an arrow would easily pierce an oaken door the thickness of a man's hand—so what this bow in the hands of this archer could do had yet to be seen.

The archers set stakes and tall shields in a line before the walls, drew out five long arrows from their quivers, and laid them on the ground in front of them, a single stride apart. Each arrow was forty-eight inches from black razor tip to red goose-feathered notch. The archers took up their bows, strung them, and stood looking out over the smoking trenches.

A half-mile away across the green sward piled high with smoking engines, shattered beasts, and other waste of war, Tynan caught glimpses of the high wood-walled palisade the Terasians had built, a wooden siege wall encircling the stone walls of Dara. The only gap in the noose was the slender spit of sand behind them, five hundred feet below the city at the foot of the massive sea cliff. The storm that had scattered the Terasian fleet and blown Septus's ship to Caledon had kept the ocean lanes to Dara open for a short time. Some at least would escape slavery or worse. Cities that resisted suffered the same fate: soldiers were put to the sword to the last man; the civilians were sold into slavery for entertainments in stadiums across Teras.

Set in the space between the Terasian palisade and the walls of Dara was a high timber platform. The Daran groom who had helped him with his saddle and tack had told him that on that platform—day by day, as the first ray of the sun shone out—the Terasians would sacrifice a prisoner taken in battle, to be used as an omen of the day's operations, then the commander of the Terasian troops would issue orders through flag and trumpet signals from atop it.

This morning, however, those on the platform did not know their peril. In a strange motion of fate such as sometimes happens on fields of war, the fogs and smokes of the morning were blown aside momentarily, and this group on the platform was silhouetted perfectly against the red sky beyond. Even at seven hundred yards, they were clearly outlined, etched in the growing light.

Tynan had heard that skilled archers could release arrows so that five of them would be airborne simultaneously, and he saw the line of archers sight their first arrow, step a full stride forward and let it race away, in the same motion picking up the next arrow, striding into the shot, and releasing it, then the next, and the final two. Tynan heard the arrows rattle and hum as they arched away through the chill air.

Then Gerald turned and signaled to the squad, starting his horse ahead at a walk. Tynan kept pace, his horse nearly touching the rider to the left of him. Light spread in the sky, thick smoke drifted in dense banks, confusing the entire field. On his right, Tynan could feel Marc's horse's shoulder, with Kiefer and Devon shoulder-to-shoulder in their turn, and so down the line, as they moved forward as one man. The strange silence, the breathing of the horses, the low thud of their hooves on the grass, the gray sky, and the white smoke created a vivid and very tense scene.

Gerald urged on to a canter, bearing left of the platform, now cloaked again in smoke. They would sweep left, then wheel right, using the platform as a pivot, driving into the flank of the Terasians. Tynan could not see any enemy on the field but pressed forward, expecting a rush of enemy infantry to burst from the smoke-shrouds at any moment.

The horsemen rode forward until they were near the command platform when Gerald called a halt. The field was completely clear of Terasian troops. They sat on their horses perplexed.

"Marc," Gerald said. "You, Kiefer, Tynan, and Devon secure that platform."

"Yes, sir," Marc said. Reining up and dismounting, they bounded up the stairs of the platform. The work of the archers was evident. There Tynan saw a strangely dressed figure lying, pierced by two arrows—his face had a look of someone who had met something unexpected. Another arrow had struck the commander himself, who also lay dead, a signal flag in his hand. Other arrows were buried deeply in the wood of the platform.

The would-be sacrificial victim was also there, bound to the table, surprised and unwounded. Kiefer and Marc untied the dazed man and led him down the stairs.

Tynan picked up one of the fallen banners and looked out toward the Terasians. From the platform, he saw clearly the wide extent of their fortifications and siege works. The tall wooden walls stretched away in a shallow arc for some two miles with towers erected at regular intervals. One hundred meters from the base of the palisades and fortifications, a bewildering array of ditches, moats, and stakes had been built, protecting the wall of the palisade itself with a network of trenches. The palisade itself was some fifty feet high; its height and strength more imposing than many stone fortifications.

But it was the widespread army arrayed beyond that took Tynan's breath away. From the top of the high platform, he saw several camps many acres square that announced the presence many legions, with uncountable banners of other auxiliary units, spreading out past the edge of his view.

"Let us be going!" Kiefer shouted. "Those on the wall will soon get us in their sights." Even as he spoke, a five-foot-long dart whistled by, burying itself in the open field behind them.

As they turned to go, Tynan saw a disturbance beyond the palisade amongst the Terasians themselves—a glittering squadron of horsemen was riding up from the east. A Terasian commander stepped forward and bowed to them. The mounted figure leading the group unhurriedly cantered up, drew his sword, and cut the commander down where he stood. A few other troopers were also struck down; then as if nothing out of the ordinary had happened, the mounted figure shouted orders, the palisade gates were opened, and the mounted Terasian horsemen rode out on to the field.

Tynan ran down the platform stairs and remounted, pulling up the rescued man behind him and handing him the Terasian battle flag.

"Form up! Form up!" Gerald shouted. "Wheel right in-line!" The line turned to face the oncoming Terasians.

"Set arms!" Tynan drew his spear from its scabbard and held it under his arm. Then Gerald gave the command.

"Charge." And they sprang forward at a gallop toward the oncoming Terasians.

As they charged, Tynan heard the hum and whoosh of arrows arcing overhead and into the Terasian ranks. The leader of the Terasian horsemen was struck and flung to the ground unmoving.

Then came a trumpet call from the city to fall back. "Back to the city! Pick up the archers as you go—each rider with one bowman," Gerald shouted.

The Terasians fired from their encircling palisade walls and rolled their siege machinery forward. Tynan galloped back to the city carrying the captured standard. The Terasian cavalry reformed and spurred after them, while masses of Terasian foot soldiers were pouring out onto the field.

As they neared the walls of Dara, another trumpet sounded. The gates opened and Tynan rode in through the city gates, which were shut behind them almost in the faces of the pursuing Terasian riders.

Amid great shouting they presented the captured standard to Aegis. The cheers were deafening.

Aegis waved for quiet. "A small victory—perhaps in capturing this standard we have a sign that the future may yet emerge in our favor. Now we must go, each taking ship to wherever the winds carry you, but most to Albion, where my kinsman rules. There we will gather and plan our return."

Suddenly a great explosion shook the city, throwing them to the ground. A large cloud and shower of rock darkened the sky at the far southern end of the wall.

"They've undermined the wall and employed some blasting fire!" shouted a guardsman.

Gerald and Aegis ran toward the breech, rallying their men as the Terasians stormed through the ragged opening.

Aegis stopped and grabbed Gerald by the shoulder. "My men have orders to destroy the passageway down to the shore if such a breach happens—you must go *now*. I command you as the lord of this city."

Gerald stood hesitating, then another tremendous blast shook them and a section of the wall before them collapsed in a rush of smoke, fire, and fallen stone—the Terasians poured in like a river breaching a dam.

Gerald was cut off from Aegis by a river of troops. It was impossible to cross over to him. He saluted with his sword, then ordered the Caledonians who had gathered around him to fall back in a fighting retreat to the opening at the top of the passage, then started down the stairway toward the water's edge. They turned and saw the Terasians coming up behind, when the captain of the gate guard pulled down a large iron lever and sent a cascading rush and roar of masonry that closed the mouth of the passage against the Terasians.

They stood there for a moment in the sudden darkness, nearly choked by dust, then someone lit a torch and said, "Let us be going." They turned and hurried down to the beach, across the sand, and to the waiting ships. They had been able to take many refuges aboard the *Sea Wind*, but heard a rumor later that Aegis and nearly all his house fell in the last defense of their city, and many strong soldiers were lost that day, who were sorely missed in the struggles still to come.

CHAPTER 9

Gray Winds

THEY REBOARDED THE *SEA Wind*, cast off, and soon passed out to sea on the return to Caledon. A wave running up under her bow signaled the first watch, who took the helm and trimmed the sails. The others went to tasks below decks, and a third watch took the first shift to sleep. Their work would be later, in the dark watches of the nights to come.

The weather was fair; the wind following and steady. They soon left the high cliffs of Dara well behind, plowing blue waters steadily. The sun was bright, the air cool. The long deck rode up and down the swells of the gentle sea aquamarine blue, spray and foam, the surface of the water a calm skin on a tranquil body. Gulls sailed behind, floating on the following airs that blew the *Sea Wind* on.

Tynan and his cadre gathered around Siwell, who unrolled a map on a table bolted to the quarterdeck. It was an ancient rendering of the countries and lands known—some hundreds of years before—as Albion. He talked and told tales of tall ships sailing, petty kings squabbling, and dark crags frowning deeply over small violent battles for control of sheep, cattle, metals, and pasture.

"So, what of these Terasians, Siwell?" asked Kiefer. "Are they the monsters the world has painted them to be, or merely men as we are?"

"Men, of course, but a fearsome, relentless foe. They began as a small obscure tribe in the mountains high above the Litonian Plains. They were small-minded, with small aims of ruling the local farmlands and hoarding the most cattle. Then he who became the first king was born. It is said he stood tall among all his people—from the shoulders up, taller than any other. In the early days of his rule, he didn't style himself as a king, only as a First Citizen, and he pretended no connections to the highborn or royal houses in his country.

"Later, though, he and his counselors created tenuous or frankly fabricated links to their ruling classes. Through murder and betrayal, he raised himself to the throne, crushing all who counseled peace, and began to build a military juggernaut. Their first victims were lands near to hand, whose small disputes were used as pretexts for conquest, then enslavement.

"That was several centuries ago. He destroyed any lands or men that opposed him—including his own brothers—and built an administration of terror, fear, and reward so thorough that an iron core of fanatical support was welded with chains linking many other vassal states. It is said that the latest descendant from that first ruler has elevated himself to be a god, and that to worship him or images set up at key centers throughout the empire is the only way to high favor in his designs; and that the day may soon come when all must fall down before a gilded image to prove their loyalty—or at least their lack of traitorous intents."

"Then we have been taught to be wary of them with good reason," said Marc.

"Indeed," replied Siwell. "They are dangerous, cruel, and predatory; driven by a religion of emperor worship, seeing it as their mission to bring all peoples under their sway, cleansing their conquests of unbelievers, and thereby saving the world. They have by threats alone subdued ignorant countries with their claim of a divine right to rule."

"Can they be that powerful?" said Devon.

"As we saw at Dara, they can be overwhelming. Rank upon rank of bronzed armor, red banners, javelins like a forest, shields advancing like a moving wall. They have rarely been defeated in pitched battle on an open field—having suffered a temporary loss, they quickly refill their ranks to continue the battle."

"Much better, then, to defeat them a small bit at a time," said Kiefer. "They have been stymied at least once that we know of, and that by our ancestors."

"Cynald again," said Devon. "Among his many exploits, he was the Caledonian leader who put the Terasians to rout—unfortunately, as with many of his other stories, this is completely undocumented."

"You mean to say, of course," said Siwell, "that the whereabouts of his records are not known, at present. There is yet other evidence that can be pointed to: place names and their history, flags, banners, and other trophies that predate Cynald, and so on. Regardless, someone from among our forefathers defeated the Terasians, keeping them from invading our land. Why shouldn't the war leader be named Cynald? Regardless, our flag, with the chain shattered at the third link, carries a symbol of our being free from the oppressive designs of Teras."

"That thinking, at least, has some validity," said Marc. "Many of our early kings kept Teras at bay, opting for a rule of mutual respect and improvement—a rule of ideas, not of arms and law."

"One thing I'm glad for," said Kiefer, "is the difficult sea that separates them from us. It is hard for a large force to land on our beaches, nearly impossible if we oppose them vigorously at the waterline. If we are strong, ready, and determined, we can hold them long. But now it seems their plans are more widely laid. They will gradually cut off those with strength, in a kind of siege by isolation, gathering local allies, then set upon the remaining resistance from several sides, breaking through at some point to drive in and conquer."

"And so it is good that we are strong and need to stay strong," said Siwell. "Indeed, we may be stronger than they in warships and have better cavalry. And our hosts, though smaller, are determined. We are not without hope, even in a pitched battle. And perhaps we can avoid that. Thus far, we have few entanglements with the countries pressed by them. We may be able to avoid being pulled into a war we do not wish. But for mercy's sake or the sake of a just cause, we may be compelled go to another's aid."

The following day, Tynan sat on deck looking out over the sea that the sun rose strangely in the sky. The sailors had become edgy, often stopping and looking across the rear of the ship at a rack of odd-colored clouds that seemed to be rising on the stern. The clear fair skies and gently swelling seas began to give way to sullen nervous gusts of wind and low dripping clouds, the winds alternating between a sultry calm and driving squalls that shredded sails and frayed nerves. Lamps were lit at noon.

"Give orders for all hands to trim her up for gray winds," the captain said to the first mate, his voice low but urgent. Tynan saw the first mate, who had spent his life aboard ships, pale, then set off quickly, calling orders to the crew. Instantly, the whole ship was alive with hurrying men, some of whom looked worriedly at the sails and the sky, flinching at a certain strange heaving of the ship.

"Gerald," said the captain. "Please go below and, if you would, confine your men to their berths."

"Gray winds, Captain?" said Gerald.

"These clouds rolling up behind us bring them. Winds that drive down the sky to the sea, sometimes smashing ships outright; ofttimes scooping up funnels of water, making dervish pillars, stirring the waters so that strong men cover their faces and weak men throw themselves to the waves for fear. Gray winds are a nightmare of every man who goes to sea."

Tynan hurried below, finding the others in their bunkroom, when the ship gave a sickening lurch down and left, then lifted like a mad seesaw, flinging them to the floor.

Kiefer got up slowly, rubbing his arm. "We must speak to the captain about his piloting of this vessel. Quite unsatisfactory."

"According to him, such things as this are not his fault," said Tynan. "He spoke of gray winds, and neither he nor the first mate looked happy about it."

"It appears that we are experiencing them," said Devon. "Though I do not find them much to my liking."

"Nor do I," said Kiefer. "And the captain would not have confined us to quarters if he did not expect some rough going and quick sea work that we would muddle up."

"I for one . . ." began Marc when a loud knocking on their bulkhead door interrupted him and the cabin boy entered.

"Begging your pardons, sirs, but the captain sent me along to see you dry and taken care of, what with the galley not cooking and these, ah, contrary winds rattling us about." The cabin boy stood easily, unmoved by the widely canting and twisting of the ship.

"Did you risk all that way topside in this buffeting just to offer us tea and cakes?" Devon said.

"Well, 'tis my duty. By your leaves, if all is well here, of course, I will be back to the pilot to see what else he may need."

"One moment," said Devon. "We have a fancy to follow you up and see what these gray winds are, as they seem to be a seldom-met phenomenon."

The cabin boy looked uneasy. "I don't know, sir. With you not being accustomed to a ship in rough weather—not that you couldn't be fine, but—um—and the captain—I don't know . . ."

"No fear," Devon put in. "We will only take a quick look out of the deck hatch and return here straight away." With that he jumped from his bunk and was instantly flung to the deck

"You see, er, how rough it is, ah," said the boy as he helped Devon to his feet.

"Lead on, good sailor," said Devon. "We shall gain our balance presently."

The boy's worried look increased, but he said, "As you like . . . but it helps, er, to keep your knees bent, stay up on your toes, and to slap your hands against the bulkhead walls as you walk along."

In this way, they followed the cabin boy to the ladder that led topside. The climb up could be difficult in any weather, but with the ship lurching unpredictably, Tynan was nearly flung off several times. As he climbed, Tynan heard an increasing roar and startling noises above him.

The boy stopped just below the hatch. "I'm going out now. Remember—just a look, then back to your cabin as quickly as you can."

Devon smiled. "We promise and thank you for your kind concern. So, on you go."

The boy nodded, pushed the hatch open, and clambered out on deck. Tynan scrambled up behind and, looking out, saw total bedlam. The wind howled ferociously, ropes and ties twanging like the bowstring of a banshee. The deck rocked wildly, pitching forward and back, rolling and wallowing until at times the mast nearly touched the water. Everywhere he looked, towering grey hills of water moved with startling rapidity, rushing at the ship from all directions. Long steaks of grimy white foam stretched out down the backs of these hills, the wave tops, towering twenty feet above thirty-foot swells, torn and shredded into white sheets of flying water. All about, waves crumbled and fell like destroyed mountains, collapsing with a deafening roar, while fresh upheavals of cascading seas towered around them, mountains of water overhanging the ship.

Tynan watched as the cabin boy, holding a safety line stretched from prow to stern, threaded his way back toward the ship's helm where the pilot and captain struggled to keep a semblance of a course and the ship from foundering. The boy was moving along the deck with ease—that he was able even to stand seemed miraculous. He was helped by the safety line, but his hand barely touched it as he maneuvered quickly along the sloshing deck.

Then a sudden lull—a complete and uncanny calm in the rage of the storm brought the *Sea Wind* abruptly around, three-quarters to the wind. A loud, rising roar off the starboard quarter behind Tynan was the only forewarning of an onrushing wave. Tynan turned and saw a breaker looming up in the mist, towering high above the mast. The wind, driving from the stern, and the wave sweeping in from the bow, forced the ship to shudder to a halt, as if it had run aground. The cabin boy was caught flat-footed and thrown headlong—his grip torn from the rope—and slid headfirst into the ship's side. He tried to rise, then slumped to the deck and lay still.

Tynan sprang out on the deck, scrabbling toward him. The next wave or sudden burst of storm would almost certainly wash the boy overboard. The eerie silence and confused seas kept the ship momentarily stationary, wallowing uneasily. Nevertheless, the deck was pitched like a steep roof, forcing Tynan to clutch the safety line with both hands. He felt the rope bite deeply into his palms. Coming even with the boy, he slid down the deck.

"Get up!" he shouted. "Get up!" The boy groaned; blood ran from a deep cut on his head. Tynan, heaving with all his strength, dragged the stunned boy slowly up the canted deck. Without warning, the ship pitched back and they were both hurled into the mast base. Tynan lay stunned, his shoulder jammed into a fitting. Through his swirling consciousness, he heard a rising roar of water. Shaking himself, he struggled to his feet, lifting the boy, hooking his arm over the safety line, wrapping the rope twice around so the boy was wedged and tied. None too soon. The *Sea Wind* lurched more sickeningly than before. A riotous wall of foam and water plowed into the ship tearing a tackle block loose from the deck, and flung it forward, smashing into Tynan; then the wave itself struck him.

The shock knocked Tynan's breath from his body and sent him hurtling through the air, plunging him into the wild, white-streaked waves. It was shockingly cold, and he had couldn't draw a breath, as the air seemed completely filled with choking water. The sea poured over him, pushing him down deep below the surface. Thrashing frantically, he struggled up to the surface, spitting out a mouthful of briny sea.

From out of nowhere a round hoop of wood splashed next to him— it was attached to a rope and floated just out of his reach.

He was numb, tossed about by the stormy pinnacles of sea. The cold and constant struggling to the surface ebbed his strength, but he floundered after it, twice having it within his grasp only to have it torn away spinning and rushing up an oncoming sea ridge. With a last lunge, he grasped it with both hands and heaved his water-logged body onto the hoop, laying half in and half out of the water. With the extreme last bit of his strength, he pulled himself up, then with cold sea slapping over and nearly submerging him as the wind roared and tossed him like a leaf in a winter gale, he felt the hoop being tugged and looked up. The rope was stretched tight and on the other end were Marc, Kiefer, and Devon heaving with all their might.

Tynan suddenly realized that he was awake. His eyes were closed, and his head and his shoulder ached abominably, but he was definitely awake and by inference alive. He had been vaguely aware of being pulled up the side of the *Sea Wind*—dragged, really, back onto the ship, scraping and bumping against the sides most painfully, having the sea water pumped out of him, then being bundled into a hammock. Fever set in and the rest of the voyage was a blur of dreams and fitful sleep and warm broth being forced down him by Marc and the others, then strapped to a stretcher wrapped in a heavy wool blanket and the clip-clop of a long cart ride.

"There's the city—into the infirmary with him," came a voice above him. Alternating fever heat and bone-crushing chill then a rush of wringing sweat and sweet sleep at last.

Tynan slowly emerged as if from a confused dream. In the dream, he was aware of lying on a rough wooden plank. He was soaked through and had no strength to rise. Nearly covered in sand and debris, he lay there breathing, hearing the waves breaking gently on the shore, feeling the soft surge of the hissing water around him. He hoped that he was above the high tide mark, for he had not the strength to drag himself further up the sloping beach. There was no wind. He was very thirsty.

A long space of time passed with nothing in it. Then he became aware of movement—a small point of light bobbing toward him. It moved up and down along the water's edge, sometimes nearer the waterline, sometimes farther inshore, but always closer to where he lay. With a shock, he realized that he was unarmed and powerless in a land of many potential enemies. He could not move, and the light was coming on steadily. Soon, he heard an oddly familiar snuffling noise, then a low bark, followed by scrabbling feet.

"Abelard, what have you got there? Stay!" sounded a firm commanding voice out of the dark. Tynan struggled to rise—his sodden body would not respond. Instant death was near if this person's intent was to plunder. He was too weak even to speak as the figure set the lantern in the sand and knelt beside him. Tynan saw him reach for something and draw it out of his pocket. Then he spoke, but not to Tynan. "Thank you for directing me to this poor soul." He turned Tynan onto his back and placed a bundle under his head. Producing a flask, he said, "Drink this." Tynan took a small sip of something warm and strong and slightly sweet. It settled his uncontrollable shivering and sent a tiny hint of warmth through his thoroughly chilled body. Best of all, it washed away the salt-taste from his mouth.

"You've absorbed half the ocean sea," the man said as he wrapped Tynan tightly in a heavy wool blanket, binding the blanket closely with heavy leather straps. "We must move you before the tide comes in." He gripped the straps firmly and pulled Tynan up the sloping beach. "I will return shortly. Abelard! Watch!"

The man moved off, taking the lantern with him. Tynan saw the dark shape of the dog—it was immense—sitting calmly in the waning moonlight. Whatever was in the flask was having a powerful effect. He felt warmth creep tingling into his arms and legs. He was very drowsy. At some point, he became aware that the man had returned, leading a small cart. He lifted Tynan in, then leapt into the driver's seat. The dog bounded up, squeezing between Tynan and the cart's side, his bulk generating the warmth of a small fireplace.

As they turned up the shore, Tynan fell deeply asleep, unable to keep awake. As he lost consciousness again, he wondered again if the drink was drugged and what the intent of his rescuer might be.

Tynan woke again not knowing if he slept, dreamt, or both. He was comfortably wrapped and was now lying on a low bed of some firm yet very soft padding. The room was shuttered though not completely dark; sunlight filtering through. In a corner was a fire, somehow quite cheering, burning brightly on a small hearth, over which a copper kettle hung. Coverings were on the floor, a small table with a pitcher and a book stood by his bed, and two wooden chairs were set against the far wall. The rest of the room, though bare, was very clean. The walls were white-washed stone, the ceiling timbered with light wood. It was quiet, save for the sound of several dogs barking nearby. All seemed clean, sparse, and neatly kept.

Tynan looked on the fire and wondered where the *Sea Wind* was and what had become of his company. His head ached, his stomach was empty and loose, his right arm heavily bound.

The door swung open and in padded a large golden dog. It sat down just inside the door and gazed at Tynan.

"You must be the footpad who spied me on the beach. Thank you," said Tynan. "And are those your relations I hear disturbing this spring morning?" The dog's tail swept slowly across the floor.

"So! You are awake," said a voice from the next room. "Half a moment, and I'll put on some tea for you." The rattling of cups and crockery made Tynan even thirstier than he had been. All the while, the dogs outside barked and the one in his room sat motionless, looking at him with keen regard.

Then, moving quickly, Marten came in, bearing a platter. "Stay, Abelard," he said to the dog, who had risen to greet him. "Good morning," he said to Tynan, placing the tray on the table. Then he pulled one of the chairs up to the cot and sat down. He looked intently into Tynan's eyes, examined and replaced the bandage on his head, then probed his shoulder and arm, which tingled and spasmed painfully. "Good. Your eyes are clear and your strength will quickly return. Your shoulder will heal more slowly, though." He poured tea into a mug and handed it to Tynan.

"Thank you," said Tynan. His voice was dry and cracked, as he unsteadily brought the cup to his lips.

"Sip slowly, then take some of this fruit. The bread take last."

"I remember Abelard from last night," said Tynan. "And I am grateful to both of you for pulling me from the sea last night."

Marten looked at him quizzically. "Four nights ago, actually," he said. "And it was your friends that pulled you from the sea."

"Ah! It was a dream then—at least the part about washing up on the shore. I've been asleep that long?"

"Needfully so. You were closer to leaving this present life than any your age should be."

Tynan was thoughtful at this, looking into the fire. Marten stood up, walked to the shuttered window and opened it, pushing back the curtains. The light of early morning, clear and fresh, was there, a pale orange sky capped with the deep blue lingering of night. There were no clouds and sweet, cool air flowed in.

"A glorious spring for strange and troubled times," said Marten.

Tynan looked closely at him. Calm, sea-gray eyes gazed out the window serenely. White hair and an equally white beard framed a face weathered yet surprisingly alert. Though somewhat bent with his long years, he looked strong and moved easily. He was clad simply in a brown woolen tunic, girt with a wide leather belt—like Siwell, Tynan thought. On the belt hung keys and a small, red leather box.

"You at least have hope of a full recovery," Marten said as he turned back. "Once the fever is gone, we'll be able to let you get back to the cadre."

"Thank you again! Good news, despite the fact that like a fool I went up on deck to see the winds—gray winds the sailors called them—and was pitched overboard for my folly. To my great good fortune, Kiefer is a very good discus thrower and was able to toss out a life ring within reach, then they all hoisted me in."

"Yes, we did hoist you in; and a more bedraggled sea rat has never been seen." Marc, Devon, and Kiefer came to the door of the room, laughing. "Sopping wet, beaten down, and thoroughly doused in buckets of the finest salt water."

"I'll let you all talk for a short while and stop by later." Marten went out as the three friends came in.

"Well, Tynan, how are you? And are they going to let you out of here soon?" Marc said.

Tynan sat up. "As soon as the fever is quite gone."

"Good! We're going to need you for that match against the Golds next week."

The Golds were the Academy's elite coupe team, all from major Caledonian families, a fact that went unremarked upon, of course, as the Academy didn't allow talk of society status, wealth, or family. All was theoretically based on merit, talent, and hard work; but some things couldn't be overlooked or hidden.

"Those lummoxes have been talking up their game a lot the past days and need to be sent down a notch or two," Marc continued.

"Yes, sir," Tynan said.

"Meanwhile, let's see what we can do about getting you out of this bed for a short turn on the grounds," Kiefer said.

The three had brought with them a wooden wickerwork chair fitted with large wheels. "This is the best chariot we could find for the moment.

Let's take it for a quick ride and see about getting some fresh air," Devon said as they helped Tynan into it.

They started off slowly. "We'll take it as easy as a baby in a baby carriage," said Marc, but soon they were rushing down a long empty corridor, pushing the chair up to breakneck speed, then careened around a corner, slipping and scrambling. The wheeled chair slewed left then in seeming slow motion tilted and started to tumble right. Devon yelled something, while Marc and Kiefer both leapt after them, stretching and straining to keep the chair upright.

Tynan was dumped out of the chair and slid across the highly polished marble floor, spinning like a top, then slowly came to a stop; and found himself looking up at a large figure, while the other three piled into a tumbled heap with the chair against the hallway wall.

A brief silence ensued. "Why am I not in the least surprised?" was all the figure said.

It was a matron. "Begging your pardon, ma'am. We've had a slight accident with the chair," Marc said.

"Why would it be anything else?" she said and moved to pass, followed slowly, one-by-one trailing behind, her customary file of students, each dressed identically in the female version of the cadet uniform, blue with long cape, long skirts and matching headpiece, their outfit completed by a dark brown book satchel slung on the right shoulder.

Tynan and his friends stood stock still amidst their tangled mess; and mumbled, "Good day, ma'am," "Good day, miss," to the matron and her group as they passed by. Her charges—ten in all—went along behind her wordlessly with a swish and a whisper of sound, turning at last at the far end of the hall into the Music Wing.

Tynan turned to Marc. "Who were they?"

"Medical students," he replied.

"Never seen any of them before," put in Devon.

"They're kept separate from us—in the old Aubrey College, I think."

"Unfortunately, I think we may have seen one or two of them before," Kiefer said. "As I am now remembering back to when we were first in this infirmary months ago, on the day of the long weed-out run."

"*That* group?" said Tynan.

"Yes—and from the disgusted look on their faces just now, a couple of them seemed as if they recognized us as well."

"Again then, we have failed to make a very dashing impression," Devon said as he struggled to set the chair upright.

At that moment, Siwell came walking along the hall from the other direction. "Ah! Very good and well met. Marten said I might find you out this way. Uh—all well here?"

"Yes, Professor," Marc said as they righted the chair and settled Tynan back in. "Just going a little too quickly around the corner."

"Of course—those wheeled chairs are tricky things. Meanwhile, I've been thinking a lot about the old galley slave's 'gift' that he gave us on the dock at Aston Quay, going over in my mind what he said about it, and was just coming to see Tynan here to ask a few more questions, if you all have half a moment?"

Siwell stepped into a side alcove and removed it from the case he carried. The metal object had been tucked in there since before the events at Dara, and was still wrapped in the cloth that the old galley slave had carried. He slowly unwound the cloth, rolling it out on a bench while the others gathered round. It gleamed in the light, a triangularly shaped figure of metal with a loop affixed to the apex, the metal beaten out and slightly rusted from years at sea. They said nothing as they looked at it and the silence grew.

"Well?" said Kiefer. "Anything come to mind?"

"The old man laughed," Tynan said. "And would have laughed right now if he could see our faces. 'You don't know what it's for do you?' he said. "And we still don't."

"What else did he say about it?" Marc asked. "Did he give any clues?"

"He said before he died that 'horsemen use it,'" Tynan replied. "Then he laughed again and passed out of this present life."

"It would have been better if he had saved more of his final breath to tell us further of its use," said Kiefer.

"To me, it seemed at the very end that he was speaking to someone—maybe that person was the great gift of his life?" Tynan said. "I don't know. But this was the greatest gift in all the western kingdoms, by his account of it."

"Horsemen use it?" put in Devon. "It does narrow it down somewhat—either something to use while riding or for the horse, tack or something, or maybe something for the rider?"

Marc picked it up, weighing it in his hand. "It's heavy, so not a small buckle or strap or some type of weapon to throw; and it's thick, with the side away from the apex flat, not round as the other two sides are."

They talked about every possible thing the triangular metal object could be or do: a signal device, a hand grip, a throwing weapon, a handle, and countless others. But nothing fit, nothing that would make it seem "the greatest gift of all the western kingdoms." Western? Likely this was something the old man had learned about in the East. He said he was a great traveler before being shackled to the galley—was there something in the East used by horsemen that was unknown in the West and gave the horseman some of advantage over their opponents?

It was a riddle that must have an answer. There was the object, gleaming in the light. The answer felt tantalizingly close—if they could just find the last piece of the mystery—a word or image or view that would be the key to open the lock. But the thing lay there mutely, unspeaking, unmoving, uncooperative; framed as always, nested as always on the oily, grimy cloth with which it was wrapped.

The cloth. It had never been looked at or studied before. They set aside the metal object and spread the cloth out on the table. Kiefer took an oil lamp from its niche in the hallway and set it on the bench, creating a bright pool of light around the oilcloth. Staring at the grimy cloth, so dirty and rubbed out, they could be seen what looked like a very rudimentary sketch of an animal.

"A horse?" Devon said.

"It's possible," said Siwell. "Some kind of a military manual page written with strange figures? It looks like a guide to horse trappings—halter, reins, saddle—but the figures are written in an incomprehensible script, the writing so vague and obscured is nearly unreadable. Nevertheless, something is here. It's unmistakable—but how to unravel it?"

Siwell continued to peer at the tattered cloth, pouring over it. "Hmm. There *is* something written as well as drawn on the cloth," he said as he stared, then he drew out an instrument that looked like a small inverted field glass and slid the cloth beneath.

"Hmm," he said again. "Yes—there is writing here and a very rough, almost stick-like figure rendering of a horse. The lettering I can't decipher—it looks to be based on a system of pictographs, completely unlike anything I've seen."

Siwell painstakingly copied out what was inscribed on the cloth, taking a long while as the others waited, watching intently. At length he straightened up and made a few extra touches.

"This is it, I believe," and slid it across for them to see.

Tynan and the others spun Siwell's sketch around and looked. The triangular shape was labeled and seemed to hang on a strap below the saddle.

"What do you all make of it?" Siwell asked.

"If a rider was sitting in the saddle and was of near to average height, their boots would reach down just about where those hang—then maybe slip them in—some kind of place to rest the feet while riding?" Marc answered.

"What good would that do?" Kiefer asked.

Marc shrugged and no one ventured a guess.

"We'll have to experiment as shown in the sketch to see how it works, if it does," Siwell said. "Field testing is the only way to be sure; meanwhile I'll take this sketch over to the Stacks to attempt to render it in our speech—they may have scroll or sample from the East that can give clues to the meaning of the lettering. Then we can work with the horse trainers and saddlers."

"Right then," Marc said. "Time to wheel the invalid safely back to his room."

"I for one would like to emphasize the word *safely* in that phrase," Tynan said. "Let's do our collective best not to dump this particular invalid in the hall again today. I've spent more than enough time recently being thrown to the ground, cast into the sea, and otherwise flung rudely to the floor to want to go through that experience again."

CHAPTER 10

Hunters' Moon

"BUT NOW," SAID POLICRATES, "We will hear your tale and how you all from, it seems, the same land come to be in the same ship and to arrive here on our shore." Tredegar stood before the king and looked directly at him without malice and without fear.

"O king, to you we owe all things. Our gratitude and service are yours to command. And your sight is keen: we are nearly all from Warrec, prisoners sold to the Terasians and rushed to row that cursed ship for some urgent errand to the Middle Sea itself. And as we have shown, we were taught to row well under the beat and lash of the oarmaster, until we were swept up in a mighty storm like the one that assailed us on our return from Dara, and by providence some of us lived to come to your shores.

"Once you hear my words, lord, if you have mercy and wisdom, you will at once place ten thousand spears by my side and send them with us to confront the Mataen hordes now devouring our land."

"The Mataens? Have they crossed the River?" Policrates said, turning to Gerald.

"We haven't heard of it, sir," said Gerald. "We'll need to check into it immediately."

"Very good," said Policrates.

"That shall be seen, of course, and can be established by our means," the Marshal put in. "Meanwhile, we will need to hear more proofs of yourself and the claims you make."

"Of course," Tredegar replied. "For my proofs, the first is my name. I am Tredegar Crottach, son of Benton Crottach, and I saw my father and my brothers fall before the Lion Gate and the standard of the Mataens lifted above the walls of my citadel. I myself am nearly unmanned because I live and can speak these words, one who would be better dead than to witness the grim shadow that has fallen over my people.

"The Mataens had come undeclared and unmarked, descending swiftly into the valley over the mountains from the south. No word of their approach came to the city, as they had overwhelmed the sentries at the frontier, crossing the river without provocation or warning, killing all that was living in their path. And they came with fire: burning farms, villages, and fields as they marched. Nothing alive was spared. They seemed intent on annihilation not conquest, else they might have swept unchecked into the open gates of our city, which was at peace with them and unaware of the threat of war, as all were at attendance at the High Council where leaders are chosen and hard questions disputed.

"I later learned that their keen timing was in no way accidental, but that they had long been exchanging messages with my cousin Orme to determine the most favorable opportunity to attack. That, too, shall be seen to.

"Up they marched, demanding the surrender of the city and the submission of the crown. My father, a strong and proud man, rejected them to their face and defied them from the city wall. In silence they turned away, and assembled siege ramparts and towers, rolling forward their engines to fling missile and stone against us. We returned in kind, with mangonels and ballistas, often slinging back at them the very material they launched at us, with the added advantage of height and greater skill. Therefore, many of their soldiers fell in those days from lethal missiles wrought by their hand."

Here he paused, barely able to contain his emotion. "For three weeks, we held them completely at bay. Then Orme, who commanded defense of the Cliff Wall on the last night, gave our city and our people over to them. It is said that with his own hand he threw down the key to the small gate at the base of the wall, thereby sealing the deaths of many. If ever I see him again, I will ask and will know if it was so. And if it is true, then the justice of heaven will not be denied.

"Nevertheless, through that gate, the Mataens swarmed in. They sent a small force which surprised the gatehouse sentries, then flung open the main gates. Their troopers rushed in, cutting down any they found. The rest of their horde flowed in behind. A detachment dashed to the citadel, hoping to surprise my father's house without a fight. This they were not able to do. We made them buy their victory at a high price. Their bodies piled high around my father, my brothers, and our household troops. In the end we were overmastered.

"I was surrounded and struck down, my helmet sheared in two. Though the axe blade merely nicked me, I fell senseless in the midst of the fighting. Some weeks later, I recovered my senses, finding myself chained to an oar in the galley from which you delivered us. My clothing was changed, and my beard shaved; and I guessed that my shield bearer had altered my appearance to be overlooked by the Mataens.

"Afterwards, we were sent on an urgent errand to the Emperor until caught up in the storm which destroyed many of the other ships in our convoy. Somehow, our vessel held together until we were windblown to your shores."

Tredegar finished speaking and sat down. The room, filled with others freed from the galley, shook with loud shouting. "Tredegar king!" "Death to Orme!"

Tredegar stood again and motioned for silence. It was some time before the shouting and pounding ceased. He spoke to his countrymen. "My brothers. You at least know that I am the heir and the lawful king," here there was much shouting again from Tredegar's people. "But my claim can be lawfully established only at the gathering of all freeholders on High Summer Day. Until then, I am not a king, but a captain. I am content. And the law of this creation will see to Orme, though I should be surprised if he goes to his grave in peace. Regarding him, twice traitor though he is, I charge each of you within my hearing to withhold from striking him down though he sits now in a bloody, unnatural place. He must be given the chance to give way by choice and then proper punishment pronounced."

Here Tredegar paused, looking down, doubt and sadness commingled in his face. "Perhaps," he said quietly, "perhaps he can be redeemed."

Some shouted, "No! Death to all traitors!" But they were drowned out by others crying assent to the rightful laws of their country. "Yes! Yes! Listen to Tredegar. Such is the wisdom and mercy of a true king."

"Thus, lord, is our tale," concluded Tredegar as he sat down. For several minutes the hall resounded with "Tredegar! Tredegar! Tredegar!"

"Have you further proofs?" asked the Marshal when the room had finally quieted.

Tredegar stood again. "Most compelling would be the ship of war lately come to your shores. That Septus was aboard her ought to be a signal that something major is afoot. Then the shouts and affirmations of these men, whom you yourself have seen to be all from the same land. The last is that I plan to present is myself and my body: lend me a sword and passage to Warrec and I will prove with my body and my life that I am Tredegar, son of Benton, son of Edgar, lawful heir to the throne of that city. How that I would be away quickly to my land, to free them or die in the effort! My soul rages within me! Regardless of what you decide, I must beg your leave to go quickly—with all who will choose to come with me—and take back from Orme and the Mataens what was unlawfully stolen from us."

At this, the entire hall erupted again with cheers, shouts, pounding fists, and stamping feet. "Aye! Aye! Aye! To Warrec! To Warrec!"

After the hall had quieted somewhat, Policrates asked, "And where do the ten thousand spears of Caledon enter this tale, if this tale be true?"

"Just here, lord," answered Tredegar. "You have seen the ship of war at your dock and have spoken with the admiral Septus. Though the law of the sea and all good men forbid it, you would have done well to sink it at its moorings and slaughter the crew. For this is but one of a thousand such vessels for war, with more than twice that toll in supply, troop, and baggage ships.

"I have seen them, as have many others sitting here. At Dara, they came to conquer what they called Albion, and then—in league with the Mataens and others—they are planning to come here. Aboard Septus's vessel, we heard them speak tales of your land, which they call Ultima Thule, where they told of human sacrifices and the drinking of blood among profane rites, headless monsters, and flying serpents. The priests of their country are seeking portents and signs from their gods by their foul methods as to whether this land—as others—would benefit from the rule of Teras.

"That their priests will receive a favorable answer from their gods is a foregone conclusion, most assuredly, as we know their deities have not as yet commanded them to withhold their overlordship from any land their Emperor deems fair, or merely free. You may weigh any of these obvious facts with several that might readily suggest themselves to you and realize that, regardless of who I might be, our common enemy is Teras and all her agents."

Tredegar sat down again. There was a long, long silence. For many minutes Policrates said nothing, his eyes closed, his hands tented before him.

"Truly," he said finally, "Your news is strong and disturbing. But not wholly unexpected. My house and those of others here have had long-standing business with Teras. We share a somewhat connected history with them and even what happened at Dara was really just another chapter in that long history of helping a friend against them.

"Fortunately, we have other friends, friends even within the dark places of Teras who pass to us information needful to protect this land from sudden onslaught. Events, though, are moving more swiftly perhaps than we had expected, and it may be that you have been brought to us to guide our ways to preserve many people alive and to prevent many evil things from happening on this earth. So, you our guests will retire to your places to rest. We will remain to gather our counsel, then determine our course."

"As you will," said Tredegar. "What I would add to what has been said is that all delay aids the Mataens, Teras, and their ilk—with each day counted in lives."

"That may be so," answered Policrates, "and your heart is in your land, as mine would be if it had suffered as yours has suffered. I know. We will choose, then take the things that are sent to us."

Smoke rose over the citadel—beyond, the Great River flowed out to the western sea. A tall bridge stood there guarded from a strong point on the near side, with a guard shed placed on the far bank. Tynan's patrol sat on their horses on the high ridge looking down on the town while, ominously, carrion birds rode the sky above the plain, circling their grisly appointed rounds, biding their time.

"The smoke we saw from a distance is this burning, then," Gerald said.

"The place is swarming with Mataens. They've barricaded themselves in," Kiefer said.

"They've barred the gates and are slaughtering, burning, and looting the city. It will last a day and they will leave back to their land over the bridge," Tredegar said.

"Not if we can help it," Gerald said. He quickly wrote a note and handed it to Devon. "Ride back to the Marshal and describe the circumstance. Request he send forward three squadrons of cavalry ahead of the foot troops. It will be a forced ride, but they must be here by mid-morning tomorrow." Devon saluted, spun his horse, and galloped away.

"I would really love to catch some of those devils in the palace—Orme especially—and cut off the head," Gerald said. "The rest of the beast then may fall. We've got about thirty of us here. Is there a way to raise such a ruckus that they will think the whole Caledonian army has come up on them from the bowels of the earth? Who knows what kind of carnage they might carry out between now and tomorrow."

"There may be another way in," said Tredegar.

"Another way?" Gerald asked.

"An old, unused, partly blocked watercourse. It's been years since I've been through it, though at one time it was passable," Tredegar answered.

"Can you lead us up that way?"

"It might be done," he said. "The old citadel was built to guard the central mines west of the river. The whole reason the city is built where it is was to maintain control of what comes out of the mines. Later, the mines ran dry, and others were discovered further north. It's said they are still worked to this day by the Mateans, the most recent of many other mine owners—mines that have been worked for gold, silver, and lead for centuries. Some of the oldest shafts, tunnels, and channels, however, have left a maze of diggings beneath the walls of the city.

"One of the slurries drains out to a covered channel below the western wall. It is gated and usually guarded, but a determined man or group of men may be able to go up from the outside and come out through a disused offshoot into a well that is open to all in the city, if one knows the way in and the way forward once inside."

There was a silence among those who listened.

"Well, we can't very well let those barbarians wreak havoc on the town while we sit outside watching our beards grow," said Kiefer.

"It is likely too that Orme has taken what remains of my family hostage and will try to carry them away with him if he leaves the city when the Mataens go."

"We must try something to get into the city as quickly as possible," said Gerald. "Let us attempt entry the way you speak of—perhaps some good will come of it."

The citadel at Warrec rose darkly above them. The moon had passed beyond the distant hills. Stars shone bright and hard against the night sky. A steady breeze from the west rustled trees and bushes, disturbing the silence and covering any rattle of stone or loud footfall they made as they slowly worked along the base of the fortress. At a midpoint along the wall, they stopped and looked up. Tynan saw or rather felt the immense mass of the stronghold raised high as a bulwark and watchtower over the river plains below. Tredegar was right: assailing this wall by direct attack would be futile. Only by betrayal—as had been done once—or escalade as they were to attempt could the key be turned.

Tredegar stepped back and fitted a shaft tipped with a cloth-wrapped iron hook to a bow. To the shaft was lashed a climbing rope. Looking up, the hard edge of the parapet was lined as if by a ruler against the starry sky. He drew back his doubled bowstring and released the bolt. It flew up the sheer wall and hit with a low thud on an unseen ledge. He gently pulled the rope back, feeling it scrape along, then the secure catch of the hook. He slung his bow over his shoulder, tugged hard on the rope once or twice, then began the slow hand-over-hand ascent up the hundred-foot cliff.

They climbed, traversing the rock face. The night grew completely dark. Slowly the small band of men threaded their way toward the shadowed stronghold, taking great care as they stepped slowly through the tumbled and broken stone that nearly choked the old footpath winding up the cliff face. In some places the path was broken and shattered completely, forcing them to leap over dark chasms with no way of knowing how far away the other side would be—a literal leap in the dark.

Without Tredegar, who was thoroughly familiar with every piece of cracked and broken stone, they never would have done it. But he knew every turning and soon they were huffing and catching their breath beneath the huge wall that rose sheer from living rock, its face nearly smooth as glass.

Stars shone out again, bright and hard against the night sky. A steady breeze from the west rustled trees and bushes, disturbing the silence and covering any rattle or loud footfall they made as they slowly worked their way around the base of the cliff walls. Tynan saw or rather sensed the immense mass of fortifications raised high as a bulwark and watchtower over the plains below. "No force could assail this wall directly and overthrow it. Only by betrayal or escalade could it be taken." Tredegar's words ran through his mind again. And escalade—an *internal* escalade—was what they were about to try.

The small group continued to make its way slowly across the steep rocky slope that ran below the walls of Warrec, skirting the abyss that yawned below them.

The field turned into a bed of larger stones; boulders, really, some as large as small houses. The stone was very cold; the wind blew across the face of the slope. They halted. Tredegar was feeling his way ahead, then seemed to disappear into the rocks themselves. Tynan quickly followed him and found himself squeezing into a narrow crack in the stone, which immediately widened into a rough-hewn tunnel that ran ahead into the darkness. Beside the opening they found torches with flints to light them, as if placed there for their use.

"The gods must be with us," Tredegar said, as he lit the first. In the sputtering light, Tynan saw they were in a fairly wide tunnel with a channel cut into the rock floor. In this channel water flowed slowly and clearly into the hill beneath the city.

They walked cautiously ahead and came to a stone-lined, water-filled grotto. Tredegar led them past, following a nearly unseen narrow path that went down to the floor of a rocky gully at the bottom of which stood shallow water, nearly stagnant, overhung by some type ancient brush. They squirmed under the hedges, handing down the packs of gear, and descended quickly to the gully bottom, then turned and followed up the narrow way toward another sheer rock face. The path was heavily covered with thick brush, some nearly as strong as young trees, and was obviously long disused, nearly choking the channel. Sloshing ahead in ankle-deep water, they were able to force a way through.

They came to a dark semicircular opening that yawned ahead of them. Tynan could hear slow-running water, a low but distinct sound as they walked straight into the cliff face, a sheer rock wall. Tredegar moved quickly right—and disappeared. Marc was just ahead of Tynan, took a couple of steps, then whispered, "It's a crevice to the right." Then he disappeared into the cliff as well.

"More torches," came the whispered command. The torches were passed up, then lit. Another passage was revealed, carved by tools, nearly level, and in some places polished smooth, shown ahead of them.

The group continued on. The ceiling started to slope down imme-diately, and the passage narrowed as well. Soon they were crawling on hands and knees, holding the torches in their teeth to keep balanced.

They came to another opening and Tynan heard more running wa-ter ahead, swiftly now, a rush of free water in the watercourse proper. Tynan turned left and dropped into the channel. The water came up to his waist—cold and strong, it flowed into the darkness. Splashing and wad-ing forward for some time, they came to a vertical shaft, water from the spring now brought to its foot via a branching channel. It was like a well within a cave, reached by a long sloping stone-built gallery, at the foot of which the spring itself was guarded by a now unmanned guard chamber.

Passing through the next section, the ceiling rose again, then the height of the passage reduced to less than four feet, then further on to only two and a half feet in height. The bottom was now a soft silt with a calcareous crust at the top, mainly strong enough to hold their weight, except for a few places where they broke through it with a sudden drop into a layer of silt nearly eighteen inches deep. They were now crawl-ing on all fours and were getting on very well, the water being only four inches deep. Presently bits of debris came floating by and they suddenly awoke to the fact that the waters were rising again.

The water was now began to run with great force, and they were crawling laid out at full length, up to their necks in it, thrashing ahead through the gauntlet of the water, each holding a torch in their mouth, the passage leaving only four inches of breathing space, though some of the time even Tynan's mouth was under water. They came to two false cuttings, and then were going in a zigzag direction when the height of the channel lowered perceptibly and forced them plunging and puffing through the water again, when at last the passage rose slowly to walking height, leading to a shaft, where they came out and stood shivering for several minutes before going on.

They continued on beside the now broader water channel. As they went, Tynan gradually perceived a growing rumble—a low, persistent, deep sound like heavy wagon wheels churning in iron grooves. They sud-denly came out into a high vaulted grotto of sorts. The channel widened into a broad pool, deep and still, while at the far end a huge wheel turned dredging up the water to a channel above.

"How does it turn?" Gerald asked.

"Far above is a team of twelve oxen that toil around the crank of a windless day and night. They are replaced and refreshed every hour; and thus the city is supplied with water regardless of season, as those who come to the foot of the great stone staircase find a constantly replenished well of water brought up from this subterranean place."

A small dinghy used for repairs was tied to the edge of the pool. They scrambled aboard and slowly paddled over to the churning wheel.

"Watch what I do, then do likewise," Tredegar said, slipping over the side, swimming carefully up to one of the moving large buckets—large enough to hold many gallons of water—attached to the waterwheel; then he gripped the side as it passed and swiftly clambered in. As the bucket reached the lip of the cistern above and swung so as to deposit the water in the high cistern, he slipped out and splashed to the side. They all followed his example and were soon standing on the edge of a narrow channel flowing swiftly now down toward a pool wider than any they had seen to this point, with a stone walk that encircled it on one side to the foot of a circular staircase that curved up toward the city itself.

"All right," said Tredegar as they gathered round him. "We are to the point. Up these stairs, along the street to the right, and follow the city wall to the East Gate. The guard will be Mataens only, their eyes should be staring out into the darkness looking for a rumor of rebels and hoping for relieving force of their own troops.

"Once the guard is taken, swing open the gate. Meanwhile, we will hurry to the Great Hall to see if we can catch that worming rat Orme before he can wriggle free or alert other troops that are nearby. Do not slay any of our people or Mataens who surrender. They shall go to the prison in the citadel and there shall be judged properly once the city is set in order."

Tynan ran alongside Tredegar. The main gate was taken in complete and silent surprise. Little blood was shed as they bound the sentries in the gatehouse. Then they hurried on to the Great Hall. As they ran, the shouting and calls in the city rose and they heard the running of feet and the clattering of armed men on the cobble streets.

"Don't engage these soldiers unless we must," said Tredegar. "Orme is our prize."

The Great Hall towered above them, built of gray stone faced with marble. A wide stairway topped by seven pillars, four on one side three on the other, wound its way into the edifice. Their appearance was more of an artistic work than any real support of the building's weight and were beautifully fluted, capped by wondrously carved capitals, standing more than twenty feet high.

They ran up the wide, sweeping stairs, not admiring the intricate detail carved and molded into the walls about them. The massive main doors were remarkable by themselves, being carved of ancient wood, with many designs of silver set into the wide, heavy panels.

"These shall be hard to beat down," Gerald said.

"That is if they are barred or locked," said Tredegar. He reached and easily pushed them open. The doors noiselessly swung back, revealing a small receiving hall, which was empty. Through the next two sets of doors, they came to a third chamber, an inner final defense, planted there long before the coming of the Mataens or Teras.

Inside was the Great Hall itself, all of white, blue, and gold—the seat of power in its time of lands across the river, the stronghold of Western Albion, designed to be the right and just place for every citizen to bring their complaints and interests to be voiced and responded to in the presence of the lord himself.

The torches pushed back the gloom and Tynan saw a rough wood throne, a stark contrast to the splendor of the hall. It had no device on it, was stained dark with age, and was not unoccupied.

There, seated in the dark, was a man—or the remains of a man— wrapped in a great black cloak. In his hands he held a crown, resting the crown on his lap. His hair was blonde and thin, his nose prominent, his lips thick, pouty, and red. He was bent over the crown like a boy over his porridge.

They walked across the wide-flagged floor and stood three paces before him.

"Orme," Tredegar said. "You are a twice-guilty traitor and by the rightful laws of all good lands, I should strike you down with my sword and leave your body under the open sky to serve the beasts and birds."

Orme glanced up hurriedly then back down to the crown he held. His eyes darted left and right. "Ah . . . I don't recognize you," he said. "Save perhaps as a rebel or a robber of my land."

"You know me, at least by reputation if not by sight," said Tredegar. "I am the rightful master of this hall, king in the place of my father, whose death you brought about."

"King?" Orme said. "We have had no king since those unhappy times. Now, our Mataen friends support and guard us."

"Support? Guard? Don't you mean bind? Imprison? Your friends are givers of bonds and jail holdings."

"Umm, it is unlikely, young man that you are, that you would understand such policies of accommodation and peace."

"Peace? Peace in the way that a desert or a tomb gives peace. Those places have peace only because all life has been removed from them."

The sounds of battle grew steadily louder. Orme shifted nervously in his seat. "All in this land are entitled to their free opinion."

"Orme—don't be a fool. You and your Mataen group are finished."

Suddenly through a side entry burst in a squad of soldiers. "All is ready to . . ." said the leader, then stopped short, seeing Tredegar and the Caledonians. "Who are these?"

Orme laughed, looking up, his eyes bright. "Ah! Lucius!"

"Lucius? A Terasian soldier?" Tredegar said.

"Maybe you didn't know?" said Orme. "Yes, Lucius. This is only a traitor and his helpers. And as a traitor . . ." he stood up from his chair, straightening himself to his full height, holding the crown above his head with both hands. "Before the true lord of Warrec, I first crown myself as king." He lowered the crown, which being made for another was the wrong size and so slipped sideways, and he smiled.

"My father's crown is ill-fitted for such a narrow head," said Tredegar.

Orme seemed unmoved. "As true lord of this land—and as my first command—I order the immediate execution of this Tredegar—traitor—and all his gang. To be carried out at once."

"You are indeed a fool, Orme," said Tredegar. "We are not unarmed, and as you can hear, the city is falling back into our hands."

Orme laughed again. "But you will not be here to see it, even if it is so. Lucius: you may strike them down where they stand."

The troopers spread out around them. The leader gave orders in a language Tynan didn't understand, but one of the squad ran toward the doors. The din of fighting was near now and very loud.

"Bar the doors!" shouted Lucius, as the trooper hesitated.

Too late. Incredibly, Tynan heard the clatter of horses' hooves. As the soldier reached the doors, he was suddenly flung back like a rag doll as a great gray horse pushed through. It was Policrates himself. Behind him, also on horseback, was the Marshal. Other Caledonian horsemen surged in behind. Lucius and his men raised their hands, dropping their weapons, and were quickly bound.

"Now. Orme . . ." said Tredegar turning back to the dais, but Orme was gone, through a hidden door hewn in the wall behind the royal tapestries which hung there. They ran quickly after him, rushing down a narrow, steeply descending passage. Tynan nearly leaped into space.

"Hold! Hold!" said Tredegar. "This is a step to break one's neck and the fall is many fathoms. There is a rope fastened to the wall. Hold onto it as we go down."

They hurried down, Orme was running ahead, cackling a strange laugh which floated up to them eerily from below. Then they were out through a small door, into the open air and found themselves on a balcony.

"He's out onto the battlements!" cried Tredegar, as they burst through.

Dawn was nearing. Orme ran along the parapet, but Tredegar and Tynan were gaining ground. Then from the other direction four archers appeared. Orme drew a dagger from beneath his robe. One bowman drew and fired an arrow, which plunged deeply into Orme's shoulder. He staggered a step, then stumbled down the catwalk, pitched forward, and disappeared into the dark.

They stopped, looking down.

"Well, is that his end, then?" Tredegar said.

"There's no way to know," answered Gerald. "He simply vanished."

The sun slowly rose and there was a silence that hung over the city.

"The battle is past," said Tredegar, looking up.

"But who has won it?" asked Gerald.

CHAPTER 11

The Mataens

THEY WARILY MADE THEIR way through the ruin of the city. Not a living person was to be seen and there was no sound but the burning citadel tower far above them. A grisly sight awaited in the main open square. Nearly a hundred bodies were there, impaled on long poles while on the surrounding walls were nailed the bodies of the king, his sons, and the members of the noble house.

"Headless—all headless—why?" Devon asked.

"The Mataens hunt heads," said Gerald. "In their gruesome temples they have niches built into walls and columns that hold the heads of their victims slain in war and use them in their profane sacrifices to their gods. According to their beliefs, they hold that the head has magical powers; and when they take them—especially when they take the head of a lord or king which is deemed worthy to be mounted in the great temple at Barduk—they gain control of those powers and in some measure gain the mastery over the enemies they took them from."

The main gate was hanging open, splintered and broken. They rode away from Warrec toward the Great River—wreckage and debris were strewn everywhere, some things seemingly cut down or ruined out of mere spite—then continued across the great stone bridge that stood unguarded, the only sound the wind whistling through the stone-built arches.

"How did they get over this and into the city?" Marc said.

"No one really feared that wild unruly horde with antique weapons, chariots, and all," Gerald said. "With their spellcasting and painted bodies and faces. As we know, it was Orme who made a pact with them inciting them to treachery and it was Orme that threw down the key to the postern gate in the cliff wall by his own hand, and through that gate they poured in to sack the city."

They crossed the bridge and rode up the far slope toward the Forest of Dean, halting on the far side to make camp for the night. They set a strong guard though it was several days at least since the Mataens had passed through, seeming to be fleeing ahead of the oncoming of Caledonians.

Continuing on next morning, Tynan, Marc, Devon, Kiefer, and four scouts more rode far ahead, seeking tracks and an idea of how far ahead the Mataen horde had gone. They cantered quickly along the forest road. The signs of the Mataen flight were everywhere visible as debris, wounded and dead men, war gear of all sorts, horses, cattle, and destroyed cartage were strewn along the road. "They care not about even their own troops or beasts," said Marc as they passed.

After several hours riding, they cantered around a wide turn and suddenly came upon a wagon, broken down, and two teamsters struggling with a heavy wheel and axel. Behind them stood a tall man holding a riding crop, shouting and beating them on the shoulders. "Mend this quick, you idiots. Do you want to meet the foul greeks? They will boil you alive in their oil and feed you to their hogs!"

At a canter, Tynan leaned over and grabbed the tall man's arm, sending him sprawling across the road. The two others shouted, dropping the wheel and lurched for their axes propped up beside the road cutting. Tynan wheeled to the right in time to see Gerald cut down one. The other staggered back, swinging his axe wildly. The third Mataen was running for his horse which was tied to a tree. Tynan wheeled his horse and held it in check, reining up, pausing a moment then sprang forward at a gallop. He drew out one javelin and flung it—then the other. Both struck home, then he drew his sword and looked for the third Mataen. He never saw the blow coming as the soldier had turned and struck him a glancing blow on the helmet.

He swayed in the saddle and warded off a second blow as five other Mataens burst out from the dark trees on the far side of the road, rushing with their broadswords and axes raised. Gerald spurred his horse, drew his sword and with a sweeping blow stuck down the first. Three other soldiers sitting on the road bank leapt up, struggling to seize their battle axes. One tried to mount his horse, two others rushed them, one striking a hard blow that caught Marc on his small round shield, shearing it in two.

The soldier took a step toward Tynan and swung his battle axe. Tynan parried the blow but was unhorsed, falling hard to the ground. The footman took another step toward Tynan, raising his axe high, and was pierced through with a javelin cast from Marc, the blow turned away, beating the ground. The third guard lunged at Tynan, who deflected the axe with his sword, then drove the point into the guard's shoulder. The fourth man gained his horse and rode wildly away, raising a call on a horn as he rode frantically away, Kiefer in pursuit.

"Kiefer!" Gerald shouted. "Hold back—look to that bridge." Kiefer reined up and looked. A half-mile ahead, the fleeing Mataen rider had reached a narrow wooden bridge and was now drumming across it. The bridge was barely wide enough for two men to walk shoulder to shoulder. On the far side of the bridge, a mass of armed Mataen troopers rested, apparently waiting for the wagon to be repaired and catch up.

Kiefer and Tynan jumped down, helping Marc to his feet. "Are you injured?"

"Not badly," said Marc. "My left arm is numb."

"Why it's hanging useless," Devon said. "Can you lift or move it?"

"I just need a wrap—we need to be after those other guards."

"Your shield was cloven in two by that blow," said Gerald picking it up and inspecting it. "Not much use now, save to be hung up over the mantel at home."

Then he called, "Hi, Kiefer! Let whoever is locked in that wagon loose and double-time—we're going to get some visitors soon." Across the narrow bridge, a great mass of troops was starting to mill about—the main body of the Mataen forces. They saw the escaped horseman ride up to the troops and gesture back at them. A sergeant shouted, rousing the rest of the Mataen troops to their feet.

"They've obviously been celebrating already," said Marc. "Many of them are staggering drunk."

Kiefer meanwhile had broken the lock on the small thick wagon door and opened it, peering into the dim cell. "Sir," he cried and waved to Gerald.

"It doesn't matter who's in there Kiefer, get them out and moving back up the road. Those troopers will waste no time in coming for us."

Kiefer looked into the wagon again—inside were three women and five children. As he reached in to help them out, one of the women stepped out and swinging an iron rod that turned out to be a fireplace sweep, just missing his head, striking the side of the wagon loudly.

"Hey," shouted Kiefer. "No need for that—we're here to help . . . to take you back to Warrec."

The woman readied another blow. "I'll help *you* into the next life if you come a step closer."

"Nan," came another voice from inside the wagon. "Please restrain yourself and help the children out of this smelly hole. Can't you see he is wearing the livery of Caledon?"

Marc and Tynan rode up. "Those lads over there are coming fast. Can we get these away—maybe fix the wagon quick?"

"We can ride," said another voice from inside the wagon. "If you have horses to lend us." And out stepped a tall woman in her late fifties—the mother of Tredegar.

Gerald knew her. "Your majesty. We are quite pleased to see you living."

"I, too, am pleased to be living," replied the woman.

"Everybody dismount and turn your horses over to the women," said Gerald as he swung off his horse, shortening the girth—the others did likewise. "Devon: take one of the children with you and lead these back to Policrates. Marc, Tynan, Kiefer: follow me."

The last who came out was a younger woman. They lifted her up on a horse in a rush—and everything slowed down for a moment as the cloak and hood she wore swept back in the wind and revealed her briefly. It was but a momentary glimpse, and Tynan concentrated on hurriedly tightening the girth and helping the others mount. The first two children they lifted up then turned to the others, girls it seemed.

"We can ride," they said and swung up ahead of the children.

"So you can!" said Devon, and the group galloped away back up the road, Devon leading the way.

Marc punched Tynan's shoulder. "C'mon! There's a few hundred Mataens we need to deal with!"

"Right then," Tynan said who to tell the truth was standing somewhat dumbfounded by these creatures, then spun on his heel and ran after Marc.

"Well, my friends," said Gerald. "We must give the queen and those with her as much time as possible to escape. If this is our end, let us make a good ending here and take as many of these devils with us as we can."

"Form up!" he said. "Those boys yonder will want to pay us a visit soon." They lined up four across the road and faced the mass of several hundred troopers gathering on the far side of the bridge. "Right now—listen up! Do not let them across that bridge. If we can hold the bridge against them, only three or four of that lot can come at us at a time. We need to get there first and stay on the bridge—then their numbers will mean less. When we reach this side of the bridge, rush forward; then halt and stand in the center—stay close together, shields up and linked tortoise-shell like."

Gerald, Tynan, Marc, and Kiefer walked forward. The mass of the Mateans had reached the far side of the bridge and stopped—there seemed to be a debate going on among them. Gerald drew his sword and turned to them. "Good luck to us; and may the heavens have mercy on our spirits."

Tynan's head still rang from the Mataen blow—he felt he could barely stand; but no matter—this must be done. Fortunately, the Mataens didn't cross immediately—a mass of them were busily working at the far end of the bridge.

The women and children safely away, they drew their swords and stalked toward the bridge. The Mataens looked at them pointing, still holding back, not crossing the bridge though they could have easily done so. There were several hundred of them, foot soldiers mainly, with a few of their war chariots interspersed among the ranks.

"It's too bad we didn't get the one who galloped away; he's brought a lot of his friends back with him," Tynan said to himself.

The bridge spanned a fifty-foot gorge wide chasm, the water roaring in a stone flume some hundreds of feet below; narrow, fast, and rushing loud was the stream below, a dark noisy grinding sound. As they approached, they suddenly could see what the Mataens were doing.

"They're cutting away the far side!" Gerald said and began to run, but as he did the Mataens succeeded, and the narrow bridge collapsed with a crashing rush into the chasm below. The gap at their feet was a sheer drop to the surging water beneath them. The Mataens immediately turned and began trotting away into the distant wood—actually running in some cases like the legions of the underworld were after them.

Gerald stopped, standing there perplexed. "Well, I have no idea why they did that. They should have overpowered us en masse—and could have done so with little or no trouble."

"They must have thought that the rest of the army was with us or close behind," said Marc.

"Well," said Kiefer. "For whatever reason they're gone. Should we wait here or start walking back?"

"We need to push over the river fast—they must have at least a hundred prisoners still with them," said Tynan.

"Do we have enough of our lads coming up?" Marc asked.

"Hardly," said Gerald. "About a hundred cavalry and five hundred infantry is all, less than half of what we see they have. More will be coming in with Policrates and the Marshal over the next few days but will take some time gathering."

"They've got two, maybe three thousand with them but they are nervous—look how they threw down that bridge at the sight of only four of us!" Marc said.

"This might be a chance to deal with them once and for all." Gerald replied. "And we must not forget Orme; he must be with them—his body hasn't been found at Warrec, so he somehow survived his fall. If he has the opportunity to recover, he will surely try to whip the Mataens into a frenzy again when he deems the time is right."

They noticed then that Marc's arm and shoulder were bleeding heavily.

"We should have you both looked at as soon as the medics get here," Gerald said to Marc and Tynan.

At the medical tent, Marc found his arm was not broken though his wrist was severely sprained from the Mataen blow, and Tynan only a slight bruise, though his helmet was deeply dented.

"You're both lucky," said the medic. "Those pikestaffs are usually deadly if they get a free swing at you."

"Yes, sir," said Marc getting down from the table. "We burst into them and surprised the guards."

"May you always have such good fortune!"

Tynan and Marc went out, Kiefer was sitting outside waiting for them.

"All well?" said Kiefer.

"All good per the medic," Marc said.

"Good news, then. I've heard we're moving out in the morning to scout the Mataens. The rest of the army will follow as soon as our engineers rebuild that bridge."

"Sir. The Mataens have stopped running. They've built a wagon laager and fortified the top of Ratae Hill with an earthwork and cut timber," the scout reported.

"Tribal levies must be coming in, then," Cage said, turning to Gerald.

Across the river a dark land had closed in, a dense forest of ancient oak and yew crowded the narrow path winding west, ripe for ambush or blind assault, toward the fastness of the Mataens, a land cut by deep valleys that held the mines that produced the wealth of that land, and were worked by slaves won in the constant wars between the four or five leading Mataen clans that struggled for supremacy.

They had ridden single file across the rebuilt bridge and to the paths beyond, where they found a dead trooper, the one struck two days before by Kiefer.

"They leave their own to their own dishonor," Gerald said.

They had cantered quickly on, going slowly, scouts fanning out on foot along each side of the path then signaling all clear and the rest of the troops would come forward.

It took them two weeks marching like this to cross one hundred leagues of that dim country, and now at last the Mataens were coming to a halt.

Gerald nodded. "For certain. Our scouts have seen bands of fighters trickling in from the surrounding areas. There must be larger groups on their way."

"No wonder they stall now and have asked to parley. They hope to delay action until they are at full strength, especially in chariots, and with all the troopers that can be mustered."

"Still, we'll need to wait but be prepared."

"Policrates is sending envoys to them—offering peace if they return the remainder of the prisoners and pledge to stay west of the Great River in perpetuity."

"I doubt they will agree," said Gerald. "They are an impetuous crew and can be downright unyielding and fierce if they get their hackles up over some question of honor or there is a matter of a blood feud at stake. Then nothing short of strong blows will stop them or get them to change their minds."

"What of this circumstance, though? They attacked over the river unprovoked and were let into the city through betrayal?"

"It has taken a great deal of self-deception to convince themselves that, doing what they did, they were in the right."

"The lands on the west bank have always been in contention; they likely have an ancient claim somewhere that has come down through the stories of the elders to say it was unlawfully taken from them in some past time."

"Also, they can't abide weakness of others if they think it's there—they attribute it to a curse of the gods or a sign of moral cowardice if a people seem weak or unable to defend themselves. They've been able to assault us for the last forty years pretty much whenever they felt the urge or weren't caught up in their own internal strife, so they may have developed a picture of us as a vassal state to their own."

"Maybe," said Cage looking at Gerald. "We may teach them that matters have now changed."

"The envoys were brought back late last night," the Marshal said, entering the tent. "Dumped outside of the outlying picket patrols: they were found tied, gagged, naked, tarred, feathered, and smeared with pig dung. Their beards were shaved and the word "no" was written in blue ink all over their bodies."

"They certainly don't seem to be in the mood to discuss the matter civilly," Cage said. "Our sentries reported that the Mataens shouted and taunted as they drove off: 'Come and take them if you think you can, you bloody sissies!' 'You'll get yours,' 'My spear longs to find a place in your guts', and other unpleasantries."

"Charming. How are the envoys?"

"They'll recover, though it will take some time. Meanwhile, Policrates has ordered the Phalanx to stand to arms. Bands of fighters have constantly been pouring into the Mataen camp and a large body of mixed infantry and chariots is coming down from the north."

"They've determined to fight then, hoping to break us, leaving the country wide open to plunder and sack. They've mainly had their way against us in the past and feel that it will be the same again if they come with enough numbers."

"Well, many things have changed since last we met in the field. We'll see who will be broken by whom," the Marshal answered.

The horde gathered across the ridge above them—spreading out to the left and right for a half-mile the line stretched. All were heavily armed and armored infantry with broad axes and long two-handed swords, helmets, and chain mail, with heavy boots and banners streaming out orange and green in the fall winds, winds that carried the sharp edge of the coming winter. They shouted and cursed the Caledonians, clamoring for battle. A small group of horsemen rode before the lines, haranguing and shouting, stirring them up to an even greater fervor.

Tynan knew their lines were at least eight soldiers deep, the distance between them equaling the swing-length of a long sword or broad axe, leaving many irregularities and gaps able to be exploited by putting in a cavalry charge. The Mataens only advantage was that they were positioned at the top of a steep slope above the Caledonians and would have gravity on their side if they charged. The counterstroke ordered by Policrates was to hold the wings of the formation and give way in the center. The horde would flow in like water funneled; then the flanks of the Caledonians would close on either side and the classic double envelopment would occur.

"We are to offer them final terms," said Gage as they sat with the council in his tent. "The king hopes to gain, if not their loyalty, at least their gratitude, and perhaps build longer spells of peace."

"I think I may know one them," put in Gerald. "His name is Magnus and he was a squadmate of mine at the Academy, and I'm thinking I've seen him among them in the last few days: an uncommonly large man with bright blond hair who leads their right wing and is part of the chieftain's bodyguard."

"I believe I've seen him as well," Cage replied. "Isn't he one of those stirring up the others?"

"I wouldn't doubt it; he's fierce and can be frightening. But he can be reasonable most of the time. If he's close to their war leader, maybe he could persuade them to parley rather than fight."

"As the king is seeking some way to resolve this peacefully, it is a path worth trying," Cage said.

"They only ride their horses to places where they dismount and fight on foot—our cavalry can sweep around them and take them in the rear. Magnus used to talk about them in strategy class. He hated that they were so quick to fight, resistant to new ideas, and often spoke about helping them see a better way," Gerald replied. "Perhaps he is still willing to talk."

They rode slowly up the sloping hillside the far side of the vale, a large flag banner on one hand and a large branch of a flowering fruit tree—the symbol of peace—in another.

The horde quieted down to a low, running, menacing sound of a quieted but dangerous sea, but Tynan knew they would explode at any time and there were stories of them rejecting attempted parleys when the frenzy was upon them by flinging the heads of the emissaries out of their camp. Out from the Mataen lines walked a delegation, men heavily armed and bearing the clan flags of the Five Nations, surrounded by a ring of large guardsmen dressed in the short, armored-leather tunics of the land, wearing ironshod boots. The two parties stopped five paces from each other. It was silent save the wind and the flapping of the banners among them.

"Well?" said the foremost soldier, a blue-crested helmet all that distinguished him from his followers. "Do you come to bargain or to submit straight away?" Those with him roared with laughter and the wind carried their words to those behind who laughed and catcalled as well, clanging their shields for several minutes.

"Neither," said Gerald. "But rather to discuss if there may be a way to avoid the needless shedding of blood between two peoples."

"Needless? It would only be needless if you and your troops turn right back round to that king of yours and leave us in peace to rule ourselves in our own land, a land whose border you crossed some miles back and so stand unlawfully on our sovereign soil."

"I see what you are saying," said Gerald, looking around him. "It is a beautiful land—one that our common fathers fought to keep free from any yoke . . ."

"A pact wrecked by *your* side of any so-called common family history," broke in the emissary. "If such things must be spoken of as unknown to those here as well as those of a more recent nature, the mines of Dovedale have been taken by Policrates rather than given over to us as should have been done."

"Only temporarily," put in Cage. "They are due to go back to you six months after all prisoners have been freed and the borders of the hostile factions of the clans are to be set further back as part of a neutral zone between us, where no man can do any harm."

"I doubt that any of that will come to be and all the while, valuable ore flows straight to the treasuries of Caerleon."

"An accounting has been given you of all that is being secured. It shall be honored when the time comes."

"Hah! That's been said before many times by different mouths and been gone back on before many times by different mouths. What difference now? What is there to cause the mouth of *this* king not to change its word this time as well?" the chieftain replied.

"The mines are not his interest," said Cage. "He'd rather have a strong friend on the border because as you may know the menace from Teras is growing steadily and may soon threaten us all with its darkness."

"Ah—Teras—that is something," the chieftain said looking sidelong. "Are they such a bad master as rumor makes them?"

"Of this at least we should be in agreement: the folly of trusting them. They will come under some pretext of lawfulness; and then they will never leave. Surely you know this? To be in league with them or to accept their aid is like accepting help from the fox to watch the henhouse," Gerald said.

"For Caledon, maybe," he said slowly. "But for our country—it may not be so. One needs friends in this world, and the stronger the friend, the better."

"We have one request," Cage said. "And that is that the twice-traitor Orme be turned over to us for the just punishment due upon his crimes and that any members of the family and household of Tredegar be returned unharmed."

"Orme has been a good helper to the Mataens, which is more than can be said of others. He cannot be sent back. And the household you speak of is from a dethroned and disgraced family, a curse to the country of their fathers. They are to be kept in custody for the safety of the rest of the peoples of the land," replied the emissary.

There was a long pause here, and Tynan looked at the bodyguard that ranged around the speaker. Near the back of the group was the largest man of all. His hair was plaited and braided long and caked in blue mud and paint. His face and body were painted and covered with figures, some tattooed there as well, others drawn with charcoal. But the eyes staring out were wilder—flowing over with animal fury, void of human life or reason.

"Magnus?" Gerald called out.

"Eh? Gerald my boy," the man answered. "So you're with that lot?"

"Yes, my duty of course. Why have you come out in arms against us?"

"Why not arms? What do you know of me? And *Magnus* was the name given me by you southern folk. I'm now called Magnar, a right northern name. But your name is still Gerald is it not? A suckling babe that hung about the men from the old days at school." The tribes roared in laughter again.

"Yes—Gerald." A silence hung there and there seemed to be nothing more to say. "Why do you fight?" Gerald said.

Magnar laughed bitterly. "I've told you before that these firebrands come through, speaking truth and stirring up men to deeds. This is our right: to fight to be free and to stay free. We'll be bound to no man and will be the masters of our own fate whatever may be. No foreign power can think it can march in here and order us about left and right. It's not natural and it's not moral, so we've got to put a stop to it here and now. *Now*!" He ended in a shout and the clan's roar swelled louder and louder at his words.

"Wouldn't it be better to band together to fend off Teras and build the land of Caledon into a great name?" Cage replied

"Caledon?" Magnar nearly spat the word. "You speak as an outsider. All I know is the Brae Mateans and the calling of *that* name is one to rouse a man to the greatest height he can obtain in this life."

Gerald spoke again. "As Aegis said when we were at Dara, 'Every life lost here will be harder to bear later.' Appeal to your lord. Give this up and strike a blow for peace."

"We'll strike a blow: for the Brae Mataens! Be gone and we'll see each other again on the field if you choose to appear." With that, the Mataens turned back to their own lines, a thundering cry going up as they stirred up the great host.

"It was well attempted," Policrates said when they had returned and reported the Mataen words. "Now they have chosen to let battle decide—and so it will!"

"Cadet! Take this order to the Marshal—he must advance up that right wing immediately, swing out, and drive his cavalry into the flank of that mass of soldiers."

"Yes, sir!"

"And remind the Marshal not to let the cavalry pursue the chariots—let the Mataens freewheel as much as they like—they are trying to lure us in for an ambush from their foot. And about those chariots: get the peltasts to charge the horses head on—they'll pull up sharply and refuse to keep going; then we can take down the driver and fighters."

"Yes, sir!"

Tynan took the written order and galloped out toward the right wing of the Caledonian troops. The thunder and clatter of the Mataen chariots was deafening—the din confused the mind and the dust confused the eyes. The drivers and fighters aboard each chariot shouted and flung their javelins, driving madly in an attempt to cause chaos among the Caledonian troops. The Caledonians stood alert, silent and unmoving amidst the clamor.

The chariots drove in all directions, circling and weaving at high speed, their javelins and spears hurled at random individual enemy targets and soldiers. They tried to break the ranks of the phalanx, charging up and working their way into any gaps in the formations. Then the fighters would leap to the ground, drawing a long sword from a sheath hung across their backs, slashing and swinging wildly to cut and hack their way through. The chariot drivers withdrew some distance to be of aid in case a withdrawal of the trooper was needed. This was the point that the Caledonian cavalry and light-armed troopers would assault the chariots as the drivers carried only small daggers and the whips that they drove the teams and were stationary. On the move, these chariots could drive at furious speeds even on steep downhills, could check their rampaging teams at full speed, stop, and change direction in a moment. Tynan saw one driver run along the pole forward to where the horses were harnessed to unwind a snarled lead, even stand on the yoke.

As he rode, a group of three chariots noticed him; and the first changed direction to charge head on, the fighter aboard yelling and shouting, cursing Tynan. At the last second, the chariot turned aside, and the fighter catapulted into the air, carrying his javelin and seeking to knock Tynan from his horse. In a flash, Tynan reined Phaeton to a stop, and the blurred figure of a large blue-painted warrior hurtled past.

Tynan rode on, Phaeton springing to a gallop in two strides. Another chariot careened toward them. As the chariot neared, Tynan drew a javelin and hurled it. The javelin struck low on one of the wheels, snapping uselessly. Tynan drew his second javelin, paused a breath, and flung it as well. This one went home, threading the wheel spokes, plunging deep in the ground, and catching the charioteer unawares as the javelin stopped the wheel like a hard handbrake, and toppled the chariot, which rolled over and over, a shattered mass of wood, leather, and metal.

The third chariot carried one of the high chieftains. It was pulled by four ponies and balanced on the platform of the metal-wrought chariot body itself was the driver, an armor bearer, and the chief himself, all naked except for a short blue cloak and metal neck and armbands, glistening with sweat, caked with the dust and grime of the field. The tumult of the vehicle was tremendous as it bore down on Tynan. He flashed across before the lead ponies, then reined hard left, leaning far over the pony teams, and slashed down with his sword, cutting the reins. The chariot plunged wildly away and Tynan rode on, twisting back to see the Mateans being rounded up the Caledonian foot soldiers.

He rode quickly to the Marshal, delivering the order from Cage. The Caledonians charged up the slope, sweeping in a wide angle, then plunging into a gap that had opened in the Mateans massed front. The Mataens turned and fled back toward the safety of their defended hilltop, pursued to the very edge of the barricade.

Tynan stopped for a moment to catch his breath, patting Phaeton on the neck. At that instant Sergeant Major Webbe rode by shouting, "Cadet! Well done delivering that order *but* you were a danged mess when you presented it to the Marshal. Try to clean yourself up a little next time *before* you come into the presence of a lord!"

"Yes, sir; thank you sir," said Tynan.

"Well—what are you waiting for? We need to hurry to catch up with the unit!"

The next morning, a group of Mataen chariots drove out from the hill fort waving an evergreen bough as a flag of truce. One of the chariots carried a bronze-bound wooden box which, when opened, was found to contain the remains of Orme, who had been ritually dispatched by the Mataens. "A traitor cannot be trusted no matter what side he is on," said the guards who delivered him.

The other chariots carried the members of Tredegar's family left alive—grimy and hungry, but otherwise unharmed, and behind came walking the remainder of the prisoners from Warrec.

"This is a message for Tredegar," said the Mataen captain as he turned to go. "To remember that we strictly observed the ancient laws of hospitality in regards to his family, and could have done otherwise if we had chosen."

CHAPTER 12

All Life Is Fleeting

Tynan was surprised to be called to Siwell's office. "I'm afraid that your grandfather has fallen quite ill," Siwell said.

Tynan felt his chest clutching. "Ill? What does that mean?"

"Unfortunately, the message says he is near to the point of death and wishes to see you and speak to you before it is too late."

"Too late, sir?" Tynan replied. "Too late for what?"

Siwell put down the message and looked away at the bright and warm fall day that lay beyond his window. Then looked back at Tynan. "Too late to say what your grandfather may want to say to you; too late to give you the chance to say anything that you wanted to say to him. To say everything that can be said is important to some at the end of this part of a soul's journey—the beginning of the next part of that same journey. Just the same, it is the end of this chapter."

"That's not very clear, is it?" said Tynan.

"No," said Siwell. "It isn't, and no one has returned from the other side of death to report to us what is actually there—at least no one that we know of. There are rumors and legends of some who have done so but the records of their experience have not been handed down to us, therefore we must be content with speculation and so-called educated guesses."

"Not much comfort in that," Tynan said, looking down.

"No," said Siwell. "But at least we can give honor to those who will soon pass that foreboding door and comfort them in body and mind where we can. To that end, you've been granted a ten-day pass to go to your home and speak with your grandfather as he requests and may use your service horse to travel there and back."

"Thank you, sir," Tynan said. Tynan left feeling odd and disoriented, a strange sensation of unrelated and shakily-focused memories flooding over him: playing with his grandfather as a young child; then trips when his father was still alive and his mother was there, then the move away when his stepfather—ill-tempered, given to drink and sometimes violence when 'fate was agin him' as he said—couldn't abide him any longer and his mother didn't seem to be able to help herself or him.

Tynan cantered steadily west. It had been more than a year since the day the messengers had appeared at the farm and he had been suddenly swept up into something much bigger than himself—a life beyond the sheep farm—in some ways, infinitely better; in some ways infinitely worse; but always interesting, and it was hard for Tynan to decide if it was better overall when the emotions ran up and down like the gray winds of earlier that year, but somehow he had stayed on his feet and now was close to completing cadre school and then being sent out to who knew where—maybe the Border Guard? No telling—but what would be, would be.

A few hours on, his horse suddenly began to limp. He dismounted and saw he'd thrown a shoe. "Bother!" Tynan exclaimed and looked around. He would have to detour through a village—and that quite slowly as he would be walking to find a blacksmith—some two miles off the main road. It was Beybury, a small cluster of buildings that he had visited once or twice but mostly avoided growing up.

Finally reaching Beybury, he led his horse into the main village lane and stopped a passing workman. "Excuse me is there a blacksmith near?"

"There is," answered the man looking at Tynan with a strange expression. "At the end of the village road that way." He waved and continued on.

The blacksmith's shop was the last on the street, small but neatly kept. Inside, a man hammering away at work on anvil. "I say, pardon me," said Tynan. "But it seems my horse has thrown a shoe. Would you have time to look at it? I'm on my way up the Vale and am in a hurry."

"Of course. I'll see what can be done," said the smith, wiping his hands on his leather apron and walking up quietly to the horse. "There you are, now," he said softly, gently lifting the hoof.

"Yep—clean thrown and a small nick where the shoe nail came out awkward-like." He set down the hoof and then applied a small ointment to the cut.

"That's a real horse," the blacksmith said as he turned to shape the shoe. "Don't see many like them come through here."

Tynan stepped around the shop, admiring the metalwork and tack. "He's one of the new army breed that's come across from the West. Good horses, not as fast as pure racehorses, but tireless and without fear."

"Ah, it's good—helps keep the country safe and borders secure."

Tynan nodded. "That's right."

"You from around here?"

"White Farm on the Vale about ten miles on near Westcombe. My grandfather's sheep farm is up there. He's gone sick and I'm on my way to see him."

"Sorry to hear that—hope he comes out well."

Tynan nodded and was about to say something more when outside on the street, a disturbance arose. Looking out, Tynan saw that three village men, talking loudly, had gathered around a young girl carrying a basket. Tynan gazed at them. "What are they about?"

The blacksmith glanced over. "No good will come of that. They're the bailiff's sons. Nothing but trouble."

"They wear insignia—are they deputies?"

He nodded. "Truth is, it's hard to tell sometimes who are the law-breakers and who are the law-keepers around here; these sort stir things up if they think they can."

While they spoke, one of the men grabbed the basket from the girl and threw it on the ground, scattering bread and fruit across the road.

Tynan stood, drew his riding crop, and walked out onto the street, stopping midway across. "That was unmannerly," he said.

One of the deputies turned and spat on the ground. "What of it?" Then he turned back and ground the bread into the mire of the street, the other two laughing as he did.

"You are ridiculous fools; and I must ask that you first apologize, then repay this girl for the bread you have ruined," Tynan said.

"Ridicu—what? That's some big word. What does it mean?"

"It means you're being laughed at because you are behaving like benighted country clodhoppers. However, it's known that manners can be taught—either with the flat of the sword or the haft of the spear, though the best way would be for you to recognize their importance willingly and forego the rod that is prepared for the back of fools."

"That so?" said one of the deputies, stepping out a little to the right. "And don't you know it's against the law in this village to carry a weapon inside the town limits?"

"I'm a king's soldier, tasked with guarding his interests at all places and at all times. And the king's writ runs even across the boundaries of ignorant places such as this."

"So—you're just a lackey for ol' King What's-His-Name?" said another sidling back, fingering a club that hung from his belt.

"The king in Caerleon is the king here; and he bids all his subjects and citizens to be safe and untroubled if they're peaceable." Tynan replied.

"I don't think you'd be talking so big if you didn't have that illegal blade strapped on."

"The king's service carries even to the limits of this place, so its authority is rightly present. Of course, such a weapon would not be used on chuckleheads like you, though, save maybe the application of the flat."

"That's some bold cheek since there's three of us."

"Thank you for that observation and for proving that the theories of higher mathematics are known to you. I'll at least need this riding crop, since I'm quite out-numbered, but that only to switch you as you run."

"That so, eh?" said the bailiffs, as they gathered themselves, preparing to spring.

"Festus!" came a thundering interruption. The three started, looking around, shuffling their feet.

"What are you boys playing at?" came the voice again. Tynan turned, and there stood one of the largest men he had ever seen, towering with dark hair, dark eyes, and a dark beard, leading a donkey and small tipcart filled with supplies. "You three get on with your business and stop bothering folk!" he continued.

"This is none of your affair, Edmund," One deputy said.

"It's my affair when you are hindering traffic in the street in front of my shop or harassing someone who is a customer."

"Well . . . we may see have to see to this later," one of the deputies said, eyeing Tynan.

Tynan bowed. "You may find me at Caerleon—which is the capital of this realm—at your convenience. There are many ways such a conversation may be concluded."

They said nothing in return but laughed and walked on down the street.

Tynan watched them go for a moment, then went over to the girl, who was standing stunned, and picked up her basket, handing it to her. "Here is a silver piece for the damage they did."

"Thank you, sir," she answered. "Why are they so petty?" then turned and left them standing there as the street went on with its business.

"Sorry for that," the large man said. "They can be downright pests."

"It was nothing, but thank you for speaking out. I'm Tynan Glendower; and who are you?"

"Edmund Blackhammar; and that's my father Raymund that runs the smithy."

They went into the blacksmith's shop itself, which was becoming a riot of clanging hammers and the beating of metal on metal as other apprentices and workers came in.

"Your shop is quite busy," Tynan said.

"There is a lot of metal in this world that needs working," Edmund replied as he unloaded the supplies.

The low, throaty, bubbling sound of the bellows provide a breath-of-life feel, the impression for Tynan that the smithy was a living beast, a breathing animal being molded and cast and plunged hissing into the water, to be born once again, hammered and shaped, refined to a unique form, then sent out in small portions to take their place in the world of the daily life of men at work.

Edmund went to the anvil and clamped the shoe with tongs. "Say Tynan, would you mind working the bellows a bit while I mend this shoe?"

"Of course."

"Just get a firm-like grip on that steer horn handle and push down slowly—the counterweight on the other side will lift it, so no need to pull it up."

As he worked, Tynan felt he was breathing life into the shop, a resuscitation of something that had lain dormant for eons of time, a silent space, a lifeless body, vast beyond knowledge, waiting to be infused with the breath of life.

"Good!" cried Edmund. "We're getting some heat now. Full heat is what we want for this tempered bronze." He struck two or three strong blows, then tapped and shaped the glowing metal, paying especial attention along the edges where he tapped rapidly, like a painter before the canvas finishing a masterpiece, his face glowing nearly gold in the brilliant light of the furnace. Then suddenly he gripped the tongs, turned rapidly, and plunged the shoe deep into a barrel of cold water, which steamed and hissed immensely, as the living metal shrunk back to cold inertness.

He placed it on a heavy wooden table while he turned and shaped another shoe. "It's best to have four fresh shoes put on together, then you know they're sound and won't risk having another throw off or unbalance the whole."

While he did, the first had cooled and Tynan lifted it. It was light yet the strength was obvious in the wholeness of the shaped metal. "Fine work," he said, turning to Edmund. "Much better than anything made in the farrier shops of the army."

Edmund nodded. "It's the extra time spent on the edges; it hardens them for secure attachment to the hoof while leaving the inner areas softer and more pliable for movement. The new technique has been invented out in these areas, but not made its way to the capital it seems."

"It is much better," Tynan said while Edmund finished with the shoes, then quickly reshod Phaeton's other hooves and walked the horse easily around the yard, studying its gait. "He looks good and should last three months or so before needing any adjustments."

"Three months? Why, we have them to the farriers twice a week normally."

"Of course—this new method helps in many ways."

Edmund carefully hammered the edges, each tap hardening the bronze, to finish the setting. He straightened and said, "Can you stay back here until morning? We'll want to test and polish them to a smooth finish, but then the horse will be stable, no uneven strides or wobbling plus you know when one wears out, they all need replacing."

Tynan frowned. "I can if I can leave at first light. I've got to ride out to the end of the Vale, then back to the Academy within a week."

He nodded. "We'll hammer them out for you quickly and have you off before sunrise."

"All right," said Tynan, then another thought struck him. "I'm sorry. How much would that be? I've only got a few day coins with me for the road."

Edmund smiled. "We won't charge you anything at all—think of it as a favor to the king—except that we'd be interested, if you were willing, to take a look at that blade you're carrying, as a matter of professional interest and all?"

"Thank you. Of course," Tynan said as he slowly drew the sword from his sheath. Both Edmund and his father's eyes lit up as they gazed on the polished bronze, inlaid with figured metal added to strengthen the blade itself.

"Ah, it's a beauty," said Edmund. "Mind if I handle it?"

"Go right ahead," said Tynan.

Edmund lifted the sword expertly, weighing it in his hands and checking the balance by perching it on the back of his wrist. "Hmmm." He said as he sighted along the edge of the blade.

"Something wrong with it?" Tynan asked.

"No," Edmund said somewhat hastily. "Not really wrong—but how sturdy are the edge and point? Do they bend or go out of true without coming back to shape?"

"As a matter of fact, they do. It's a problem the military armorers are trying to solve."

"Hmmm. It's the same problem as with the horseshoes," Edmund said looking at his father.

"Yep," his father said taking the blade. "Fine edge to start with but needs the finishing hammering to cure it like."

"Can you do that to this one?" Tynan put in.

Edmund's father looked startled. "Well . . . it's government material and all . . ."

"I can give you my permission," Tynan said. "If your technique works and the weapon is improved, the armorers can learn the technique; if it doesn't work, no harm done—it's in the same shape it was."

Edmund's father brightened. "I'd love to! Always wanted to work on something made from the best material." He bent to the task, Edmund assisting at the bellows and striking skillfully with a large hammer on the blade at places his father indicated by touching with a small ball peen hammer.

"Leave it in the sheath for a day or two to fully harden, then see if you notice the difference," he said as he handed it back to Tynan after cooling and polishing it.

Tynan slept that night in the straw at one side of the smithy floor. It was clean and dry, and he slept soundly wrapped in his riding cloak and a wool blanket courtesy of Edmund. He awoke, ate a bowl of porridge and hot drink as they polished up Phaeton's shoes, and rode out of the village he had limped into the day before, soon cantering smoothly on the main road heading west.

It has been almost a year since he had left his grandparents' farm. The letters there and back had been sporadic, with many interruptions and long periods of not being able to sit down for more than a few minutes of scribbling, and then the post was sometimes poor at best with parts of the kingdom almost out of reach except by personal courier. He rode though with eagerness, the weather fine as he went west, looking at the land with a now more military eye—which was the only way he could describe his new way of seeing—sketching in his map case as he went, noticing narrow places, wider stretches, areas to bivouac large bodies of troops at need, places where water and forage for horses was plentiful, towns near the road—some maybe friendly, some of unknown allegiance. Many parts of the country were still in upheaval, and like his experience at Beybury, caution needed to be taken in showing the king's colors too brazenly.

He came at last to the familiar turning, marked by two stone-built pillars on either side of the road set with metal engravings of sheep and the shepherd's life. He rode along the road and the rising reddish-yellow dust of the way brought the memory of it all back to him in force, not a completely bad set of memories, but a mixed feeling of happiness shot through with loss and regret.

The farmhouse looked much the same as the day he left it with the two troopers, now several lifetimes ago it seemed. A loud cry of dogs raised at his approach and the first one out was old Cap. Tynan leaped from his horse and smothered the dog with hugs—a laughing, rolling tumble of great joy.

"So—this is how the great soldier comports himself?" came the loud unpleasant voice of his stepfather from the porch. "Stand up and try to stop making a fool of yourself."

"Yes, Stepfather," Tynan said, standing up and dusting himself off, then he looked directly at his stepfather. His stepfather had grown seedier since he'd seen him last, and his face bore an irritable unpleasant cast, slightly jaundiced.

"Do you feel you're something special in that getup?"

"No, sir. It's standard issue in my cadre," Tynan replied.

"Standard issue? Paid for out of the pockets of hardworking common folk, more to the point."

"Maybe, sir. But everyone benefits it seems from what the king builds: roads, armies, laws."

"Talking like you've been taught, no doubt."

They stood looking at each other without speaking for several moments, then his mother and grandmother came bursting out the door.

"You've come back!" they said, hanging on to him as they pushed their way past his stepfather and pulled him into the familiar kitchen.

"They allowed me a leave as soon as your messages arrived at the Academy." Here he paused, waiting for them to speak. Then said, "How is grandfather?"

His grandmother looked away. "Not so good, son; not so good."

"What is it—what's wrong with him?"

"What is it," she repeated. "Just the turning of the seasons and the accumulation of old wounds and hurts not quite healed, it seems."

Tynan nodded. It really didn't make it any easier to bear, but he had seen the same in animals before—the years suddenly seemed to catch up to them—one day nearly spry as a newborn, the next day hardly able to move, and the breath rattling slowly in and out of them.

"They allowed me to come because the messages seemed to say he may be departing this life . . . or . . . or close to it."

"That may be; that may be," his grandmother said. "We aren't sure about how long he has left but are sure he wants to talk with you while he still can make sense of his words and yours."

Tynan nodded, though his eyes were clouded over, and his throat clutched at him at the thought of what she meant.

His grandfather was propped up in his old bed in the far room. Tynan had rarely been in this room when he lived in the house, and he paused for a moment at the door. It was a plain room with few furnishings, simple and mostly made by his grandfather and his grandfather's father, handed down through each generation of the life and heritage of the farm, which mostly was about sheep and wool but at other times had raised cattle and even—many generations ago—horses that had not done well in the cold of the high winters, but had led unexpectedly to the farm producing some of the best long grass for horse grazing in the country, and even some inquiries from places outside of Caledon had come of late but the disturbances on and across the Narrow Sea had limited exchanges of good as well as travel, and so the fortunes of the farm in a way rose and fell with the fortunes of Caledon.

One thing Tynan now saw however was a large book, leather and woodbound it seemed, that was on a table by the window, with two chairs nearby and seemed a place where his grandparents could sit together and talk or read—they liked each other, which was no small thing, and often spoke of their marriage as a 'lifetime of talking with each other.' It was something Tynan hoped for in his own life, should it ever happen.

Tynan knocked gently on the doorpost and went in, sliding one of the chairs over to the side of his grandfather's bed. His grandfather looked thin and pale, his skin seemingly translucent. He had aged much in just over a year's time. But it was the sickness or ailment that was doing it, eating away at his lifeblood and strength. Could Marten do something? Tynan thought suddenly and was on the verge of standing up; when his grandfather stirred.

"Ah, Tynan my lad," he whispered. "How's that blackthorn staff working out?"

"It's doing well, Grandfather. Ab is using it to guide the sheep."

"Very good!" He seemed to collect his thoughts and his strength; and sat up straighter in the bed. "How silly of me to forget . . . but these past days have been like that. But what of you—how is the Academy?"

"It's hard but good—never a dull moment, at any rate! Just a little more time to go, and I should be assigned to a field unit—hopefully in the cavalry."

"Cavalry? That'll be good for the horse market." Here his grandfather paused and seemed to be searching for the right words to say something.

"What is it, Grandfather?"

"Well . . . it's just this. . . . You wouldn't consider, would you, to come back and run this farm when your time in the army is over?"

Tynan was shocked. "Me? But what of mother and stepfather—wouldn't they be the most rightful ones?"

"It's in my power to leave things as I choose. I've spoken with your grandmother, and she agrees. Your stepfather is all right in his way—but I'm not sure if I trust him. He has his own farm to run, and he's not in the hereditary line—something your mother gave up when she married him—but that's the way that it is. If it's not you, it's likely to be them, or even to someone else who buys the property."

"Well . . . I really don't know what to say. I'll have two or more years of a service commitment once I graduate. What would happen meanwhile?"

"I'd work out an agreement with someone that could work the flocks and fields while you completed your time, could be Ab or anyone."

His grandfather smiled and looked at Tynan.

"Let me tell you about your father. I expect you don't know much about him since he died when you were young."

"Was killed, don't you mean, in the fight against the Mataens?"

"Mortally wounded by them and passed from this life three days later. There's a letter from the commander himself in the pages of that book yonder that speaks of it, but before that he was one of the best men in this county—loyal and kind to all—though he could drink more on occasion than was good for him but never suffered anything permanent from it. Just the same, you should be warned that ale, cider, and all is bad for our family and more than one relative has been ruined by a taste for them—stay clear of it altogether if you can. But here's a story about him that tells you more than anything else.

"When he was a lad no more than seven or eight years old at most one of our lambs went missing. Your dad heard us talking about it, wrapped a piece of bread and some cheese in a cloth and went out looking for that lamb by himself without telling anyone. He was gone four days and we'd just about given up on him making it back when he come dragging himself back home half froze and near drowned, carrying the lamb in a sling he'd made for it.

"He passed out on our own kitchen floor, but revived and when he did, we asked him why he did it and he said, 'I couldn't stand thinking of that lamb out there all by himself and had to take him a blanket and bring him home if I could do it.' That was all he said, though he was laid up for a month himself and never really got over the chest problems that came of it. But that was your dad: he cared—and he cared most about you and your mother."

Tynan nodded. "I can remember that about him—I'm not sure how, but it comes through."

"Yes," his grandfather said. "You were a lot like him in that way when you went after Bwlch to get him back from the catamount. And you'll see in the letter about the battle that he could have saved himself—got away unhurt—but he went back and fell with the rest of his company around their commander and the standard. All of them fell together—but it delayed the Mataens long enough that our reserves were able to make it up to the Gap and so the Mataens were beaten and turned back when it seemed like they would break through. And that *is* the truth."

His grandfather stopped speaking, lost in thought. Tynan sat there as the silence lengthened. "It's the same story that the recruiting officer told me when I got to the Academy; and I am glad to hear it's true. It makes him more real to me."

"That's well. I wanted you to know before I went to be with him."

Tynan looked up. Age rested heavily on his grandfather; and he couldn't speak in reply.

"For now, I'm fine, but need to sleep, as I seem to most days now. I love you, Tynan. Being a good man is a hard thing to do—an art and a craft, they say—but you can do it if you try."

"I love you, Grandfather," Tynan managed to say. He hugged him briefly and turned away. At the door, he turned back to say something more, but his grandfather was breathing gently, already asleep.

"Well, boy, what did he say to you?" his stepfather said when he came out.

"He told me about my father; what he was like and how he died."

"That all? Did he say anything about the farm?"

"Only that everything would come clear later on," Tynan answered, feeling angry that his stepfather would ask him about such things that didn't matter at all, especially now. "If you don't mind, I'll lay down for a while."

"Your room is where it's always been."

"Yes, sir." Tynan really didn't want to say anything more. The constant baiting and browbeating were tiresome beyond words; and he turned to his grandmother. "Write when he goes. It seems like it won't be long, weak and sick as he is."

She nodded. "I'll miss him." She struggled then, not able to speak, and covered her mouth a moment with her hand, looking down, tears coming silently. Tynan handed her a clean cloth and she took it. "Thank you, son." After a few moments, she said. "We've had a lot of good years together—happy ones at that, with a lot of laughter mixed in, so it helps."

Tynan nodded and hugged her a moment, silent as well, looking out unseeing through the kitchen window toward the green-spreading land.

CHAPTER 13

A Winter's Mission

IT WAS A CRISP winter's day and the light was of that special kind reserved for winter, filtered to a thin brightness, and the days were growing shorter—but there was much to do.

Wind gusts and snowstorms were the norm, the snow driven across the grass and parade ground, bare tree limbs, yellow and brown, fixed against the sky, and flashes of fast-moving sunlight, then clean blue light illuming the damp earth.

Tynan stood with the others in the frozen courtyard. Even wrapped in a fur-lined leather riding cape the cold was bitter and the wind hissed across the flagstones driving snow rills before it—outside the protection of the walls, the wind at this time of year could be devastating.

An officer from the Marshal stood by Gerald's horse, whose breath steamed and smoked in the early morning air. Gerald's groom was there as well holding the horse's reins, bundled as well against the cold.

Gerald came out into the courtyard, saluted. The officer saluted back and handed Gerald a large pouch.

"Deliver this sealed pouch to the hands and eyes of Kendric alone," the officer said. "Remain with him until he writes a reply; then bear the reply back to the hand of the Marshal only and no other. If more than thirty days pass, you are free to return, and we will have to assume Kendric has rejected our terms and will plan accordingly."

"Yes sir—understood sir." Gerald took the pouch, slinging it across his chest, then mounted up.

Webbe was shouting: "Shields 1 through 5! Report to the east warehouse—hurry up! Horse and field kit for seven marching days."

Tynan, Marc, and some forty other cadets gathered, standing by their horses with their field gear before a large warehouse as Webbe came out. "At ease! We are assigned to deliver twenty-five cartloads of high field wool to our trading partners at Duris. In exchange, we are to return back to Caerleon with forty barrels of lamp oil and assorted other goods contained in the king's manifest.

"Gold Team! Blue Team! En route, you will compete in attack and defense, guarding the baggage train as well as counting coup for touches and strikes with javelins and lances. We're going to be using real, full-weight weapons furnished with leather buttons and wooden tips. It's time you felt the weight of an authentic weapon and feel how it operates just a whisker from true battle. Night attacks and ambushes will be included—just like you're marching through hostile enemy country. Seniors versus plebes and no legal holds barred.

"Form up! Form up! Road guards out in front; scouts along each wing; rear guard behind."

The convoy was soon ready, and the heavy-laden carts rumbled toward the main east road, the drivers shouting and cracking their whips as the mules strained beneath the weight. The days were filled with instruction and field exercises, with Webbe's voice providing the background. "Keep a watch out on those bluffs that parallel the road. Make sure you halt the cart train before entering a forest or narrow cutting; wait until the scouts come in with a report of all clear before moving through. *Always* station a guard of three or four horsemen or foot soldiers upstream and downstream when crossing a creek or river—it's a prime moment to be attacked."

The column rumbled down the central road to the crossroads, then turned east on the snow-covered road, riding with a bright sun rising ahead of them, turning the world a brilliant blue-white of transcendent purity it seemed and the sound of the wind dying to a soft sighing in the bare trees that stood thick on either side.

They continued on from the waymark, the fresh snow unmarked before them, just a dusting on the road itself, deep hummocks and hollows of snow with drifts eddying up in small knife-edged ridges spread out in the fields beyond. The sun was soon fully up—a clear day, its light casting shadows out long behind them. A deep sky above blue and bright and no wind; a calm muffled day that rolled away behind them into the west.

"Now listen up!" Webbe was talking as Tynan's Blue Team had gathered round. "The Gold Team is crafty—Smith and I go way back and know each other pretty well. They will for sure set up a diversion: fire, smoke, or some obvious troop movement to get our attention to draw it away from the direction their main force is really coming from, then they'll pounce: surround and ambush us to secure our unit flag. We will not let that happen! Not only will we deny them our standard, we will so plan as to take *theirs*. Stay alert, keep moving, don't stay still long enough for them to get a bead on you or map our positions because we're standing around like herons in a creek. If you're doubting what to do, keep pushing forward a little further, swing a little wider out on the far flanks, make another move—any move!—don't hunker down, don't dismount to rest; eat in the saddle *on the move*. Keep circulating on the perimeter, not in some mindless, repetitive, predictable cadence like a clock. Not regular but staggered timing, again nothing repetitive, nothing predictable. Investigate anything and everything you notice: a dust cloud, a startled flock of birds, a breaking sound in the brush. It's the small things that will give away where they are and what they're doing.

"The other thing about this group is that they can be a little overconfident—comport themselves with a little too much cockiness and self-satisfaction. Sure, the Academy is set up to treat everyone as an equal but we're up against those who might be thought of as the first among equals. The Gold Shield it's called by us, but it could be called the Royal Shield and everyone in it has a connection to the Caledonian royal house or one of the great families—a connection and loyalty that will outlast anything that happens here in school. But don't be intimidated! I'm just telling you this now because it's a weakness in their psychology that we may be able to exploit in this field exercise.

"Another thing. They can't just shoot at us with bows or throw javelins from an ambush. They've got to capture us without spooking the ox carts in order to secure the cargo, so they'll need a place where both things can be set up: a diversion blocking the road or what not, and an open flat area from behind or the opposite side of the road where they can conceal a squad that will spring out and take advantage of any of our inattention.

"Take a look as this sand model." He pointed with a stick to the ground, inscribing a line as he did so. "There's a place about eight miles down the valley that even includes a river line crossing right before. It could be a good location for an attack. We'll want to spot them and set up a counter-ambush if we can guess correctly. That place, would be ideal, so keep especially alert when we're getting close. Any questions on this?"

Four hours later that day, a glint flashed on the hillside above him: they were there. Tynan reined up, his eyes riveted on the ridge, and saw first one then a short string of silver flashes. Polished helmets—too polished—they should have rubbed mud on them for the mission; now the helmets' flash showed even through the thick trees that lined the upper road.

Those horsemen were the diversion—something was coming up from the right flank almost certainly, and as they were fast approaching the sweeping left bend in the river valley Webbe had spoken of, it was likely the attack would be coming from the south, where a wide, sandy flat covered with willow and scrub oak spread out toward sloping heights would be perfect for an ambush or a counter-ambush.

Tynan turned and signaled to Devon, who in turn passed the message down the line to Webbe, who called the squad together.

"They're feinting left and coming hard from the right as we expected. We need to appear to them as if we're heedless of what's going to happen—let them think we're taking the bait on the left. Squad 1: that's your job. Canter out in front on the far left side of the road single file and keep veering left. Squad 2: you will counter-ambush the Gold Team force that will likely come up through the sandy scrub oak flats. Swing far out to the right to outflank them and come up from their rear. If all goes well, they will be so concentrated on what's happening on the road they'll never know you're there until you're touching them with your coup sticks."

They carried out Webbe's instructions and soon heard Junius's patrol riding down the road to toward them.

"Hold and surrender your flag!" Junius shouted as he led his troop onto the road.

"On the contrary, we request that you hold and surrender your flag—look over there," Keifer replied and pointed to the right.

Junius glanced sidelong and saw the second ambush brigade taken prisoner with Marc and Tynan standing guard. The rest of the Blue Team closed in a circle, their javelins at the ready.

"We yield," said Sergeant Major Smith riding up. "Maggerle, surrender the flag." Maggerle rode out and flung down the gold standard.

"Thank you—it will do nicely in my outer portico," Webbe said. "Though you would do better to bear it with honor even in defeat." He lifted it from the ground with the tip of his javelin and caught it in his free hand.

Gerald rode up as well. "The exercise is declared complete. Gold Team will form up and proceed back to Caerleon under the command of Sergeant Major Smith. Blue Team will form up with Sergeant Major Webbe and act as the guide squad for the cart train of wool and proceed to Duris."

Then he reined around and rode on without a look back up the trail toward the head of the column. Tynan swung onto his saddle and cantered after him along with Marc, Devon, Kiefer, and the others. As they went Tynan felt the eyes of Junius and his squad staring after them.

Smith ordered the Gold Team to stand to their horses and Webbe was shouting at Tynan's cadre: "Hurry up! Why are you moving so slow? Fan out ahead on the *double*! Drivers whip up the teams—we need to have this cargo to Duris tomorrow!"

They pushed on, riding through the night, and were weary as the sun rose before them in crystal orange fire and there—oddly enough—was the sea, snow fallen right to the edge of the silently heaving water, calm for this time of year, thought Tynan, when they suddenly came upon a small guard post—two squat structures straddling each side of the road with a barrier lowered between them. Several soldiers swathed in heavy cloaks armed with spears and a few with bows hallowed them to a halt.

"Halt and say your business," called out one of the soldiers.

"We have brought the wool from Policrates to Kendric and are in haste to deliver them in exchange for oil," Gerald answered.

"Policrates, you say? We thought he was dead—killed at Dara."

"Not so," Gerald said. "He lives and sends word as well of his plans and hopes."

"Right, then—carry on to the city gates." They lifted the barrier and the Caledonians rode through and were met at the gates by other guardsmen, who led them on foot into Kendric's main hall, an arched, gray-stone, rather cold affair, more a military post than a royal residence.

A man appeared in full battle dress, armed as if to ride out to a battle.

"Sir, we bring you messages from Policrates—his greeting as well as health wishes to Kendric and his household," Gerald said.

"Thank you," said the man. "And our returns to the compliments of your lord and our gratefulness to your news that he lives and had not fallen at Dara as we had erroneously believed. Kendric is at sea today but meanwhile, Egbald here will settle you and your men, as well as show you the way to the warehouses for the exchange of the wool and oils."

Egbald bowed slightly. "Follow me this way," he said.

As they walked the wagons and horses slowly through the streets, Tynan saw the sky change from pale fresh-washed blue to a brighter deeper azure and a breeze came up, ruffling the flags on the wall top. He also noticed many armed sentries there, carrying arms and in uniforms identical to the guardsmen they had met at the border of the country. There were also many guard stations scattered around the city, each with its alert watchmen, intent on keeping watch.

So many troops—Tynan wondered why they needed such a heavy hand to keep the people in order especially as their law forbade the carrying of weapons in the town limits by any other than the military or law enforcement—there were a lot of policemen about, traveling in small bands with stout staffs or poles, as well as a few on horseback. Something felt wrong about it all; he just wasn't sure what it was.

Egbald led them to a compound that was bounded on one side with warehouses, winches, and tackle for the handling of freight, while the other side was a series of barracks, stables, and various temporary housing for visitors and travelers.

As the unloading began, Tynan and his cadre went with the horses to make sure they were stabled well, rubbed down, foddered, and draped with padded stable blankets against the windy damp and cold.

"These mariner men may be good tenders of ships and know the secret ways of the seas and all that swim in them; but they look to know little about horses and their needs. This paddock is barely tolerable," Devon said.

"Is that a Terasian ship anchored out there?" Tynan asked, pointing to the flag that flew at her stern.

"It is," Marc said.

"We're surprised to see them, maybe?" said Kiefer.

"Only that Kendric's folk usually don't have such awkward guests such as us and the Terasians here at the same time. There's a bit of—competition—between us that can strain the moment," said Marc. "They must have been delayed, and hopefully will be sailing out over the next day or so."

Later that day, Kendric sent a message delivered by Egbald to the Caledonians—it would be a few days for his council to review the messages and compose a reply, and would they be pleased to rest in the guest lodgings that the four heavily armed guards would be happy to escort them to?

They were led to a small compact building in the far corner of the royal grounds, which was surrounded on two sides by the towering city walls and at the end of a narrow lane. Not quite a prison cell, thought Tynan, but quite close to house arrest, and the quantity of guards seemed out of proportion to his and Marc's ability to make trouble.

"Kendric is a strong man," Gerald said as they settled into their quarters. "He rules all the eastern seaboard and guards the approaches to it. It was his coastwatchers that intercepted and escorted Septus's ship to Aston Quay. Kendric himself was reluctant to come to the city to meet the ship, though he finally appeared. The question was why the hesitation? It has been felt by many that he styles himself to be a rival to the throne—not openly, for he loves peace and wishes to see the rise of Caledon to a place of greatness, but it has been whispered that Terasian agents have approached him with gifts and promises of much greater span of rule if he sided with them and turned against Policrates.

"It's not out of the question. Kendric has a reputation as a fierce, proud, independent ruler and would not take kindly to being crossed or arbitrarily ordered about by Policrates or anyone else within his own borders. The letters from Policrates are likely requests based on mutual lineage, heritage, history, and the place the future might hold for all of them if they stood together. Nevertheless, his father's father had formed a pact with Policrates's grandfather for mutual defense and trade arrangements—the bounty of the sea for the wool of the high fields—and all have mutually benefited. Kendric though is made of hotter blood and sometimes has gone off with anger or just on a whim, inflicting unintentional harm on himself and his people."

"Sirs, would you be so kind," said Egbald as he unlocked and opened the lodge door and let them enter, following behind. "Let me light the fire for you and the lamps." The place was soon lit and beginning to warm.

The furnishings were made with a dark heaviness, a dark coldness of the sea, and again barely concealed the aggression of the soldier and the feeling that the room could be converted to a barracks or cell at a moment's notice. Two high windows with thick dark oak shutters let in very little of the late winter light, which was fast waning to dark. The unsmiling Egbald lit the fire in a brusque mechanical way.

"Do you require anything further for your comfort?" he said tonelessly.

"Thank you; we have everything we need," Tynan said.

"Very good." Egbald saluted and left the room, shutting the door softly. Tynan and Marc waited a moment, but all they heard was footsteps crunching away in the icy snow.

"At least, not locked in," said Devon said, trying the door and looking out.

Wordlessly, Marc pointed to the walls where two guards paced, then down the street where another two sentry posts could be seen in the moonlight. Between was a straight narrow windowless alley with no doors or gates branching out.

Kiefer went into the room and sat on a couch that seemed to be made of black bear fur. "Which is one good thing, though this couch looks like it could stand up and walk away on its own. If you ask me, the whole décor of this place feels like it's intended to strike fear in the hearts of the guests."

Tynan was sitting on a chair that was tawny colored with a lion's head for a pillow. "Rather like an exotic hunting lodge seen in a fevered dream."

Indeed, their quarters were something out of a hunter's nightmare. Between the stuffed bears, sea creatures, lions, and the fantastic art in the form of large wall paintings showing the kings and princes of Kendric's land doing battle.

They walked down a narrow hall to a small room. "What's this?" Tynan asked

"It's called the seat of ease—the waste drops directly into the water below," Marc answered.

"How revolting!" Devon said.

"Of course—though better than a pit in the ground. And there's more. See that jarred pot next to the seat? Liquid waste goes there and is collected every day. These folk use it to clean their clothes."

"Clean their clothes with *that*? Seems a contradiction in terms," Devon said.

"And so it is. To compensate, they rinse everything in salt water that gives their clothes both that faintly pungent fragrance you may have noticed wafting in the air around Egbald and some of our other friends, and the board-like starched crispness of his attire that, in its own way, looked quite neat," Marc said.

"I thought the air about the place was a little closer than most, especially as it has warmed up, and was thinking they had cats that had been at work, both mousing and marking out their territory," Tynan said.

"We'll likely continue to be treated to a unique delicate blended fragrance of all those things," Marc replied. "Not to mention the grease of the leviathans they hunt is used to make their soap cakes, which have a fishy scent in their native state, though they add pine, lemon, and lavender ointment to some versions that they trade to other countries. Compounded on top of that the oil of their lamps in its most unfiltered form can smell like a summer fish fry; and there you have it."

Tynan grimaced. "Well, I guess until the baths at the Academy, I wasn't the cleanest or best-smelling cadet either. 'You still smell like 'em,' Webbe said, meaning the sheep, the first day I met him, and he was right. I shudder to think how else or what else I smelled like that day."

"These whalers believe it to be a badge of honor, a sign of success and prosperity and good fortune that the leviathan has been caught and made to serve them with all its parts and that the fishest smelling houses are to be found among the wealthiest and highborn of their people," Gerald put in. "We buy their oil for our lamps. It's prime and the most expensive on earth, giving forth the cleanest, brightest, longest-lasting light of all the oil. We trade our wool to them for it and they weave the wool into their great rain shawls. They ride to the winter hunts in them, so they're fond of us in their own way, though privately I'm sure they think we're too clean and smell too much like cheap perfume, a sweet smell of a sickly type."

"Have you noticed all the major figures in these pictures look alike?" Devon said. "Maybe ancestors or something—and are complete with violent hunting scenes, as well as the occasional hand-to-hand combat or depiction of the conquerors and the conquered? There seems to be a large quantity of blood and guts shed, which lends an extremely lurid or ghastly feel to the place."

"Bloodthirsty in the extreme, don't you think?" said Tynan.

"Yes," Marc said looking round. "But no weapons hung on the walls or displayed otherwise?"

"Hmmm—so they may not be used by unhappy guests?" Kiefer said.

"Just so. The whole feel of the place is a threat: obey the master or pay the price of being made a trophy hung on the wall and displayed as a warning to others," Tynan said.

"Decidedly uncomfortable," replied Devon as he examined a side table made from the leg of some massive beast.

"More so, Kendric and his folk don't seem to be keen to talking."

"We'll have to see, but the stories told about them say that most of what their talk is shouting or the roaring drinking songs of the sea—or angry silence."

"They are all hunters of the leviathan," Gerald said. "They harvest all they can snare or harpoon, turning the sea red with the blood of their prey."

"What is the leviathan?" asked Kiefer.

"They are the creatures in many of these images, an ancient beast from the depths of the icy sea," Gerald said. "They emerge from the extreme depths of the ocean—no one has discovered from where whence or why—a year or twenty or a hundred will pass between sightings or appearances. Their odd thin, flattish, very long shape comes it's thought from the weight of the water on them over the years of their growth. As it is, they come in after the whales, so the feud with them is bitter."

"Sounds much the same as our feuds with wolves, bears, and catamounts; all that would devour our shepherds and ruin our flocks. It just cannot be allowed," Tynan said.

"Not very encouraging. But what is our need of Duris in this business with Teras?" Devon asked.

"They can be the shield of the kingdom against them," replied Gerald. "Or they can be the hammer of the Terasians against Caledon. Even if they merely stand aside and do nothing to oppose a Terasian invasion force, it could deliver a blow difficult to recover from. If they stand against Teras, then we will have a stout defense and even the means to strike a blow in the other direction, as Kendric's ships constantly patrol up to the very shores of the continent. Besides, the oil of every lamp in Caledon and much of the western world comes from Kendric and his people, so there are important reasons to keep them as friends."

The night passed without a sound, and in the early morning they were awakened by a polite knock. Opening the door, they found Egbald standing there with a fine-smelling breakfast tray and a note from Kendric: Would they care to join he and his other guests that evening for a dinner and entrainment if they were quite refreshed from their journey?

"What do you think?" Tynan asked.

Marc shrugged. "It's part and parcel of ambassadorial work, though I'm sure from the look of these we may be garroted between the soup and the salad, like as not."

Gerald turned and replied in the lingua franca that they would be most pleased to attend though they would be limited to wearing their travel clothes. Egbald nodded and backed out of the room.

"Whatever else happens, this breakfast at least looks good!" They had barely finished when another polite knock at the door and there stood Egbald again, accompanied by two footmen carrying several sets of decent dinner clothes accompanied by a note that Kendric was pleased to furnish their need.

"Perfect fit," said Marc. "Though I look like a cross between a sailor and a woodsman."

"Yes," said Devon. "Even though it means we are being *very* closely watched and observed, and even measured from head to foot."

That evening, they filed into the Great Hall. Gerald was leading and stopped abruptly at the entrance. Along one wall to the right of the king's raised dais central table sat four Terasian lords, glowering at the Caledonians.

"The chickens have invited the fox to dine in their hall. Or in this case the fish have invited the fishermen," Kiefer said.

Gerald entered, and the Terasians stood and bowed silently to the Caledonians, who bowed in return, then made their way to their seats along the other side of the hall.

"May we remind our guests that this hall is neutral ground," spoke a man who sat near the center of the high table. "All hostilities were checked at the door when you came in as, of course, the courtesy of the hall demands peace and good behavior."

All agreed pleasantly but Tynan felt the strain between the sides seething just below the well-mannered surface.

"Your choice of who you share the fellowship of your hall in this case is a little surprising. These are the sort of guests that may be supping at your table while they measure the accommodations for a fit to them-selves," Gerald said.

"We have many friends, some of whom are less friendly to each other than we are to them." This last from Kendric, who now entered, all his people rising in his honor. "Of course, you know the old phrase 'if you're an enemy to my enemy, you're my friend.'"

"Ah! Then is the reverse of that coin true as well, if you're a friend of my enemy, then you're my enemy?" Gerald replied.

"There may be a third way! I'm told of a friendly enemy, someone who can be a friend or an enemy depending on the circumstances, who keep an eye on the main chance, the thing likely to be most profitable for them. These of course can't be trusted much because it's a hazy guess about what may be the most important thing to them in a situation."

"A friendly enemy! I like the idea; it leaves one with more options, more freedom to maneuver," spoke up one of the Terasians.

"But less likely to find help in time of need, when friends are most needed," Gerald said.

"Help? We help ourselves and stand or fall by that," the Terasian replied. "Trusting to friends—so called—can leave one dead on a battle-field somewhere, or shackled with chains on his feet and wrists, and neck, bitterly regretting his choice of friends."

"Well-spoken from both of our guests!" Kendric said as he sat down. "Let us all agree that for this evening, at least, to set aside these weighty topics and enjoy the hall!" and he ordered the dinner to begin.

The hall itself was built in the shape of a long ship and the walls rose up in wide curves from the floor to a high, flat plank ceiling. Large fish, sea eagles, kraken, tiger seals, and sharks—all stuffed and mounted in a lifelike state, figured as when living—adorned the walls and took the place of statues in various parts of the hall. Woven tapestries of ships and men at war with creatures of the sea and other sea-faring peoples, the largest showing a huge dragon-like creature wreaking havoc on a score of ships and one man with a harpoon in hand poised precariously on the bow of a small hunting boat facing it, were hung there as well.

At the high table, Kendric sat surrounded by all his great lords and closest friends, but especially Reger, with whom Kendric had the closest of bonds, as they had grown up together and had sailed together in many hunts. Stretched above on the wall behind the table was a banner some three yards square, a wine-dark field upon which a huge dragon or snake-like creature undulated.

"A song of the West! Give us a song of the West!"

The call was taken up throughout the hall. Kendric laughed loudly. "A song of the West would be welcome! What say you, our visitors from Caledon? Do you know any songs?"

"This is your cue," Gerald said to Tynan as an aside, and stood. "Thank you, our friends, for your welcome! It so happens Tynan here is known to play a few songs, if we can but find him a pipe to play."

"A pipe! Aye we have some of those in our seagoing land," Kendric replied. "Bring the boy a pipe and be quick about it!"

Tynan nodded. "Thank you," he said to their ever-present Egbald, who brought him a set of pipes, half-bowing and extending it to him holding it in both hands. Tynan took it and examined it closely.

"It's well-made." He didn't recognize the materials or the handiwork but was able to tune it with the turn of a few knobs, adjusting the pitch, then played out a single long note, then a brief melody. An immediate hush fell on the company—it was a tune that moved them all to silence, the ale forgotten for the moment.

"Maestro, do you know this music, 'The Song of Kenton'?" Tynan called to the concertmaster.

"'The Song of Kenton'?" he replied.

"How do you know this chanty?" Kendric interrupted. "In our language it is called 'To Follow the Sea' and is a song of our old longfathers, not often heard outside of our own land. It amounts to our national anthem, if you will."

Tynan shrugged and bowed slightly. "It's also a song from the West of where I live." He paused. "It was thought that we had written it!"

The hall erupted in laughter. All knew the words, and all stood—except the Terasians, Tynan noted—and took up the tune, singing with great energy and feeling. The last note hung in the air as the song finished and the hall broke out in applause.

"Another!" they called. Tynan struck up a lively tune, one of the dancing jigs of Caledon and the whole room was stamping their feet and pounding the tables in time with the music. He ended with loud applause.

"We shall have more of this!" Kendric shouted. "The men from Caledon have a soul!"

"Nicely done!" said Marc as Tynan sat down. "They at least will feel the worst for it if they cut our throats or fling us into the sea so soon after being given such a good entertainment."

Tynan laughed. "Good point! Though like all of this place it is a cold comfort and below all the seeming fellowship, there runs a deep current of anger or distrust—suspicion and I would say fear—as though all outside their land and city are to be rightly suspected of plotting their overthrow, enslavement, or destruction."

"They've likely had some bad experiences with so-called allies in the past and are warned against becoming too friendly too quickly," Marc replied.

"I agree," Tynan said. "And would be inclined to feel the same in their circumstances or given their history. They've been invaded at least twice from the West and multiple attacks from the sea including at least one major incursion in the last generation—so says Siwell," he ended sheepishly as he noticed Marc staring open-mouthed at him.

"You are an encyclopedia!" Marc said.

"Well done!" called Kendric again, hurling his plate to the floor and smashing it to bits. The rest of the hall did the same, a crescendo of crashing dishware and crockery. "You are welcome again and if you would learn to handle a harpoon, sit still in an open boat, and have a mind to, we'd be pleased to take you with us onto the sea tomorrow."

"We'd be honored to be included," Gerald said standing and bowing to Kendric again. "Though we are poor oarsmen compared to you all. And we'd like to raise a toast to . . ."

"Hold a moment!" shouted Kendric again. The raucousness died down, and into the hall an old man dressed in a tattered whaling cloak hobbled slowly down the center aisle of the room.

"Welcome, Maon!" Kendric said. "A stool for the Singer!"

Then came forward Maon the Singer. The sight of his eyes were dim; yet the sight of his mind was long. He was the greatest poet—some said seer—of that day or possibly of any day. As he took his seat on the stool, the hall grew completely silent. In his hand was a small harp and he strummed softly and sang of Bran and his struggle to keep the kingdom whole with rebels breaking away in many places and the sails of strange ships often sighted off the coast.

Maon's voice wove a spell of golden threads that drew the tale from the art and form of the hall itself, weaving all the long history, life, and times of Duris into the hunt for the leviathan, whose likeness and power linked all together.

In the midst of his tale, he suddenly paused and bowed his head for some moments. Then he spoke. "Greater disasters than those of this tale shall befall our land in our time, weighing most upon the house of Kendric and his present descendants.

"We have guests!" Maon continued. "Though I can't see them, we have messengers from *both* Caledon and Teras here now, likely bringing us promises and requests?"

"You have seen clearly," Kendric replied. "One asks our help, to be a shield to guard against a growing threat in the East; and the other asks for our assent, at least not to hinder, the rolling forward of a tide rising from the East."

"Ah! And let me guess that it's our visitors from Teras that speak of the tide as peace, prosperity, and order; while it's our friends from Caledon that urge us to join the resistance against that tide, as the prosperity and order that is promised comes with the price of servitude?"

"To the general nature of the debate, you have spoken correctly, without adding the question of whose time has come, that is, who or which idea will prevail regardless of what we do or don't do; want or don't want."

"It is so," said Maon. "Not a simple nor easy path in either direction."

He paused and seemed to be looking into the heights of the hall, listening. "And what will be the reply?"

"Our reply has yet to be fashioned, but the couriers of both must leave shortly with our answer and the time is passing quickly."

"Our time is our own, on that count," the old man said. "Caledon is unknown to me," he continued. "But they stay behind their borders and trade well with us. That much is good."

Gerald stood. "It's a matter of Teras, sir. With apologies to our fellow guests, they are making encroachments everywhere. Our intelligence has reported they are building a great invasion force beyond the Narrow Sea. To keep them back, we must stand together or likely we will see all lands, one by one, entangled in their net."

A Terasian stood. "My lord, we must insist this is not the place for these matters to be discussed, though many of our friends in other lands would say the so-called net that has entangled them has lifted them out of polluted water to the fresh stream of a higher way."

"Entangled in a net, you say?" Kendric said. "An apt choice of words for us mariner men here, as we know that nets are means of the capture of fish, their freedom forever gone. Here, we here live by the laws of the sea, which bend to no man.

"The oil of the leviathan is the wealth of our country, as well as the fishing and the control of trade in these waters. Protecting what is ours by keeping off those who would encroach or prey upon it or yoke it to their purposes—whether they be purposes of the East or purposes of the West makes no difference; they are not *our* purposes, and therefore we lose any governance over what may be. As right as those purposes seem to those who hold them, they belong to them and not to us, so we must weigh the balance of the scales that we hold in our own hands and measure their weight against those that are held in the hands of others."

"Many scales can be calibrated together to balance the mass of the world as it now stands and so preserve for all of us something to be weighed or balanced in the scales for the good of all, measured out in our own view, in our own time, by our own hand, and not at the behest or the hands of others, either as command or as benefit or favor bestowed," Maon said.

Kendric sat silently for a moment. "Regardless of all this, tonight we are here to honor the sea. Tomorrow we will render our decision and send you back to your lords."

Moan also sat unspeaking, his head bowed, then his face transformed. "The leviathan is here!"

"The leviathan . . . ?" Kendric began.

Suddenly, an alarm sounding like the ringing of a claxon bell, a marine call to arms, rang through the hall.

"Hi! Hi! It's the leviathan!! All hands to the chutes!" Kendric shouted, then turned to the Caledonians.

"You're welcome to go in the third boat, if you have a mind to see something worth seeing. We hunt in pairs with the first to strike, the second to back it up. The third boat is for finishing the beast and haulage—also safer in case the beast bursts the lines or stoves in the other boats."

"Of course!" Gerald answered and they followed after Kendric to the chutes.

The crews vaulted into their hunting boats, the boats held to at the ready by heavy ropes, angled down the wooden launch chutes poised to be cut away and rushed down the chutes some two hundred yards steeply to the water below.

The third boat was a larger vessel designed to provision and support the two prime hunting craft with harpoons, rope, and be alongside to rescue any crew or wrecked boats from the water and to tow in the hoped-for catch of carcasses to the harbor or cleaning area.

Into this boat, Tynan and Marc scrambled, thumping down at an oarlock, lashing a leather belt across their front.

Suddenly, Kendric himself joined their boat, taking the rudder. "Strap yourselves in snug-like, and don't touch the oars or the rudder," he said.

A sailor handed each of them a twelve-foot long, razor sharp harpoon, the wooden shafts wound with tarred rope, fitted with a four-foot bronze dart fluted at the tip like a large arrowhead. "Hold these points up," he said. "Be careful when you uncover the tips of these pikes, as you can lose a finger—they're that sharp—and hand them for'ard when they're called for by the harpooner."

"It helps when the boat is rolling with the sea or skipping when pulled by the leviathan to pick a spot just above the horizon and keep your gaze fixed on it; it can be a lifesaver, I assure you," Kendric said as he limbered up the rudder. "What you see may be startling—something not seen by mortal man for nigh on a hundred years or more, something to fix in your mind and bring to your remembrance when you feel you've seen it all or have nothing left to see. These are creatures that, seen in the light of the sun, may warrant being called something new under the sun."

Tynan lashed the leather strap around his wrist and gripped the harpoon tightly.

"All secure?" Kendric shouted.

"All secure!"

"Cut us away!"

"Cutting away!" The dockhand brought down an axe. A loud whack sounded, and they were off, tilting steeply down, rushing faster and faster, the spars and frame of the chute rattling and banging against the craft as they went.

To their amazement, Reger stood in the bow of the boat, his feet wedged under the gun rails, holding a harpoon above his head with both hands and yelling wildly. Their speed and the rate at which they sped up took them by surprise, and Tynan found out later that these ready boats were sheathed under the waterline with highly polished bronze, oiled—appropriately enough—using the oil of the leviathan and burnished to a fine smoothness. They hurtled behind the others toward the darkened water below. With a whoosh and a heave, they struck the water, skipping across the dark surface and sliding far out into the bay.

"Oars out!" Kendric shouted. The crew swung out the oars, rowing hard, hoisting a small steering jib sail that caught the sheering wind, fairly lifting them across the water's surface.

"Finback to port!" called Reger, pointing to the left.

"Finback?" Kendric said. "Are you certain?"

"Aye, Kendric. It's a finback for sure." Reger replied. "And coming fast!"

The great fish bore down on them like a rampaging water-born killer creature, cleaving the sea, sending up huge spray like a massive plow furrowing the water, casting the spray high and curving to each side as it came on.

"Uncover and hand up the spikes!" Kendric ordered. Tynan and Marc stripped off the covers and prepared to hand them up, when a great tail swept across the boat, sweeping Reger away and shattering the prow of the boat. The beast paused a moment and raised its head, peering down. Tynan and Marc didn't have time to think, they stood, hefted the harpoons like a spear and cast them at the beast. Both of the harpoons struck the bulbous eye that looked down on them, and the monster reared up in the water, roaring deafeningly, setting the water to a boil, writhing in its death throes.

A silence settled on the sea, as their hunting boat, slowly taking on water, bobbed gently next to the mountainous carcass.

"It wasn't a leviathan at all, as bad as that would have been. It turns out that was a bloody rorqual, and a green one at that," Egbald told them as they sat by a fire in their rooms later that morning.

"Rorqual? You all seem to have an endless stock of sea monsters and other horrifying specimens of the deep. Where does this one fit in?" Tynan said.

"A rorqual—a razorback or finback—is a leviathan that has gone through some unnatural changes in the extreme depths of the sea; at least, so it's speculated. It's a throwback to other kinds of sea monsters or sea dragons that are supposed to have stopped living long ago. Even then, rorquals are said to be red. This one was *green* and only one other green one has ever been seen or heard of."

Egbald pointed to the pennant in the rafters. "That pennon is one that represents a green rorqual; the only one ever seen and hunted, as happened some five hundred years ago. Hunted but not caught, mind you, destroyed all the boats sent after it and then disappeared into the depths." He stopped a moment and looked somewhat sidelong at them, smiling crookedly. "Legend has it that they really come to hunt boats, not other fish, as a sort of judgment of the hunted on the hunters, so we've done a great service to us all by slaying this one."

"Well, truth be told, I'm glad we didn't know more about *that* beast before we met it and also very glad we were able to help you in the hunt," Marc said.

"Aye; and though you may not have noticed, the Terasians were not in it. They took their leave of the hall as the claxons rang and weren't seen again until this morning at the breakfast table," Egbald said.

"I've always said those Terasian boys live with an eye to the main chance," Kiefer said. "And so they will always prove to do."

At that moment, Gerald came into the room. "Let us go to Kendric and hear the outcome."

They were escorted to a small side room off the main hall, where Kendric sat with only a small group with him, looking as fresh as if he hadn't spent the whole night of the previous night on the open water. He stood, smiling. "Welcome again, Caledonian friends! And especially to you who were in the rorqual boat. Quite a message from all that guides the cosmos that it was by the aid of your hand it was felled, wouldn't you say, Maon?"

Maon was hunched in a corner, looking uncommunicative. "Some might say so, Kendric. Others would say naught but a fortunate coincidence."

"Coincidence? That from our great seer?" Kendric replied. "I would have expected a deeper reading coming from you."

"It's a safer path to say too little than to say too much," Maon replied.

"That I'll at least agree with," Kendric said. "But now to business."

"Kendric, there is a second message from the Terasian envoy," interjected Reger, bandaged and looking haggard from his encounter with the rorqual. "He is demanding that it be delivered into your hand and read by your eyes alone." He reached into his cloak, produced a rolled parchment, and handed it to Kendric, who carefully studied the heavy black wax seal for some time before he broke it and unrolled the leather. For some minutes he read silently, only the crackling of the central fire could be heard. Then he looked up, smiling slightly.

"As you know, the Terasian ship that we sent to the bottom that day at Aston Quay bore a famous personage—Septus, known to many of us as an admiral and sometime governor of certain lands. Our Terasian friend claims that it was inadvertently blown into our lands, by the adverse winds of the gods. He says—as a side note—that his nation has no interest or intent to ever come here . . ." At this, the entire room erupted into loud laughter.

"He goes on to request reparations in the form of gold or similar currency for the losses of their ship, men, and slaves, as this recompense will be viewed as a pledge of our acceptance of their offer!"

"Two messages in the space of a single day: one from the sea, one from the East. Doubly spoken . . . doubly certain." Kendric leaned back in his chair and looked at Gerald.

"As has been said, as reasonable as those purposes seem to those who hold them, they belong to them, not as clearly to us, so we must weigh the balance of the scales that we hold in our own hands and measure them against those held in the hands of others," Maon said.

"Many scales can be calibrated together to balance the mass of the world as it now stands and so preserve for all of us something that can be weighed in the scales at all, measured out in our own view by our own hand not at the behest of another."

Kendric sat silently for a moment and nodded. "Well said, Maon. What say you all here?"

Reger spoke for the group. "It seems that Caledon purposes to be a friend but not a master; while Teras can only be a master and never a friend."

"I think that phrase says it as completely as it can be said," Kendric answered. "We will send a polite refusal to the Terasians, keeping the language as open as possible for future discussions." Then he took up a pen, signed two pages, sealed them, and handed them to Reger, who gave them to Gerald. As Gerald put them in his courier bag, Tynan saw Kendric crumple up and cast away another set of documents—they had a refusal written out as well.

Kendric caught the expression on Tynan's face and laughed. "Don't be surprised, young one! We had many words and much language prepared and may have refused the offer of Caledon. But as it is, we are glad now that we have accepted."

Gerald nodded. "We are glad as well and will return these when Policrates and his council put their signature to them."

They saluted, bid them farewell and were led out of Kendric's ship-like hall.

"Did you follow everything that was said or not said?" Tynan asked as they sat on their horses waiting for the final barrels of oil and other goods to be loaded on the waggons.

"I think Kendric told us," Marc replied. "That he has signed the treaty to cooperate because he was convinced somehow that we will be a true—or at least better—friend to his country than Teras and that Teras could never be more than a fickle master at best, by their nature they would always be the ruling partner in any agreement, quick to assert its overlordship when it felt beneficial to do so."

"Kendric had a refusal drawn up as well, as I'm sure you noticed?"

"Of course. They had to see all possible words on paper for it to be real to them; and they have to protect themselves. We have no ill intent toward Kendric, but one can't be too sure even when all seems pleasant and friendly."

"And as a negotiation they had to let us know they were considering other options?"

"Certainly," said Marc. "It's the same stratagem used when a seller lets a potential buyer know that there are 'other interested parties.'"

Tynan nodded. "Right, then. What will be our next movement?"

"For us, we'll hear fresh policies, which I am sure will be forthcoming soon. I'm guessing they will be satisfied for now with a plan to send a delegation to Kendric in the spring to hammer out the details, especially guard the coast and to provide a land force to drive off any hostile force that gets too near the eastern seaboard."

Tynan nodded again as Egbald came up.

"Thank you, Egbald," Marc said. "You have been most kind to us and though you haven't spoken many words, we're sure you've listened much."

A very small though pleasant smile crossed Egbald's face. "My pleasure, young masters."

Just then, Webbe's voice cut the frosty morning. "Squad forward at a canter! What are you standing around for?"

They reined round and, with a salute to Egbald, rode out with the wagons, the sun rising to meet them.

CHAPTER 14

The School of Social Graces

TYNAN WALKED TOWARD THE walled garden. The quadrangle of neat-mowed grass—where he had spent much time and extra duty manicuring—smelled fresh and sweet, a swelling up of new growth, bordered by cherry trees with dark purple trunks thick from years of steady tending by Academy arborists, bearing clouds of pink and white blossoms just on the cusp of the fruit itself.

> *Meet me in the special garden by the fountain if you can, just before the late afternoon bell. E.*

The note was short; and the words had sent him back to the day he had gone early to the Music Hall, looking for a spare reed for his pipes.

As he rummaged in the storeroom, the most delightful music started up, coming from the string section of the hall, the player hidden by instruments on the stage. It was as if a dream had woven itself into waking life; as with his pipes, a flow of images came forth like water flowing, fresh breezes, blossoms, the song of birds, the still water on the surface of a lake under the moonlight. He stood transfixed, just listening as the notes swept over him. Then the music paused, and Tynan found the reed he sought, and turned quickly to go. He stumbled and knocked down a music stand, which set up a domino-effect as one after the other of twelve of them toppled over, clattering loudly in the acoustic hall.

"Who's there?" came a voice from the string section, the speaker hidden in the recesses of the stage.

"Er—no one," answered Tynan as he grabbled to set up the music stands.

"No one who?" came the answer.

"Just no one. I'm sorry I disturbed your playing—it was very good," Tynan replied.

Footsteps sounded and from the string section of the hall walked a female cadet.

"You've been standing there all along *spying* on me?"

"I'm sorry," he answered. "No—just admiring your music."

"You really shouldn't spy on people," she said and walked past him and out of the room.

He hurried slightly—dinner in the dining hall was prompt and they were out for a steeplechase training ride that night with Lydia—when the thought flashed in his mind that he hadn't fared well with Ellen at another time.

Tynan had been obliged to take the hand of the girl across from him in line. She turned gracefully to her left and extended her right arm hand palm down toward him, fingers spread slightly, eyes focused ahead not looking at him. Tynan was just a step behind the music, he pivoted on his right foot and took her hand—too tightly, and she grimaced shaking her hand free.

"Cadet!" Webbe shouted. "This isn't a wrestling match! Lightly! Gently! We want none of our guests having to go to the medics because of you!"

"Yes, sir," and he lightened his touch.

"And palms up! Let her grip your hand—a gesture of mutual respect."

His partner seemed so far to have not noticed his discomfiture save for a slight smile and they walked on.

"Now," commanded the sergeant. "Make *interesting* small talk!"

"Sir, what would that be?" someone asked.

"Does no one in this unit have the slightest idea about anything except mucking out stalls and the latest heroes of the stadium?"

"Sir. No, we don't. Sir!" the cadets shouted in unison.

"For once, I agree with you!" he bellowed. "Start by introducing yourself, using a phrase such as 'I'd like to introduce myself. My name is *blank* and I'm very glad to make your acquaintance.'"

The entire unit repeated his words verbatim, including the 'My name is blank' phrase. The girls broke up hysterically.

"Are you complete idiots! At the part 'my name is *blank*,' say your *own* name." Webbe was by now an incredible shade of mottled purple and red, and Tynan thought he would literally be spitting nails shortly. "*Your* name isn't blank is it? No! Though some of yours *ought* to be blank—I wouldn't put it past you, and how I pity your mothers."

Tynan turned to his partner. "I'm very glad to make your acquaintance. My name is Tynan."

"Then go on: 'May I inquire as to yours?'" Webbe continued. "*If she is able to overcome her contempt of your clumsy efforts so far and answers you, do your best, will you, to make some reasonably intelligent observations about the weather, or the room, or the company. Keep it courteous and keep it clean!*"

"May I inquire of yours?" Tynan said mechanically.

"My name is Ellen," had come the answer.

By that time, the music had ended, and they had arrived at the doors to the dining hall, preparing to go in two by two, as though the dance would continue at the meal.

"Now! As you approach the matter of dining, here are the words to use," Webbe said.

"'Shall we go in to dinner?' 'May I help you with your chair?' These are the formalities of courtesy and are not *questions* but emblems of etiquette displaying the honor and respect of one person to another."

The cadets seated the girls and then themselves.

"Remember!" Webbe's voice cut across the room. "The only part of your body to ever be seen *on* the table is your hand, and—for the love of all that is good in the world—*use* the fork."

That was all to the bad, he thought as he hurried on. But three weeks after his return from the mission to Kendric, something that seemed better had happened.

He was working in the Stacks and was high up one wall on a ladder, restocking manuscripts when he heard a voice below.

"Excuse me. Excuse me—library worker?"

"Yes?" he answered without turning.

"The Warden sent me to you. I need help finding a medical text by Ascepilus. He said one of you would know how to help."

"Linaes and his people are the best," said Tynan. "But I'll help if I can." And he started down the ladder, which was one of the rickety narrow types used for the high shelves. Just near the bottom, his foot slipped, and he slid down the last several feet, crashing into a heap of scrolls at the bottom. As he struggled up, she laughed.

"Why it's you: Mr. Music Spy and Mr. My Name Is Blank!"

Tynan laughed. "Normally, I'm a little more coordinated and able to speak up intelligently at need, but yes, it's me. Tynan."

"Well Mr. Tynan, I don't know if you remember, but my name is Ellen. I hope you're not injured too severely; and if you're not, do you know the way to the Ascepilus?"

"Of course. I believe it is in the chained-text alcove. Follow this way."

The garden was off the far end of the quadrangle and near to the grand windows of the library. A little reluctantly, Tynan turned off from the bustling activity and went into the shaded coolness. The gray walls lined with close-set ash trees and the thick ground cover bordered narrow dark gravel paths that wound pleasingly through the garden, creating the illusion that the garden was much larger that it actually was, giving one the feeling that they were alone in distant solitude, away from the world. The silence was enveloping, and the coolness of the place made it one of Tynan's most enjoyable.

Ellen was already there, seated on a low bench before a fountain shaped in the form of figures riding water horses, crafted to near life-like size, capturing the moment of escape from the sea or the plunging out of a deep river ford. She wore a slim blue student gown, the headpiece set beside her, her auburn hair pulled back, close-braided, her green eyes sparkling in the dim light. One hand slowly swishing the water of the fountain. She looked up briefly as he approached then turned back to the waters of the fountain.

Tynan stopped a few paces from her somewhat awkwardly, as she didn't speak, and her face held a serious expression. Not knowing exactly what to do, he uneasily assumed a kind of "at ease" posture.

"Hello. Marc gave me your note and here I am."

She looked up as he stood there—for a moment looking very bright and somehow uncertain or undecided. She nodded and smiled, though still with an unusual tentativeness; she was always so confident—why so uncertain?

"I hear you're likely going away with Gerald in the fall."

"Um—yes, if we all graduate, some of us will be named to a new company: the Silver Shield. We'd be going in as Gerald's personal subaltern staff."

Ellen didn't reply, so he continued. "It would be a great honor and Gerald personally selected us . . ." his voice trailed off lamely as Ellen remained silent, the silence growing more uncomfortable by the minute.

"It's just that, well, I just found out I may not be here when you get back."

"Oh?" Tynan said.

"I finish this term, then I'm to go back to Hereford."

"I see," Tynan said.

"You could be gone for months and the truth of it is I'm not sure I want you to go."

"Don't want me to go?" said Tynan puzzled. "I really doubt I have a choice in the matter, short of deserting."

"I know you must; but it still doesn't have to mean that I want you to go."

Tynan had to admit to himself he was not understanding what was being said . . . and being said in plain speech by someone he thought he knew. He stood there looking down at his feet, hearing the fountain and a breeze rustling the trees of the garden, and he couldn't put his finger on his feeling or his thoughts—they scattered from view when he tried to look at them directly, but from the corner of his eye he discerned something important was going on here, hovering just beyond the fingertips of his mind; and that it was important that he understand.

"What are you afraid of?" she asked.

Tynan stopped fidgeting. "Afraid of? Well, many things. Large, fast-moving people with malicious intent would find a place high on my list, though broccoli or especially brussels sprouts would also vie for the top spot. Mataen chariots . . ." his voice trailed off weakly as he saw she was not happy with his answer. "Is that what you mean?"

"No—those are trivial things."

"Trivial? Have you ever seen a . . ."

"Someone with the intellect of an ox can face them," she cut him off. "The mind of any kind of large blundering animal can deal with those. What are you afraid of—here? Now?"

"In this garden? I fear nothing," he answered. "In many ways, this place is my fortress, my refuge, my place of peace in troubled times."

"Then why is fear written all over your face and the jitteriness of your hands and the shuffling of your feet? Am I a large, fast-moving person with malicious intent?"

Then she laughed—a laugh that Tynan at that moment believed was the most beautiful laugh ever laughed in the history of Caledon. He felt at that moment that if Ellen asked him to do anything for her, he would—whatever it cost him, even all he had—just to hear her laugh that way again.

Tynan laughed long and naturally at that. "Large? No, no—definitely not large. Fast moving? No, no—but swift to help others I'd say. Malicious intent? No, no—more like serious or deadly intent, though directed at me or someone unwittingly like me, caught somehow as the object of what? I'm not sure."

"Fairly said," she replied. "Won't you sit down?"

He sat on the other side of her headpiece which lay on the bench. The distance seemed safer somehow with the hat between them, and he felt he could breathe more normally.

"That's better, isn't it?" she said looking up directly at him and smiling.

"It is," he said smiling back. "But as you are my friend, I know you didn't mean to undermine my going with Gerald. My other friends are going, and it would be a betrayal to them to stay behind."

"Of course!" she said. "Whatever gave you the idea you shouldn't go? I only wanted you to know that I didn't want you to go but would rather have you stay here."

"Stay here?"

"Yes."

"How can I do both?" he replied. "I could be sent anywhere."

Another long silence followed, and the fountain suddenly seemed oddly clamorous. It was the sound of her voice above all that intrigued and worried and entranced and excited him. It was completely unforced, unexpected. He remembered it, and at times it would come unbidden to his waking mind, a voice like no other he had heard before. A welcome sound that dispersed the silence or rather hushed the incessant chatter of his own mind and calmed him in a strangely exciting way—not to lull him to sleep but rather to summon him. It seemed the birds and indeed the world stilled their own voices and leaned in to listen.

"I'm just not sure I want you to go or what I want you to do."

Tynan looked up. "What do you mean?"

"I don't know—but I think I like your company."

"My company?"

She nodded, swishing her hand in the fountain.

Tynan smiled. "That is well."

She paused for a long time, the only sound the fountain's bubbling and spilling out to the small stream that ran through the bottom of the garden. "Do you like mine?"

That brought Tynan up short and he paused for several moments. "Well—honestly, I don't believe I'm understanding what you're saying."

"Then you'd better just go—you're nothing but a typical lunkhead."

She stood up, flung the water from her hand, and walked away through the garden gate not looking back.

Tynan sat there for a few minutes, staring after her, not moving as if he was a carving of stone. He looked down. She had left her head-piece there and he picked it up, holding it even more awkwardly and, not knowing what else to do, stood and walked back toward the quadrangle. As he emerged from the garden, the evening bell rang, and he stopped just outside the gate.

"Tynan!" shouted Webbe who was hurrying by. "Get a move on!"

"Yes, sir," Tynan said, and he ran from the garden himself. It was a long time before he was able to think about her perplexing words. He locked them in the back of his mind and hoped some light might be shed on their meaning and would present themselves to him, but he wasn't sure of that ever happening.

Nevertheless, he felt strange as he packed his field kit for the steeple-chase training ride. Ellen's headpiece lay somewhat disconcertingly on his bunk, carrying to his room a strangely pleasant scent drifting up that reminded him of Ellen's eyes and hair and the very tone of her voice that made him feel even more confused.

And there the headpiece continued to lay—blue and long, with a cincture in the back just like the dozens he had seen others wear save for a strand of her hair and the oddly moving scent.

Suddenly he heard Marc and the others in the hall, talking loudly and shouting for him. He took the headpiece and stowed it in the bottom of his gear trunk, wrapping it with his spare tunic, thinking he would return it to her later. His feelings and thoughts though were odd to him. He felt edgy now and somewhat distracted, his thinking drifting unaccountably back to her in unguarded moments or pauses in his constant duties. As a subaltern, his sole focus would be on Gerald: the person and work and movements of Gerald would be all that mattered. It was Tynan's duty and mission to Gerald, the king, and the country. But he felt now a tug of regret, which he quickly put down, though his thoughts were mixed up and disoriented.

"Tynan," Marc called. He leaned in the door. "We're due to muster in ten minutes—are you ready?"

"Nearly," Tynan said.

"What's wrong?"

"Well, nothing I think—I'm actually not sure—though I just had the strangest conversation with Ellen right before chow."

"Oh? What was it about that note from her I gave you?"

"Yes—and no. It didn't make much sense what was being said and it ended with her being quite upset, calling me names, and abruptly leaving the garden."

"How odd," Marc replied. "Yet girls can be difficult to understand at times—or so I've been told."

"How would someone know?"

"I'm guessing, of course. My sisters, though, can be downright inscrutable."

Tynan nodded. "My sister too. She's lived with my mother and step-father for the most part, so I haven't been around her as much to know how to read between the lines."

"Who can say?" shrugged Marc. "Anyway, we best get over to the steeplechase course. Lydia is meeting us there for some final coaching and we'd better not keep her waiting."

"Not that one, for sure," Tynan said, and they hurried out to the stables.

The team steeplechase was the last equestrian competition of the Final Games of graduation. In it, the four riders of each cadre had to race over a series of jumps, obstacles, and water hazards on a three-mile course, finishing together in under ten minutes. Lydia was there at the starting point of the course with another rider sitting on their horses when Tynan, Marc, Devon, and Kiefer arrived.

"This is Jen," Lydia said. "She is a friend who can keep quiet and has an eye for terrain." They walked their horses ahead on the course. It started in the West Field of the Academy, then plunged into a narrow, twisted route through the old forest, after which it opened into wide vistas of open fields—many of which stretched to the edge of the river itself—crisscrossed with hedges, fences, and stone walls.

"The only rule is to get to the finish first as a team without going off the course," Lydia said. "You can pick any line across the jumps and fields. If anyone of the team falls, the whole team must wait and continue on as a group—you must cross the finish line together."

Near the midpoint they came to a series of jumps and water hazards, the highest of them rose several inches above their heads as they dismounted and stood studying it.

"How do you get across that one without breaking your neck?" Kiefer asked.

"I'll show you how to do it," Lydia replied.

As she remounted, Tynan looked over at Jen and a vague recollection came to his mind.

She noticed him looking quizzically at her and laughed. "Yes! We *have* met—on the kitchen doorstep of the king's house."

"I thought I remembered that you were there," he answered. "When I first came in the city to play the pipes to ease the pain of the king's mind—and he was eased, though he nearly skewered me with his spear to the wall of that small room where I first played; grazed my shoulder but no major damage done and he felt better for another day."

"I don't remember that, though my father is often at the palace."

"Your father?"

"The Marshal is my father. Lydia's my older sister."

"I was the grubby urchin boy on the back stairs, and you brought me a plate of food—for which I've not had the chance to thank you, and I do so now 'thank you.'"

"You were welcome, of course. I'm glad it was a good first meeting."

Tynan laughed. "Well, actually you called me—rightly so—a grubby boy and doubted whether I knew how to use a fork."

"How ridiculous of me!"

Tynan laughed again. "No harm done! I had been sleeping in the woods and riding through all weather for three days before, so I'm sure I

looked grubby and likely didn't smell very agreeable either. Though Lieutenant Ross said at the time that we must clean ourselves up as we were
reporting to the master himself."

"The master himself," she said. "My father is the Master of the Horse
and a great man in his own way." She paused. "I'm so glad you've at least
had the sense to clean up a bit since then!"

"The Academy forced him to clean up," put in Marc. "One of the
unexpected benefits they are pleased to provide all cadets! But here
comes Lydia."

Lydia had circled back and was galloping toward the triple line of
jumps, cleared the first then the second.

"Nicely done!" they shouted.

The third obstacle in the set was a monster—the Academy Barrier,
standing in four tiers like an artificial mound some one hundred feet
high. The rider and horse climbed the steep uphill, having to jump low
fences at each pause, then down the other side, with the downhill pitch
by far the hardest and most dangerous.

"Most teams will dismount and walk their horses on the downhill
side of the Barrier," Jen said as Lydia reined up for a moment, planning
her path. "To win, you'll need to *ride* down. Watch how Lydia does it."

Lydia spurred her mount into a gallop, the horse going at full
speed within ten yards, and urged up the steep slope to the first plateau,
smoothly jumping the first fence, then up to the second plateau, leaping
the fences set there, then the third, and onto the fourth plateau. Without
skipping a stride, she and the horse leapt off the downhill side of the
Barrier. She was leaning so far to the rear that her back was touching the
horse's hind quarters as they plunged down the slope at more than breakneck speed, then were out on the flat and angling for the next fence. Lydia
slowly reined her horse to a walk, patting the horse's neck, and turning
back to where the others waited.

They stood in a stunned silence.

"How did you manage that?" Devon managed to say at last.

"Thank you," she said.

"Of course. How did you keep your seat on the downhill?"

She laughed. "I was riding before I was walking and since my father
is the Master of the Horse; I would be a grave embarrassment to him if
I weren't an expert rider. He wouldn't be able to show his face in public
and so forth."

Lydia dismounted. "It does take practice, but the best riders will do it that way. The key is to lean back, hold the reins with one hand and let your other arm extend behind you. It balances the horse and helps it to keep its footing on very steep downhills." She paused a moment to take a drink of the water Jen handed her. "Any other posture will cause the horse to slip and both it and the rider will soon be a tumbling nightmare."

"I don't know," Kiefer said. "It looks very tough."

"You're a big boy," Lydia replied. "Which can be against you in this competition, but you do have two weeks to work out how to do it, so it's not beyond your skill if you have the nerve. You can be sure that the only other team that will try to ride the downhill will be the Gold Shield. The rest will certainly walk it, which will give you four to five minutes to the better."

"My only remark," said Jen, "Is that when you reach the bottom plateau of the Barrier and head toward fence 14, you'll gain another minute if you cut the corner by crossing that shallow brook rather than go up and around on the path."

"Is a minute going to make that much difference?" Tynan asked.

"The last six or seven steeplechases have been decided by less than that, so every second can mean the difference," Lydia said.

"We have our work cut out for us," said Marc as they spread out on the turf for a break.

"And only field rations for today, ma'am," Devon said, looking down at the unidentifiable food in his tin. "Sorry we can't offer you any better for all the help you've given us."

"Ma'am-ing me!" she said. "I'm no *ma'am*, Devon, and you know it."

"Of course, of course. Pardon me," he said.

"And as for payment for my help, I believe in the future I may need you and your little friends here to escort me on rides from time to time for my protection; as well as to run for water or hay or other trifles for my friends and their horses."

"We'd be most happy do so," Marc answered for the group.

They paused then, as they ate and looked away to the west. The hill fell sloping down and the Great River glittered beyond its feet. Tall hills rose again beyond the river to a darker green belt of thickly forested hillsides, with ridges sweeping north. The hills themselves walked toward a dim blue haze, dissolving at last into nothing at all. But the haze remained; in the far, far distance, a line of highlands and crags rose toward the land of the Mataens; and beyond that the Narrow Sea and the specter of Teras.

CHAPTER 15

The Lodging of the Colors

PASSING DOWN A LONG corridor, they entered an interior courtyard, and were met by a squad of sentries who knew their names and immediately admitted them to the rooms beyond. Two other guards were there flanking a heavy oaken door. On the door were two shields, one blue and the other silver, blazoned with winged horses.

"Please listen to me," said Webbe. "This new Strategicon is a busy man. When he was the Marshal, he sent the letter asking for you as a piper and seems to want you to be part of this new command, but as the Strategicon, he may not remember all of the details and he certainly won't have a lot of time. Be crisp, be respectful, call him 'sir', and don't mumble."

"Of course." Tynan smiled weakly and worked to get his belt arranged properly.

"And above all *do* try to stand up straight," said Webbe, then he knocked once on the door and entered without awaiting a summons.

They marched briskly in, halted three paces from a massive wooden table, and saluted.

"New cadet graduate candidate reporting as ordered, sir," Webbe said.

"At ease," said a polished Caledonian cavalry officer faultlessly attired who sat in a chair to one side of the table. Next to him sat a somewhat disheveled figure in a plain brown robe girded with a leather belt who said nothing but wore a look of mild amusement. A third cavalry officer, as well-dressed as the first, stood a little behind, looking through a sheaf of documents.

He looked up—it was Gerald. "Tynan. Good to see you again. It's been a bit since our little excursion over to Dara, wouldn't you say?"

"Yes, sir," Tynan answered, his eyes focused on the far corner of the ceiling beyond.

The Strategicon, sitting at the table, stamped the parchment he had just signed, leaned back, and looked up, seeming just then to notice Tynan and Webbe standing there.

"Cadet Tynan," the Strategicon said and turned to the others. "Gerald it seems you know. This is Lieutenant Colonel Cage—he commands this training post; and Siwell, the headmaster of the school that is part of this Academy. Through their efforts, we have combined the military and the academic arts to form a new kind of officer, a cadre of leaders that know how to fight and how to think." He paused. "The time at the Academy has gone well for you, has it?"

"Yes, sir."

"Very good. Do you have any regrets or reservations about continuing on in the service?"

"No, sir."

"Very well. Siwell?" He looked at the stocky man.

Siwell nodded. "He has a questing spirit and a reasonable way with words."

"Cage?"

"Only one comment says no—we have a direct word on that," Cage said. Cage referred to the file and read: "'Cadet unqualified due to lack of pedigree and breeding.'"

Gerald grinned at this and said to Tynan. "Cadet, does that rather awkward—not to say unflattering—comment anger you?"

"Sir, no sir. It may be true of my past but not of my future."

"Very good!" Gerald replied. "As the Strategicon has given us a free hand to build this unit, my own thought is that lack of pedigree and breeding might honestly be one of the best qualifications to succeed here, so I think we shall set that remark aside; most courteously, of course."

"Of course," replied Cage. "The rest of the cadet's record is fairly good, leaving out some minor details of having to guard the quadrangle on numerous occasions for relatively small infractions. While we still need to complete the Final Games and the Lodging of the Colors—barring anything grossly insubordinate or very much out of line, I would recommend bringing the candidate in as a provisional with the cadet brevet rank, and review in a year's time."

"Right then," the Strategicon said. "Cage and Siwell rarely agree on anything so easily, Cadet, so don't be put off by their commentary, some of which is directed at each other, and some directed at this new world that is taking shape around us. Life in the service can be very tough but if you choose to listen, Cage and men like him will make you the best officer and man you could ever be. And Siwell and his brethren will teach you how to ask the right questions and think for yourself."

"Sounds fine, sir," said Tynan.

"This new corps will be all volunteer—we are looking for men who want to do this. What do you think?"

Tynan felt at that moment that walls were closing in while at the same time the entire world was opening out.

Then he said, "Thank you. I would very much like to join. Sir, one worry I do have is that my grandparents' sheep farm will be hard to take care of if I don't return to help. My grandfather passed away earlier this year; my grandmother is left alone to manage the place."

"I'm glad you mentioned that, as we did have one other piece of news to pass on to you." The Strategicon paused and shuffled through another stack of parchments on his desk, selected one, and handed it to Gerald to read.

> *Every man that was part of the Fifth Foot Volunteer who fought and fell at the Battle of Monroe Pass was by royal decree granted lifetime immunity and debt relief for himself and his family of all tax and levy labor in return for their selfless dedication and service to the land. The Battle of Monroe Pass occurred eleven years ago, and it has just come to our attention that Eason of Westcombe, a sturdy man and foot soldier, was a member of the Fifth Foot Volunteer and gave the ultimate self-sacrifice for his country, and yet due to an oversight, was somehow overlooked when the decree went out at the time from Policrates.*
>
> *To remedy this, a writ will be issued for the return of eleven years' taxes inadvertently paid by his survivors during that period, and a copy of this declaration etched on a bronze tablet will be issued that declares all the holdings of Eason and his family to be freeheld for all time.*

Tynan had a difficult time taking in what he was hearing. It meant a new lease on life for his mother, his grandmother, sister, and even his cousin. "Thank you, sir," he said. "Why . . . I . . . I can't express my gratitude. Thank you for deciding this way for my family."

Gerald smiled. "We're pleased as well and very glad to correct the oversight."

"Very good," said the Strategicon. "If that eases your mind, what say you to the honor of continuing to serve your king?"

"I would be most happy to, sir," Tynan replied.

"Right then. Cage, do you have the document?"

Cage stepped to the desk and placed a parchment on it. "If you choose to sign this," he said. "You will be bound to the king and his service for three years and one day, during which you will receive a payment of one sesterce per month minus costs for your uniforms, horse, equipment, and room and board provided by the crown. Should you choose to withdraw from your assignment prior to that term, then you will be detailed to whatever work pleases the commander and returned to your home following the completing of the standard period. Do you so agree?"

"I agree," Tynan said.

"Since you have agreed in the presence of these witnesses, please sign here."

Tynan signed, then Gerald, Cage, Siwell, and finally the Strategicon also signed.

"Very good!" said the Strategicon. "You will have very little to worry about if you work hard, think hard, and never quit."

"Where shall he be assigned?" Cage said.

"Any preferences, cadet?" the Strategicon put in.

"The Border Guard would be interesting," Tynan replied.

"Border Guard? Gerald, that's your area," the Strategicon said.

Gerald paused, looking for a moment at Tynan. "I think that would be a good posting for this cadet, though there is a lot of interest in the unit. We'll see what can be done."

"Very good. The Border Guard it most likely will be. Good luck, cadet. Do your best," the Strategicon concluded and immediately turned to the next vellum stack on his desk.

From the corner of his eye Tynan saw Webbe straighten to attention and draw a salute. He did likewise; and they were dismissed.

It was all coming down to Marc's ride. Junius had finished, as had Egan, the third rider in the final competition. After two weeks of Final Games, three teams were tied—the Silver, the Gold, and the Seventh Shields. This was a circumstance not seen for generations, and it took the game umpires some time to decide what to do.

Finally, the directions were published: an ancient contest known as the champion-of-arms would determine the outcome. The champion-of-arms was contested on a figure-eight course, strictly timed, and set with targets—some for the javelin, some for the lance, and some for the sword, including the very last one which was a hundred-yard ride at full speed, testing the limits of a horse's endurance and the rider's skill at the spearing of a series of three-inch golden rings each suspended on a leather strap hung from unevenly spaced gantries and a final taking of a tent peg driven into the ground. Every section of the course would be done at a canter or full gallop and was a mighty feat, having been officially recorded at the games only four times in the past, with two of these being highly suspicious and controversial accounts, two years in a row naming the crown prince at the time as the champion.

The course design hadn't been seen in the past hundred years, but the plans and rules were unearthed from the Stacks and were laid out in the central arena under the blaze of torches set up for this purpose, as sunset was coming and the games, by tradition, must be concluded by the last hour of the final day.

As Tynan, Kiefer, and Devon watched leaning over the top of the arena barriers, Marc cantered to one side of the arena, scanning the course as he rode. The start was set by two white stones connected by a line of chalk drawn upon the arena soil. He slowed as he approached the start line and stopped, his horse tossing its head eagerly. The chief umpire leaned from the umpires' platform and waved the start flag. Marc drew his sword, saluted the king, and rode forward at a canter along the first line of combined jumps and targets.

He smoothly cleared the first jump, then moved from the sword-engage to the sword-in-line position, his arm fully extended, urging his horse to pick up the pace as he skewered the first target: a melon set upon a seven-foot-high wooden post. He cleared the second brush jump and cleanly sliced the second target: a lemon, set on the top of a wooden post as well, sliced so the bottom half remained unmoving on the top of the post.

Still maintaining a canter, Marc resheathed his sword and drew his first javelin from a side saddle scabbard as he swung in a right-hand circle, approaching the next line of targets. He cleared the first brush jump, in mid-flight hurling the first javelin at a man-sized dummy to the right of the course. As it pierced the middle of the target, Marc drew his second javelin, leaped a second brush jump, flinging the javelin at another target dummy positioned on the left, striking it full on, actually knocking it flat to the ground.

Marc continued his canter, swinging again in a right-handed circle toward the center and final line of targets while drawing his lance from the left saddle scabbard. Grasping the lance firmly and tucking it under his right arm, he urged the horse to a full gallop, aiming his lance at a hollow ring some three inches in diameter suspended by a cord from a narrow wooden gantry. The lance pierced the ring, snapping the cord, and Marc carried it forward on the lance head, aiming for a second identical ring, carrying that also, then three more; and finally lowering the lance to his boot level, aiming the point at a tent peg buried in the ground, he caught it up with his lance then rode ahead with all six targets balanced on the lance tip across the finish line.

"Time!" the chief umpire called out. "Within tolerance."

"Noted! Time accepted," answered another.

"Well done, Marc!" Tynan, Devon, and Kiefer shouted.

"Thanks," he answered, wiping the grime of the arena from his face. "Hope it turns out to be good enough for us." Then they walked back together in the cool darkness of the early evening to the stables.

Three riders thundered into the wide oval arena, their armor and leather glittering in the bright sun. The leader rode a little ahead of the other two, one carrying the royal Caledonian banner, the other a long brass trumpet. They reined up before the royal box and the lead rider called out in a loud voice, "Lord! May we have your permission to lodge the colors?"

The silence that followed was immense, stretching out like the breathless arch of translucent sky that hung above their heads. The king then answered in the time-honored form.

"As Lord of the Colors, you have my permission to lodge those that are worthy."

Tynan and his cohort were near the front of the column, just a few rows behind Gerald and his household troops and Cage with his administrative troops and staff. The fanfare of the king started, and a ripple of anticipation rolled through the throng seated in temporary wooden bleachers surrounding the Academy parade ground. Along one side of the stadium viewing platforms were the female graduates and their matrons, while higher up in the stadium were special places for the families of the graduating cadets.

Just ahead of the main column rode a group of seven horsemen—all highly decorated troopers—holding aloft the seven banners of Caledon, the trooping of the colors so called, an ancient event meant to accustom the troops to seeing the colors as a rallying point in the chaos that battle could produce across a field. There was also a specially armed escort, fifty of the best riders and graduates of the years gone by, prepared and turned out to greet the king and provide a mounted escort of riders in additional to his household band, who accompanied him everywhere and provided a steel ring of bodyguards, messengers, and personal retainers whose sole duty was to protect and serve the king as he traveled the land or rode out in battle.

As he sat upon Phaeton, Tynan thought of his first encounters with the Academy and the first question: did he have the spirit and the will to endure the training and attain the standards that could make him and others the wall and shield of the land? That he was here on this day at least validated the hopes that Gerald and others had for him, to this point. *"Audacity in the moment grows from a self-confidence built on the individual's trust of himself, his cohort, and his leaders."* One of Webbe's many sayings, the crux of the rule being that there shall be no acceptance of anything that is in any way second rate. What may be good for other units was not good enough for the Academy—a place that instilled a desire to work tirelessly for perfect execution of drill and practice that developed high achievement in the unit and a self-discipline and esprit de corps that lasted a lifetime, creating a living tradition that preserved the great achievements of the past that might serve to inspire similar deeds again.

As they rounded the far end of the parade ground, the shadow cast by the massive triumphal arch stretched long over them. This was a memorial carved in dark gray stone of a solid single piece in the shape of a stepped building ringed with the mounted likenesses of the first five kings of Caledon, who looked down rather grimly and somewhat slightly displeased with much of the modern trooping of the colors and the general feeling that the modern cohorts lacked the discipline and toughness of their bygone day. Regardless, Tynan felt full of life, and his spirit soared to be a part of the company, as they slowly left the shade of the five kings behind and turned to approach the reviewing stand.

Marc gave the commands: "Silver Shield! Echelon, ten shun! Present arms! Eyes right—right!" Miraculously and as one man their squadron drew their swords and swiveled their eyes right. Devon bore the standard of the Silver Shield, which was arrayed with the awards and decorations won by the unit at the Academy. As they passed the royal box, he ceremoniously dipped the colors in honor of the king and the other leaders there present, holding the standard in one hand extended perpendicular from his side.

Tynan saw then the king himself, who stood impassively there before his high seat watching them go by, a grim and determined figure, arrayed as a cavalry officer, his sword drawn point down touching the ground, both his gloved hands resting on the crosspiece on either side of the pommel, then he stood to attention and saluted the passing echelon with his sword as a shout of "Caledon" was rung back at him from the five hundred new troopers and a massive cheer went up from those present in the stadium.

Tynan, though, felt uneasy as they filed back to the stables. He was happy yet at the same time knew that another decision awaited him: what to do now? Likely, he'd get orders for one of the units—the Royal or Household Guards, or maybe the Border Guard if Gerald was able to grant his request—but he had the right to turn them all down to go elsewhere in the service if he wanted to; or separate altogether and go back to his grandparents' farm. It was the blessing and the curse of always being a volunteer: the decision about where to go or even signing up for the next stint.

"So, what are you going to do?" Marc asked as they removed the horse's tack and brushed them down.

"You must have been reading my mind," Tynan answered. "I was just thinking of that very thing. How about you?"

"I don't have a choice," Marc said. "Seven generations of guardsmen in my family, so I'm in for a lot of pressure to join either the Foot Guard or the Household troops. Seven generations of my family in one or the other, which adds up to nearly 150 years. If I go in for cavalry, I'd be the first and would be breaking with tradition in a way—though I can't see going anywhere except with Gerald and he'll be in the new Border Guard. My family will approve it only after having gone on quite a while with much added historic gas about the *old service* and how *that* was the best that will ever be; and these new units are mostly amateur boondoggles, wasting time and crown treasury resources, and so forth. No need to worry about it for a few weeks though; we have four week's leave and our orders will be sent to our homes, with the usual specifics around what unit, where to report, and so on."

"I'm sure it's the Foot Guard or maybe even an infantry cohort for me," Kiefer said. "If I'm lucky, my post will be on the northern line. I speak the dialects from up there so there'd be a solid benefit to going there. Like our friend Magnar, though, the difficulty is my family has a history of getting restless every twenty years or so and are prone to following the same likes of the traveling firebrands that sweep the glens. They've ended up on the wrong side of some pretty nasty border disputes."

He grinned at this thought. "Not that I wouldn't mind slanging around some of your sort from time to time—all in the best of spirits, of course; but the present powers-that-be may get nervous having me too close to the literal home fires."

"I've put in for the Guides," Devon said. "Seems I have a knack for scouting—also known as slinking around unseen in a skulking manner. They like my field sketches and say they are good and accurate and help the planners see enemy troop movements and fortifications and so on. I never thought my artistic bents would be put to such a use; I actually find it quite satisfying.

"I grew up riding—we raised horses but maybe more importantly sought out new breeds. My father is something of a genius along those lines and is able to see how two or three generations of an equine mix will produce characteristics of speed, endurance, and strength. Our horses are sold all over the country and there has been a couple of times when the crown identified them as national treasures or 'critical defense assets' and allows no one outside the country to buy them—and no one inside the country except certified Caledonian military tribunes."

"No wonder you're such a fine rider," Tynan said.

"Some are born to the yew, I'm born to the saddle," Devon said. "And was almost born *in* a saddle. My mother had gone riding that morning, an activity which seemed to precipitate my arrival into this world. The doctor had to come three miles out into the country, so I was born under an ash tree with my father and my father's men all about us, standing guard in a most courteous way with their backs turned to the happy occasion. The horses were there, a handful of inquisitive cows, and a few hunting dogs—a regular stable scene! But I've loved being around horses all my life; and I think I learned to ride before I learned to walk. Fortunately, the horses seem to approve of me as well, so it looks like a good path."

"A true Caledonian cavalryman!" Marc said.

"May it long continue!" Devon reached over and slid the saddle off, hung it over its wood frame, then turned to start brushing down the horse. "Take care of these first, and they will take care of you. Nothing like a horse—or perhaps a dog—for loyalty. They act like you're one of them; and since you feed and water them regularly, as well as provide them a reasonably warm and usually dry place to sleep, they think you're the king of the world."

"You still haven't said anything, Tynan," Marc said, as they closed the stable doors and walked back to the barracks room.

"I'm not sure how things will turn out," Tynan replied. "I've put in for the Border Guard as well, but with all the intrusions and threats from the Mataens and the Terasians, and the constant slinging around from pillar to post on missions, who knows? At home, my grandmother isn't getting any younger and my uncle isn't the best businessman I've ever known or the easiest person to be around. I'll have to see how things are there and if they need me."

Marc nodded. "If you stay in, at least you'd have the king's coin to send to them!" He paused and looked round at them all. "Anyway, I hope we all stay in—it would be exciting to ride together again someday in the future."

"What are you all standing around here for? You've got to be cleared out of these quarters before dinner mess—there's another crop of plebes coming in tonight!" Webbe was shouting as he walked by in the hallway. "Everybody: hurry up!"

They watched Webbe go for a moment, then looked around at each other, and burst out laughing.

www.ingramcontent.com/pod-product-compliance
Lightning Source LLC
Chambersburg PA
CBHW051134020726
47501CB00005B/1501